# CRIMEUCOPIA

## *Rule Britannia*

## Britannia Waves the Rules

### A Murderous Ink Press Anthology

**********************************

# CRIMEUCOPIA

## *Rule Britannia*

### Britannia Waves the Rules

First published by Murderous-Ink Press
Crowland
LINCOLNSHIRE
England
www.murderousinkpress.co.uk

Acknowledgements

To those writers and artists who helped make this anthology what it is,
I can only say a heartfelt Thank You!


*The Case of the Burqa-ed Busker"* first appeared in *Windward, Best
New England Crime Stories* (Level Best 2016*)* and can also be found in
Gerald Elias's collection of short crime fiction, *It's a Crime!*
*The Hand That Feeds* also appears in *Crimeucopia — The Lady Thrillers*
*A Student Deferment* first appeared in *Eclectica Magazine — August 2018*


And to Den, as always.

Contents

A return trip to the land of his ancestors is about to turn deadly for one whistleblowing Chicago banker.

When financial executive Bob Vanags takes a job at ominous Turaida Bank in Latvia, he hopes to learn of his heritage and to fight economic fraud in Eastern Europe. Instead, Bob finds himself pulled into a world of political intrigue, blackmail, and murder.

Aided by his son David, his beautiful colleague Agnese, and a fearless Latvian journalist named Santa Ezeriņa, Bob begins to unravel his employer's darkest secrets, discovering their sins and conspiracies beyond his wildest fears. Secrets that Turaida wants to keep hidden, even at the cost of Bob's life.

Now framed for murder by Turaida operatives, Bob must go on the run to clear his name, protect his family, and reveal the plot to the world before governments topple and war ignites in Europe. KGB Banker is a pulse-pounding international thriller spanning the globe from Latvia to Iceland, Moscow to America, Ukraine to the Estonian islands and back again.

— Paperback ISBN 9781620066690 — Kindle ASIN B09GTBX6ZQ —

# Alright My Son, Say No More, Leave It 'art!
## (An Editorial of Sorts)

As I best recall, it was one afternoon here at MIP Towers – must have been a touch after the start of tiffin, so around 4.35pm – when some smart young cove decided to politely call attention to himself by saying he had a proposal:

'Why can't we do an all-British Crimeucopia?'

And, bless my soul, after several pots of tea — Darjeeling (mid-season second flush, naturally) the general consensus was a resounding:

'Why not indeed?'

From there was born this anthology, containing, we hope, stories that, should you have the desire to cut them in half with a knife, they would flash you their Union Jacks without a moment's hesitation.

So, first out of the pavilion, and lining up with leg stump is *Daniel Marshall Wood*, who knocks us into London in 1966, with his **Triple Crown**. At the other end is *Gerald Elias*, who comes in with his **The Case of the Burqua-ed Busker**.

In reply, *S. E Bailey* takes us even further back in time to just post-WW II, and shows he has **A Talent for Killing**, before *Alexander Frew* replies with his **Ring, Ring** — which bounces on the 21st Century boundary for a solid 6.

*Kelly Lewis*, who assures us that the feminine version of a jockstrap is called a jill, flips one left field with her **The Hand that Feeds**, and after a short pause to change nationalities, *Carew S. Bartley* wades in with a devious piece in the form of his **The Uniform Simultaneous Death Act**.

**Murder at St. Bott's** from the deft story spinner, *Madeleine McDonald*, shows that nothing is sacred, especially at the Rectory, which allows *Edward Lodi* to add an extra spoonful of humour with his **The Big Dig**.

***Everything Money Can Buy*** gives *Michaele Jordan* to go a little wild, before *J. Aquino* — with his ***Murder at Elephant & Castle*** — and *David Rich* — with his ***A Student Deferment*** — tell us tales of a very British, Harry Palmer meets George Smiley, world.

*Kelly Zimmer* bobs up mid-stream with her ***Incognito***, and *Sharon Richards* explains why ***Karma's a Bitch*** — before we then start stepping into a very British Noir part of *Crimeucopia Town*.

So perhaps it's just as well that *Maroula Blades* returns to hold our hands as she takes us through her ***Urban Wasteland,*** before she passes us on to *David William Johnson*, who tells us all about his ***Porcelain Angel.***

The final end of the line stop on the Crimeucopia Noir Train network is *Harris Coverley*, who lets us know in no uncertain terms, that ***If You Can Smell It, You're Probably Already Deep in It.***…

Gawd blimey, guv'nor, now ain't that a feast for your mince pies?

And as with all of these anthologies, we hope you'll find something that you immediately like, as well as something that takes you out of your comfort zone – and puts you into a completely new one.

In other words, in the spirit of the Murderous Ink Press motto:

*You never know what you like until you read it.*

# *Triple Crown*
## *Daniel Marshall Wood*

*London — 1966*

"I'm thrilled you'll be here soon, Nigel. It's been ages. We'll celebrate with some bubbly ... Where are you staying? ... Call me when you settle in, Nigel. And give my love to Aggie. Cheerie-bye." Dahlia returned the phone to its cradle.

"So your cousin's back in play? I'm surprised." Adam Canfield held little affection for his wife's family, especially Nigel. Though quite handsome, the loathsome, loquacious, narrow-minded Nigel had sponged off them for several years before a convenient loveless marriage to the titled and wealthy Anglo-French Baroness Agnesse. The very vague Nigel was some sort of lesser diplomat to some lesser country, appearing to be perfectly suited to whatever it was he actually did. Adam couldn't remember the name of the former British colony. There were so many, all blurring together. The Empire was crumbling; indeed, it was.

"I told you a month ago Nigel would be in town, though I'd almost forgotten myself. I haven't checked my diary as closely as I should. Please give him some slack," Dahlia pleaded. "He'll only be around a few days, I promise. And let's not let get into politics, even if we disagree with his conservative outlook. We don't want a family tiff while he's visiting."

"If only I could convince Nigel the error of his ways," Adam began. "If he could only see the injustices of the current system for labour..."

"It's after 4:30," Dahlia interrupted, on her way to the drinks tray. "Time to get things started."

"You definitely know how to deftly change the subject. Make mine a double."

Ice rang against crystal. Splashes. Stirs. Plops of lime.

Dahlia sipped. "Oh, that's good." She handed Adam a matching gin and tonic — heavy on the gin — in an appropriately heavy crystal glass.

"Just what the doctor ordered," Adam quipped.

"Are you certain? I thought the doctor ordered less gin and more tonic, not that I did."

"Next year, I promise." Adam took more than a sip. "Exactly when are Nigel and Lady Agnesse gracing London with their presence?"

"A week from Thursday, but only Nigel. Agnesse is staying on in Paris with her mother. It'll be lovely catching up. He's my favourite cousin."

"Your only cousin."

"But he is my favourite, even if we don't see eye-to-eye on everything." Dahlia checked her watch. "Must dash soon. Bridge club at half-past five. I was late the past few times. I really must make more of an effort from now on."

"Again?" Adam scratched the chin of a purring grey tabby that sprang onto a corduroy lap. "You've played so much bridge the past three weeks. I'd hoped for a quiet evening with Markle on my lap and a home-cooked dinner."

"I'll get take-away. Chinese or Indian?" Dahlia mixed another drink.

"Your choice, dear." Adam folded his newspaper and lit a cigarette. "Why don't you ever include me? I'm an all-right extra man." He flicked ashes onto a gold-edged porcelain dish bearing the face of Queen Elizabeth II.

"I can barely manage, and I'm spades above you. The club president would eat you alive as she out-trumped you."

"I'll steer clear of the battle-axe, then. Markle and I will purr contentedly until your return. Make it Chinese. Something chicken. Lamb curry would be too spicy for Markle."

*****

*Three weeks earlier*

Inside No. 24 Fitzroy Street, Pernilla Makepeace re-straightened already orderly stacks of documents. Order held priority in all aspects of her life.

Citizens' Reform for Other World Needs. CROWN *was* her life. She had no call for twaddle like a demanding husband, sticky-fingered children, yipping pets or constant gardens.

Until four months previous, Pernilla had been second in command at a hard-line group loosely affiliated with Russian Communists. Then some rather unsavoury characters began vying for leadership. Pernilla and several loyalists broke rank to form CROWN, but they struggled to sustain the new entity. Notices posted around town yielded several souls curious about their cause, but few returned. She couldn't understand why. Shouldn't everyone believe this was the best way?

CROWN needed something — someone, perhaps — to shake things up so the media and general public would know they existed. An episode involving a government official would be perfect. After that, the Communists would come to her, begging to coalesce.

If she were still the pious Catholic her parents had raised, Pernilla would have lit a candle and prayed for a saviour.

With no one to witness, she smiled, an indulgence rarely allowed.

*****

From the Warren Street station, Dahlia had followed Fitzroy Street, stopping before an impassive stucco-fronted townhouse at No. 24, the grim Art Deco façade an ugly stepsister to a fanciful red brick late-Victorian neighbour. She rarely came to this side of town, now a bit down on its heels, faded from the glory days of the 1920s as a fashionable place to live near a now-overgrown park.

A small poster tacked up outside the market had caught her attention yesterday. CROWN, the organization was called. Dahlia couldn't remember the words forming the acronym, but the mission for reform around the world seemed just and forthright, similar to organizations she had supported at university. Sit-ins, marches and other protests had been rather fun. That's how she met Adam, painting signs in neon colours for some urgent cause she could no longer recall.

What was Dahlia in for? Her search for purpose, to feel needed now that her son was at Harrow, had brought her to this scarred black metal door on a street where she tried not to look over her shoulder too often, so as to arouse suspicion.

Dahlia had told her husband she was in a new bridge group, thinking it best to first look into CROWN and its mission. Adam might not understand her need for inclusion, he seemingly happy with his banking career and fusty gentlemen's clubs.

A hesitant press on button 3R was quickly followed by a deep-throated buzz, granting admission. Dingy linoleum, differing colours on each level, lined her upward path to the flat. The hallway's bare hanging bulbs washed out her artful mod makeup. No matter. Only the meeting ahead was important.

At the top of the stairs, a door placed at an odd angle stood open. A sturdy woman in bilious green tweed beckoned her in.

An hour later, Dahlia all but skipped back to the Underground station. CROWN was her new cause.

*****

Pernilla wasn't sure what to make of this creature appearing unexpectedly at No. 24. If enthusiasm were the only requirement, Dahlia could lead CROWN's parade. This slender woman who might have once been a model was nervous at first, prattling on about her darling husband, a son at school, travels abroad and a precious tabby with an unusual name — a type generally abhorred by Pernilla and the cause.

Dahlia came across as an aging debutante with good intentions and too much time on her hands. CROWN hosted no annual charity ball, if that was Dahlia's bent.

But in further conversation, Dahlia's background held promise. She might prove useful, after all. CROWN needed a spark, something to put it on the map, so to speak. Something that would let the country — nay, the world — know that it existed and was primed for action, a new heavyweight in the political arena. What if an "event" — Pernilla wasn't sure what to call it at this point — could be so sensational so as to set the country on its ear and announce CROWN's arrival?

Pernilla's mind whirled with possibilities. Could she pull it off with the assistance of — dare she even think these words? — a fluttering angel sent from heaven?

*****

Entering their Regency townhouse, take-away in hand, Dahlia debated telling Adam about the CROWN meeting, but decided he might think her too quickly swept up, even if they shared liberal points of view. She tossed her latch key onto a table, removed her hat and went downstairs.

Adam joined her in the kitchen. "Do I smell Chicken Yung Foo?" Adam asked. "Yum Foo."

"You do, Adam, Yum Foo. I'll set things set out in a jiffy."

"How'd it go?"

"Very well," Dahlia answered, placing a bowl of rice on the table. "I was the star of the evening."

"I'm so pleased for you, dear. You really like this new group."

"Oh, yes," Dahlia said. "We're of the same mind and play quite well together."

"Brilliant," Adam said, feeding Markle a bit of chicken. "By the way, I just had a call. I won't be able to meet for luncheon on Tuesday, after all. A client is coming in, so we'll go to the club. Ghastly boring, but I must play that game to stay in the game."

"Just as well. I forgot about our date and signed up for bridge both Monday and Tuesday." Dahlia slipped a morsel to a delighted Markle.

*****

Now that almost a month had passed since Dahlia's initial involvement, Pernilla thought it time to test her intentions. At the end of Monday's meeting she took Dahlia aside. "May I speak with you about a vital mission?"

"Of course," Dahlia said, eyes wide with interest.

"An important official will be visiting London later this week. He could be useful in our struggle."

"That's very good news."

"Will you work with one of our representatives to take care of him?"

"Certainly. I'm excited to help the cause in any way." Dahlia beamed. "I enjoy meeting new people. I've been told I'm an excellent hostess, making guests feel welcome. I'm happy to show him around, if you like."

Pernilla snorted. "It's a very different kind of mission you'll be participating in, but still a very important one.

"An operative called Kingfish will ring you tomorrow at one o'clock at a phone box on Old Queen Street at Cockpit Steps. Use the name Quant."

"Quant," Dahlia repeated.

"The mission will take place Friday morning." Pernilla turned toward her desk. Today's severe tweed suit matched her grey hair, twisted into a tight chignon.

"That's it?" Dahlia expected some details, more intrigue.

"Kingfish will provide particulars. Not all of us should be privy to the finer points. You understand, of course."

"Of course," Dahlia said softly.

"For the good of the cause," Pernilla remarked.

"For the good of the cause," Dahlia echoed, shuddering slightly at the task ahead.

*****

*Won't he ever stop talking?* Dahlia paced outside a red phone box. A few moments later, she tapped on the door glass. The scruffy long-haired young man inside caught her glares, responding with an offensive gesture using a middle finger. Exiting a short time later, he shouted obscenities.

Dahlia looked round the street, turned up the collar of her Burberry trench coat and entered the phone box. How thrilling to play agent! She started upon hearing the sharp *brrinng-brrinng*.

Coins plunked into the slot. "Quant here."

"Kingfish." The echoing voice was deep and distant, disguised by an electronic garbler. "I've been trying to get through for ten minutes," he barked. "Our target arrives in two nights. A deputy head of mission from Zambia, staying at the Exchequer."

Quant dropped the phone. She hoped Kingfish wouldn't consider her a sloppy operative and boot her from CROWN.

"Noted." Quant turned into a terse and efficient operative.

"At eleven on Friday you will rendezvous with agent Marquess at the Lamp and Quill on Prince Albert Street. At the appointed time, Marquess will follow you into the hotel and linger in the hallway as you knock on a hotel room door. This is why we need you: the target won't be suspicious of a female voice asking if this is Mr. Smythe's room. You will then step away. Marquess will take care of matters from there. Disappear from the hotel as quickly as you can and then call me from a phone box as soon as possible. You'll be given the number."

"Who and when will I get the number?"

"Just know that we'll provide it. Got that?"

"Got it, sir. Kingfish, I mean, sir."

The line went dead. Dahlia trembled, deep in thought. What had just transpired? From whom had all that information come?

A rap on the side glass of the phone box via the umbrella of an impatient elderly woman in a bright orange hat festooned with birds and feathers brought Dahlia back to a troubled reality.

Dahlia held the phone box door open. The woman adroitly slipped a small envelope into Dahlia's hand before closing the door.

Halfway down the block, Dahlia tore open the envelope, revealing a seven-digit number above the drawing of a crown and a simple fish. Kingfish! This was the number he mentioned. CROWN's operatives were apparently everywhere and well disguised.

*****

"I'm seeing Nigel for lunch." Dahlia held a red and purple floral mini dress in front of her, assessing the look in a mirror.

"I'm not surprised," Adam said.

"About the dress?"

"That you're meeting Nigel at his hotel."

"Will you join us?" Dahlia pulled on opaque white stockings.

"Too busy, dear, even if I had the mind. I'm expecting an important call around twelve-thirty. I'll just make a sandwich, though I'd rather be lunching with my bride."

"Poor dear."

"Please give Nigel my regards."

"Do you really mean it?" Dahlia slipped on a matching silk coat lined in navy.

"I'm just being civil." Adam tossed her a wide-brimmed navy hat trimmed with a wide red, white and purple grosgrain ribbon around the crown.

"I thought so, but I'll let Nigel think you'll miss seeing him." She twirled. "How do I look?"

"A floral vision in red and purple." Adam ogled his bride of twenty years. "And white. Those long legs are still gorgeous." He hesitated. "You could be late, I suppose..."

"Watch it, lad. Tonight, perhaps." Dahlia kissed him and floated from the room.

*****

Down a curving alley a block from the pub, behind an empty haberdashery, Dahlia reversed her coat to navy. Less conspicuous for Quant. Had time been available, she would have dyed her hair auburn. Dahlia added dark glasses and slid the hat behind a rusted black drain pipe, trusting it would remain until her job was finished. If not, could she bill Kingfish or Marquess for a replacement? The hat wasn't inexpensive, even marked down at a shop on the King's Road.

At this time of day the pub wasn't crowded. She hadn't had the presence of mind to ask for Marquess' description. As an experienced agent, Kingfish should have automatically provided it. Quant certainly would, on future missions.

Dahlia surveyed the room. The flirtatious dandy in a clashing plaid suit and checked shirt? A balding workman in a stained brown boiler suit? The platinum blonde barmaid with heavy aqua eye shadow? She settled into a booth with a direct view of the door. Quant would let Marquess come to her.

"May I make your *a-quant-ance*?" The smooth masculine voice lilted over her shoulder.

"Marquess my word, you certainly may," Quant said, always ready with a snappy comeback.

The middle-aged man in a smart banker's grey pinstripe suit and double-cuff pink shirt fastened with cufflinks fashioned from old coins slid into the booth, smiling.

"What if I wasn't Quant?"

"Then I would have apologized and moved on to the next-best-looking woman in the room."

"That bleached blonde? She could never pull this off."

"I imagine she's pulled off many things in her life."

"Oh, you're smooth, Marquess. I like your style."

"You're not too shabby yourself."

"Do you always dress like the proper squire I'm sure you're not?"

"I've learned to portray every role appropriately," Marquess said. "This costume can take me almost anywhere. I'm all but invisible in a sea of gents swimming about in matching suits."

"And other portrayals?" As a newbie to the intelligence game, she wanted inspiring war stories from a seasoned vet of undercover intrigue she knew only from books and the cinema.

"Let's see. I've been a lorry driver, an art appraiser, a chimney sweep and a beggar, to name a few. I was quite convincing as a priest. The things I heard during last rites!"

"Thrilling," Quant said. "I'm rather new to all this, if you didn't know."

"So I've been informed," Marquess said, "but you're doing brilliantly so far. You seem to be a natural to all this. You come across quite well."

"Actually, in my gap year during the war I did some underground field work for, uh, various causes."

"So you have a past," Marquess said. "I'm impressed. Ever kill anyone?"

"If I told you, I'd have to kill you." They both laughed.

"Now let's get down to business." Marquess' tone sobered. "Others have put themselves on the line for you, so you'd better come through. Are you up for on-the-job training?"

"That's why I'm here." Quant's smile disappeared. "There must be sacrifice for the good of the cause."

Marquess glanced at this carefully put-together creature he wasn't quite sure was up to the daunting task ahead. Pernilla's influence — definitely. "I admire your dedication to the task at hand."

Over barely-raised pints of dark ale, Quant and Marquess detailed the scheme to reach the target's room at the Exchequer.

"What if there's someone in the hallway? A maid or room service waiter?" Quant needed all angles covered.

"Then I'll walk past you or turn down a cross hall and return when the coast is clear." Marquess' experience clearly showed.

"What if the target happens to open the door just before I start to knock?"

"He won't."

"He might. Then what?"

"Then I'll take charge, push you aside and shove him back into the chamber before he knows what's what." Marquess knew his stuff. He pulled a pocket watch from his waistcoat. "Let's get going. I've never been late for a job."

"Maybe this time you should, just to change your routine. I've heard that's sometimes a good thing, to put the adversary off his guard."

Outside the pub, Quant turned right.

"This way to the hotel, my dear." Marquess began walking in the other direction.

"Follow me. I stashed my hat so I'd blend in more. Now I need it so I won't look the same."

"The same as what?" Marquess appeared puzzled.

"The same as I did to someone who may have seen me before," Quant explained matter-of-factly.

"Clever. Kingfish said you'd be a quick study." Marquess fell into step with Quant.

Street traffic was sparse and the alley was unpopulated.

Quant beckoned. "Down here. Come on." She nipped into the alley ahead of Marquess and retrieved the hat.

"Pretty hat for a pretty lady," he said.

"I'm glad you like it." Quant smiled and then looked toward the street. "Who's that coming into the alley?"

Marquess turned.

From her coat pocket, Quant pulled out a sharply pointed silver letter knife and thrust it into the back of the unsuspecting Marquess. He lurched and twisted, wide startled brown eyes questioning her as he plummeted, cracking his head on the worn cobblestones.

"If anyone takes out my cousin, it'll be me." Quant removed the knife, wrapped it in a handkerchief and placed it in her red Lucite box-shaped handbag. Her next stop: the Exchequer.

*****

Twenty-five minutes later, Quant slipped out of the hotel by a side door in the oak panelled bar. In a thankfully empty phone box two blocks away, trembling white-gloved fingers dialled.

"Kingfish." This time the garbled voice was higher pitched.

"Quant."

"Yes?"

"It's been taken care of."

"Brilliant. I expected nothing less."

"What next?" Quant caught her breath when she saw a Bobby coming her way. Had the body already been found?

"Let's meet this evening."

"Where and when?" Quant froze as the policeman stopped outside the phone box.

"Eight o'clock at the Twisted Stick. I'll get a table in the back room, under the name Crown. Bring your husband."

"Isn't that risky?"

"It's best if your life appears normal. We'll find a way to speak quietly. You can send him out for cigarettes."

"Fine." Quant was about to hang up but spoke again. "How will I recognize you?"

"The vermeil fish pin on my lapel. The eyes are sapphires." He rang off.

Quant stepped from the phone box and breathed relief as the Bobby entered a chemist's shop.

*****

"Look who's here, darling. Your long-lost cousin, Nigel."

Adam's shrill tone when Dahlia arrived home late that afternoon wasn't unexpected. Dahlia placed her hat and handbag on the foyer console.

Adam gave Dahlia a quick kiss. "It was beyond surprise when I opened the door to Nigel a short time ago."

"Your Adam looked like he'd seen a ghost," Nigel said. "Perhaps it's because we haven't been to the seaside in some months."

"Nigel! So lovely to see you!" Dahlia leaned in to kiss Nigel's cheeks. "I'm so sorry I had to cancel luncheon at the last minute."

"What?" Adam said.

"I'll explain later, dear. But I asked him for drinks to make up for my rudeness."

"I forgive you," said Nigel. "Now we're together, at long last. You look scrumptious — not a care in the world."

Adam led their guest into the lamp-lit drawing room, comfortably furnished by Dahlia and a series of decorators over the past ten years. "May I offer you a drink?"

Plopping onto a floral slipcovered club chair, Nigel said, "A nice claret, *s'il vous plait*."

Dahlia sank into a down-filled sofa cushion. "Claret for me, as well, dear."

As Nigel accepted the wine, Adam said, "If you want to rinse out that spot on your sleeve, you know where the cloakroom is."

Nigel glanced at a small stain on his jacket. "No need. It's nothing, really."

"How's your stay going?" As soon as Adam settled into a needlepoint covered wing chair, Markle jumped onto the newly-available lap, chin tipped up for attention.

"So-so. My afternoon meeting was called off," Nigel said. "So tiresome. If I had known, I wouldn't have come to London."

"Do you like the Exchequer?" Adam asked. "It has quite a history."

"Quite comfortable, yes, though I'm not sure it would be up to Agnesse's standards. My wife is rather picky when it comes to where we stop."

Adam swigged gin and tonic. "You've been away from England for some time. Anyone call on you at the hotel?"

"Since this was a short visit, I didn't have time for anyone else, unfortunately, even though several chaps from university are in the area. I only let Dahlia know I would be in town."

"And we're so glad you did, dearest Nigel." Dahlia smiled. "Don't let it be so long until you return."

Over the next hour, the three chatted amiably, though Dahlia thought Adam a bit cross at times. If only to please her, couldn't he make more of an effort?

"Where should we dine?" Nigel asked, emptying his second glass.

"It's already taken care of," Dahlia said. "The Twisted Stick."

Adam looked up. "I've heard of it. Rather posh. The back room is considered best."

"A friend from bridge club recommended it. He might be there, in fact."

"It would be lovely to meet someone from the group that has all but taken you hostage," Adam said, rising. "I'm feeling the odd man out these days. Do I have a rival?"

"Pish posh. You're the only ace in my hand." Dahlia kissed him.

"Nigel, would you go ahead and get us a taxi? At this time of evening it may take a while. Go round the corner to the Fulham Road. Should be better pickings there," Adam said.

"I'll get your coat, Nigel," Dahlia said.

"No need, dear. I'm closer." Adam pulled out a tan balmacaan.

"It's been lovely having you here, Nigel." Dahlia hugged him.

"See you in a bit. I'll rustle up a taxi and hold it like our lives depend on it."

"Let's not tarry, dear," Adam said after the door closed. "I'm looking forward to dinner." He took Dahlia's coat from a hanger and helped her into it.

Adam donned a charcoal grey Chesterfield.

"You look very smart, dear." She kissed him, brushing her cheek against the coat's lapel. "Ouch."

"Sorry, dear. Did that scratch you?"

Sapphire eyes set into a vermeil fish gleamed ominously.

"You're Kingfish?" Dahlia slapped Adam, the sting resonating across the foyer's marble floor. "You bastard!"

Kingfish raised his hand but stopped. "And you're Quant!  You didn't finish the job, though you said you had."

"You set up Nigel!  I should have realized, since I never mentioned the Exchequer to Pernilla. And I didn't tell you I planned to have lunch with Nigel at his hotel, though it was in my diary. You gave her all that information!"

"Of course. So you can imagine my shock when I saw Nigel at the door. He was supposed to be dead!"

"When it came down to it, I couldn't kill my cousin, not even for the good of the cause." Dahlia's voice broke.

"But you could kill Marquess? He was one of our best agents."

"It was the only way. If I hadn't killed him, he'd have taken out Nigel."

Adam grabbed Dahlia by the shoulders. "With your sudden change of heart, I'm the one who'll take the blame for this debacle. I trusted Quant."

"And I trusted my husband."

"Now I'm in danger." Adam's hands fell away. "*We're* in danger. No telling what they — Pernilla — will do to me — to us — now."

"We'll figure something out," Dahlia said quietly, "but now we've got to meet Nigel, go to dinner and pretend everything's okay. I'll get my key."

Dahlia opened the red handbag. Adam reached into his pocket.

*****

Nigel hated waiting — always had. As a child he'd been impatient for birthdays and Christmases to arrive. And his diplomatic career was moving at a snail's pace. He had now held a taxi for an eternity of fifteen minutes.

"Can't wait forever, guvnor." The driver took another drag on a precariously short cigarette. "Time is money, if you know what I mean."

"I'm not sure what's keeping them. Guess I'd better check. Go on," Nigel said, handing over a few notes.

*****

"St. Alban's Church," Nigel told the hired car driver two days later as he left the Exchequer Hotel. He unfolded *The Telegraph* to an article headlined "Double Funeral for Couple's Tragic Deaths."

"You an angler?" the driver asked into the rear-view mirror during a wait at a stop light.

"Not really. Why do you ask?"

"The pin. Thought you might like to cast the rod, like me."

Nigel patted the recently acquired vermeil pin set with two small sapphires, identical to the one worn by Kingfish.

The plot against him had been easy to pick up. Nigel was tapped into British intelligence as well as a labyrinthine system of former agents, street informers and double agents from all over.

Nigel had hoped his cousin wouldn't go through with the plan, but he couldn't be sure. When Dahlia alone arrived at the Exchequer, he instantly sensed her change of heart. He learned about Marquess later, poor chap. Marquess was known to have been a great operative. Oh, well. Collateral damage.

What Dahlia hadn't known was that Nigel had no such qualms about killing her, had it been necessary. Of Nigel's many cousins, Dahlia was his least favourite. He actually preferred Adam's company to hers.

But he had had no need to off Dahlia and Adam himself. Ironically, they had — most unnecessarily — taken care of matters quite swiftly and neatly on their own, though it required more time and trouble on his part. A crew had to be despatched to clean up the bloody crime scene. Their "coroner" had entered asphyxiation as cause of death, despite multiple stab and gunshot wounds. A quick cremation wrapped things up quite tidily.

After a period of mourning deemed appropriate for a bereaved British diplomat, Nigel would return to Zambia with Agnesse and continue with his *real* vocation.

"Here we are," the driver said. "St. Alban's."

Nigel entered the nave to sit in the family pew, ready with a few halting sobs and quick dabs at his eyes to imply grieving. Too bad Pernilla wasn't around for the send-off of two of her agents.

Pernilla Makepeace, known to be the best double agent around, had taught him well over two decades. Too well, perhaps. But she had set him up to be an exemplar for CROWN's mission.

With unexpected pleasure, Nigel had personally taken out Pernilla at No. 24 Fitzroy Street, before drinks with Dahlia and Adam that fateful evening. Pernilla's vermeil fish pin with sapphire eyes was his reward for a job well done. For the good of the cause.

# *The Case of the Burqua-ed Busker*
## *Gerald Elias*

Let me explain, if I may.

It was a humdrum evening. Rush hour on the Tube. The usual chill rain. Most of the passengers in anoraks, heavy jerseys, a hat of one sort or another. Young people, glazed and oblivious—what we've come to expect from that generation. Wearing their headphones. Gazing vacuously into their glowing mobile devices. Occupying seats reserved for the elderly. Elderly standing obstinately, staring in any direction but into another's eyes. All too typical, regrettably. All too typical. Ethnic diversity rampant, but a few like us, still: stolid, trench-coated Englishmen clinging to their way of life as tenaciously as to the train's handgrips, I dare say.

The train rounded a curve and the crowd swayed like a school of sardines in a tin, if you can picture that. Among them was a solitary figure dressed head to toe in a burqa. You see more and more of that kind these days. She carried a black, zippered shopping bag. One assumed it was a woman, of course, but how many times have we heard the BBC report Taliban rascals eluding NATO troops by hiding themselves underneath women's drapery? Cowardly, if you ask me. Terrorists capable of committing the most heinous atrocities. With impunity! But God protect our ill-fated soldier who would bare a woman's face by lifting the veil of her burqa.

That's neither here nor there. As the train lurched to a halt at Old Street station, the woman momentarily lost her balance and glanced against the chest of the Englishman standing next to her. She recoiled. He averted his eyes and, as we English so often do in awkward circumstances, pretended it hadn't happened. The train doors jarred open and she left hurriedly. He remained, no doubt relieved that the jihadi husband wasn't present to witness this unpardonably adulterous act. For all the Englishman knew, his life had been in the balance.

Despite the dark drizzle, the woman shuffled slowly, entering a Best Kabob restaurant two blocks from the station. It was no different from any of the other thousand Best Kabobs that have sprouted amongst London's immigrant working class. No one took any notice when she entered. Wet from the rain, she found the lone restroom and locked the door behind her.

When the door opened a miraculous transformation had occurred! The dour chrysalis of the burdensome burqa had been shed and a brilliant butterfly had emerged. Behold! A rosy-cheeked, young Englishman, sporting a full head of tousled hair, patched jeans, and dashing smile! The zippered shopping bag, reversed into Tartan plaid, slung rakishly over the young Adonis's shoulder. He ordered curried lentils and a yoghurt and cucumber salad with pita bread. A quick takeaway because, you see, he didn't want to be late to the concert at the Royal Academy of Music. The Kronos Quartet was performing a twentieth century program of Pärt, Lutoslawski, and Jimi Hendrix, starting at twenty-hundred hours.

*Ten PM? Isn't that late for a concert?*

I beg your pardon, dear. Eight o'clock.

Rohan Rothschild, for that was the young disguise artist's name, was in fact a promising violin student at the Academy, a student of the eminent György Pauk. You and I actually heard Pauk perform Mozart quintets last April, and if I remember correctly, we enjoyed it considerably. Rothschild was the son of a Jewish merchant whose fortunes had taken a turn for the worse, and of a mother of solid and ancient English milkmaid stock. (Hence his ruddy complexion.) It was not surprising that with his agile wit and tactile dexterity, young Rothschild excelled in his studies. Evidently, though, he wasn't fully sated by his academic challenges because, you see, he employed those very same skills with similarly efficacious results to relieve unsuspecting Tube commuters of their purses, using the impenetrable folds of his burqa to ensure his safe transit.

Rothschild was a thief with a conscience, I must say, judging by his MO. After pocketing the cash he immediately posted the wallets back to their rightful owners, using the addresses he found within. He attached a note claiming to have found the wallet lying on the sidewalk, and expressed the sincere hope that nothing had been stolen from it. The owners mightn't even have had time to file a missing property claim with the police and, relieved to have the wallet returned, would conclude that any missing cash was a small price to pay.

Of course Rothschild never signed his name to his letters, at least to any that I have seen. *"From A Good Samaritan"* sufficed for his purposes. He was also astute and modest enough in his ambitions not to try to profit from someone else's credit cards, preferring to stay safely below the radar. On the other hand, he was not averse to pawning the occasional bauble—a pocket watch or cigarette lighter—that he purloined. The rewards weren't great, but neither was the risk.

Rothschild had a lover named Baiba Salaam. Baiba was also a student at the Academy, a cellist of no small talent. Born in Tunis, she had worked her way up the Iberian Peninsula into England without a passport to her name. Lithe and scorchingly beautiful—I must admit— the young lady charmed our diligent immigration service into believing she would only be in the U.K. for a week to bear witness to the royal wedding. That was three years ago. Baiba was unable to attend the Kronos performance with Rohan because, you see, that particular evening she was engaged in her own line of larceny.

Baiba had a routine to which she was rigorously dedicated. After completing yoga exercises at dawn she headed off to Starbucks coffee shops located in the shadows of pricy international hotels. When she spotted a suitable—to be read as wealthy—foreign tourist in the queue, she was side-by-side with him before one could utter the word, "cappuccino." By the time she was served her chai latte—she didn't drink coffee—*abracadabra*, the unsuspecting dupe had already offered to pay for it and a dinner date set.

These flirtations lasted only until her starry-eyed suitors left town or became overly amorous, whichever occurred first. Baiba, being a good girl, rebuffed anything more passionate than a peck on the cheek. Perversely, the greater her resistance to lustful advances, the greater was her would-be beau's resolve to shower her with evidence of deflected affection. It didn't take Baiba long to become adept at psychological profiling; ergo, maximizing the balance sheet. She was the recipient of quite lovely and expensive gifts of jewellery, perfumes, dresses, and innumerable three-star dinners, all of which cost her no more than her animated conversation and brilliant smile. Like her boyfriend, Rothschild, she pawned all of her earnings and never gave her real name.

As a result of their efforts the two lovebirds sat on a nest egg of almost £17,000. Distributed in seventeen different bank accounts throughout the city, they were under the false impression they could avoid detection if none of their accounts exceeded a thousand pounds.

Rohan and Baiba did have a legitimate enterprise. Well, at least semi-legitimate. Between classes, concerts, and capers, they busked for the masses at the marketplace next to Covent Garden. Called themselves the Dynamic Duo. Maybe you've even seen them. They put on quite a show. Baiba played her cello standing up, the scroll of the instrument wedged behind her left ear. This she did in order to dance with her partner as they played. Ingenious really. A dancing cellist! One moment it was *Eine Kleine Nachtmusik* and in the twinkling of an eye, the theme from that desperate bore of a film, *Titanic*. They also sang with great gusto, all along playing and dancing, and in between numbers engaging in witty banter. Like the old music hall days:

*"What's happened to the rest of our quartet?"* Rothschild would ask with feigned alarm.

*"The second violinist forgot his instrument."*

*"What about the violist?"*

*"He forgot how to play."*

And sometimes it verged on the ribald:

*"Why do you hold that cello between your legs?"*

*"Because it's got a longer endpin than you've got."*

You get the idea. Good fun, it was.

The Dynamic Duo were the darlings of the tourists and, I should say, the Academy. No surprise there. Audiences soaked it all up. Charming, captivating, young, impetuously exuberant. Their open cases clinked with cash happily donated.

We're not sure exactly how long, but at least for months, their activities continued without a hiccough. The night of the Kronos concert, though, all of that changed. You see, it had been another of those humdrum days, and Rothschild, in his best burqa, had pinched a ring-sized jewel case from the pocket of an elderly English gent of nondescript bearing. He wore an expensive Loden overcoat and had pulled its collar high up against his face, ostensibly against the chill. He should have known better.

Rothschild returned to his Spartan flat, having thoroughly enjoyed the concert but understandably fatigued by the day's exertions. Baiba was still out and about, so after scrambling himself an egg he went to bed, leaving the jewel case on the kitchen table. Sometime later he was awakened by the sound of the shower running, after which he felt her by his side. This is how the transcript reads thereafter:

How'd it go? he asked her. The German again?

Mm.

What did he give you this time?

A lovely Swiss watch. Would you like to see it?

In the morning, if you don't mind. How much did it cost you?

Three hours of listening to the political philosophy of the New Right. Germany for Germans.

I hope you didn't bring his attention to your skin color.

It was highly theoretical.

Good.

You know what I need right now? Baiba said.

*I think that is sufficient detail.*

Of course, dear. I'll skip ahead.

Afterwards, Rothschild remembered the jewel case. He thought he would make his lover a pleasant late night gift. But when he opened the case he discovered it contained no mere bauble. On the contrary. It was a most brilliant and valuable ruby set in an antique gold ring.

What to do? What to do? Rothschild said. He paced around the kitchen table, its surface barren but for the damned, accusing ring.

We must think, said dear Baiba. But first, won't you please stop fidgeting and sit down!

She poured two glasses of brandy to calm them.

Do you know the owner's name? she asked.

Of course not.

Should we have it appraised?

And tell the appraiser what? That it's the family jewels? Not very likely.

What if we just pawn it, like we've done with the rest of the lot?

And what would we ask for it? A million quid? No raised eyebrows there, what?

In the end they decided to do nothing. They would wait and see what transpired, not an altogether bad strategy. Perhaps the owner would come forward and make the fact of the missing ring public. Then Rohan and Baiba could claim they found it, duplicating their *modus operandi* with the stolen wallets, and perhaps even receive a reward for returning it. With that hopeful thought they endeavoured to return to their studies and their busking, but placed a moratorium upon their less legitimate activities. Not a moment went by, though, that the young lovers were not looking over their shoulders. Their *joie de vivre* faded, replaced by oppressive anxiety.

Two days later their limbo ended abruptly. Returning from a listless master class at the Academy, Rohan found an unmarked envelope taped to the door of his apartment. Inside the envelope was a typed letter:

*We know who you and your girlfriend are.*

*We know where you live.*

*We know where you study.*

*We know all about your busking.*

*We know what you have.*

*We are coming to get it.*

Like Rohan, the author left no name.

*****

I awaited their arrival at the police station. They brought the ring and dutifully handed it over. More than dutifully, really. As if it were radioactive. They also gave me the letter that had been fixed to their door. I examined it with great intensity and put it in my brief case.

It took a mere hour to coax their version of the story from them. They were refreshingly forthright, only marginally embellishing their history of petty criminality in their effort to lessen the term of incarceration they were certain they were about to receive. That was only natural, after all, and I didn't hold it against them.

Upon their conclusion, I thanked them for their candour, and told them they now had two choices.

"We can prosecute you for the crimes to which you've just confessed," I said, "in which case, Mr. Rothschild, you will most likely spend five to ten years in prison. It goes without saying your ill-gotten bank accounts shall be confiscated. You are still young, though, and…" I let the thought play out. Rothschild hung his head, hardly consoled by such a bleak vision of his future.

"You, Miss Salaam, will be deported and never permitted back into the country. But it's a big world out there, and being a talented and enterprising young lady…

"I fear, though, that while awaiting trial and deportation, both of you will be vulnerable to attack from the ring's owner, whomever it is. Judging from the tone of the letter, in my professional opinion I have little doubt your lives may be in considerable jeopardy. You have certainly stepped on a hornet's nest. I advise you to tread very, very carefully."

"Couldn't you provide us protection?" Rothschild asked. Optimism in his voice was negated by desperation in his eyes.

"Sadly, no," I replied, shaking my head slowly. "I can understand and sympathize that that was your hope when you came to us tonight. But we have no way of knowing how long the threat might continue. Our resources are limited, and to be perfectly honest, when we do provide protection it is for victims of crime, not its perpetrators."

"You said there was a second choice," said Baiba, with backbone I found admirable for someone in her straits.

"Ah, yes," I said, perking up. That was the cue to which I had been directing them. I quickly rattled off the "second choice."

"The alternative is, the two of you can work for us. Your crimes shall be expunged from the record. Your bank accounts shall remain intact. Your academy tuition shall be paid in full and eventually you shall be provided a comfortable salary, with benefits and superannuation." Silly. What do young people care about retirement whilst still in the bloom of youth? More to the immediacy of the moment, I added, "We shall also see to it that your persecutors are neutralized. You would have nothing to fear from them again."

"Who is 'us'?" Rohan asked, once he regained the power of speech.

"'Us' is who you think 'us' is," I said. "The pair of you have the natural skills we look for, but you are rough around the edges. With proper training you have the potential to serve our country well. You would end up doing similar things to what you have been doing, lo, these many months—your busking will make a first-rate cover—with two differences: It wouldn't be cash and trinkets you'd be the recipients of, it would be information. And you would be doing your work far, far away from our hallowed shores; which work, I might add, would no longer be subject to prosecution under Her Majesty's laws."

I waited a moment for the ramifications of my proposal to take hold. I glanced at my watch, desiring to return home as quickly as possible.

I cleared my throat. "Which of the two options do you choose?" I asked. "You must decide now."

The anticipated answer was expeditiously forthcoming.

As they were being escorted out to begin their new lives, Rothschild turned to me and asked, "Haven't we met before, sir?"

"I highly doubt it," I said. "And we will unlikely ever meet again. Good night."

*****

"Well done, sir," Montgomery said, once Rothschild and Salaam were gone. "Well done, indeed."

I barely looked up from typing the bloody report. The hardest part had been getting to the police station ahead of the young lovers. We had alerted local constabularies to anticipate Rothschild and Salaam's plea for protection, but it arrived sooner than anyone had expected. When the call came in to Brooks, my domestic liaison officer, I had barely time to rush to the station, hang my coat on a hook where Rothschild wouldn't see it, and pretend to look calm.

No, in truth that had only been the second-hardest part. The hardest was prevailing upon Scotland Yard to refrain from arresting the couple months ago, when we first detected their criminal activity. It took considerable trading-in of favours by Whitehall to convince the Yard that observing the Dynamic Duo in real time would be the best assessment of their skills. Our recruitment of agents has been woefully in arrears. Competition from high-paying multinationals— Ah, I see your eyes glazing over. In any event we needed time to set up a proper scenario for the couple's acquiescence. We wanted them to come to us of their own volition. Ultimately, in the name of patriotism, the Yard agreed to play the game, but only after our assurance that we kept Lady and The Tramp on a short leash.

"Will they ever be told you had them under surveillance all along?" Montgomery asked me.

"We know more about them than their own mums, don't we?" I replied.

"Unless their dear mums also monitored their boudoir, I would say more than their mums would care to know."

"Yes, that's for certain. Well, we'll keep that our little secret, don't you think, Montgomery?"

"Yes, sir. And what shall we do with the ring, sir?"

"I'd say that on the black market it would fetch at least a good ten pounds. Not exactly the Crown Jewels, is it? Looks real enough, though."

Montgomery laughed and saluted. "Wonderful ploy," he said. "Wonderful." I excused him for the night and finished my report. On the way out I put on the lovely Loden overcoat that you gave me for my birthday, and returned the contentious gem to my pocket.

And there you have it, my dear. The whole, unadulterated saga why my anniversary gift to you was unavoidably delayed.

*Oh, Malcolm! I applaud you for a very clever story, but you needn't worry so. I forgive you for forgetting. After all, it wouldn't be the first time.*

But, dearest, by Queen and country I pledge it to be God's honest truth! How could I ever overlook our fortieth? I'd selected the ruby at the jewellers—I'll show you the sales slip if you insist—and taken your grandmother's gold ring there to be set. It was to be a great surprise, don't you see? I was returning home with it on the Tube while keeping that young rogue under surveillance.

*Malcolm, are you telling me that you, the legendary chief superintendent of clandestine affairs, allowed a violin student disguised in a burqa to pinch something that precious? From your coat pocket? Go on! You can't think I'm as gullible as your lapdog Montgomery!*

Shameful indeed, but true. Perhaps you're right, dear. Perhaps, after all, it *is* time for me to hang it all up and ride off into the sunset like those American cowboys. But of course I couldn't confess to Montgomery and the others that I had been victimized by a novice. But you must admit, in the end I did get the ring back and the service got two promising recruits. Design flaw into design feature, I'd say, and a pretty bang-up job I did of it, too.

*Of course you did, dear. Of course you did. All's well that ends well. Shall we celebrate with a cup of tea? Or is that not what you "need right now"?*

# A Talent for Killing

## S.E Bailey

*Sometimes, in dreams, the faces of people I've killed come back to me; more vividly now than any time in the eight years since the war's end.*

*The war gave us reasons for killing, even lent nobility to it.*

*But those notions were as bogus to me as ideas like 'King and Country' or belief in the God they'd all given thanks to when it was all over.*

*I missed the V.E Day parties and parades. I wasn't even in Blighty, some people's wars carried on.*

*When I did get back home to the East End the jamborees in blitzed out streets were finished. On the surface I fitted back in, no-one even asked about my war. I wasn't anyone's image of a war hero.*

*Even my S.O.E medal was dished out in what they called a private ceremony because people like me are living proof of the dirty secret every government wants to hide; which is, there's nothing noble about killing people.*

*I wasn't an instrument of higher justice. The ones I'd done in over there weren't all rabid Nazis.*

*The first one wasn't more than a boy, no matter what uniform he wore. A kid who'd had no more choice about finding himself in the middle of French woodland than I'd had.*

*Number five was a woman — a shopkeeper in Arles - someone in the network thought she'd been informing. I'd been the one to do it. There was even a half chance she'd been innocent…as much as that word applies to anyone.*

*Did they deserve it?*

*They'd shared the same fate, at the same hands, as all the bad 'uns I'd sorted out. So where does 'deserve' come into it?*

*What was that quote some booky toff said a few years back? 'After Auschwitz no more poetry'.*

*I'd second that and for good measure I'd also throw in…no more stories about justice and righteousness…no more notions of heaven and hell…no more looking for reasons in things.*

*Life's not a picture show and you're not the star — you're an echo in a cave, a sandcastle at high tide, a snowman at sunrise.*

*Bleedin' Hell… now I'm sounding off like a poet.*

*The truth is I'd somehow really known all of this already - wartime only confirmed it. The big show just gave me the chance to find what I was good at.*

*And I do mean really, really good.*

*That's why, when it was all over, I went into my current line of work. With all that training and my talent (if I do say so) was I supposed to just go back to Civvy Street? Yes sir…no sir…very good, sir.*

*My current work pays very nicely and offers the nearest thing to the old excitement I've found so far.*

*But it's not noble. I work for criminals…hard people; you still get exceptions, a few who aren't cut out for this game. My current employer for one — and he's finding out what an unforgiving industry he's in. I, on the other hand, am very much cut out for this. I have now become, I suppose, a criminal myself.*

*You can't work for them, do their bidding and pretend you're not part of it.*

*But consider this.*

*Anyone I do in now really is a bad person, there's no grey area, so no hypocrisy. Don't tell me that this time I'm doing wrong just because some toff won't pin a medal on me, like they did for (amongst other things) killing that boy in the forest or the middle- aged lady shop keeper who'd gossiped to the wrong people.*

*And the pay's better. And these tight spots I get into?*

*That's not the down side. It's what I do it for.*

******

"You know," says Frank Cross, "I've always said that these days I only kill my own kind…people who chose the same game…but with you. Well, you're the nearest thing to an innocent man we have in our line of work…Alfredo."

Frank's faux sympathy is intended as mockery and he pronounces 'Alfredo' pointedly. His cockney accent makes it sound all the more foreign. It's a calculated insult because he knows that Alfredo Farrugia has styled himself 'Alfred' since his family arrived in Britain from Malta in the early thirties.

But twenty years living in London means nothing to born and bred Eastenders like Frank Cross. He could probably trace his pure cockney ancestors back to 1066 and Alfred was sure they'd all be psychopaths and murderers to a man.

Alfred was bound to a chair, every part of him in pain. Even his ears smarted from the beatings.

He couldn't see well, Cross had smashed his spectacles and his right eye was swollen shut. He'd lost at least two teeth. He couldn't tell if it was more — every bit of him hurt, he couldn't quantify which parts might ever look normal or function again. That's if he lived through tonight, which was unlikely.

If he told Cross the things he wanted he'd be dead already. That was the only way he'd held out so far. Alfred wasn't tough; although he hid it well, he hated violence.

Frank Cross was probably right. Alfredo Farrugia was in the wrong line of work. Not that it would matter much longer. He thought about Gwen and the twins, he managed to stifle a sob.

Cross had imprisoned, then tortured, Alfred in a large empty room that felt old and somehow rustic; there were beams on the ceiling and a large, unlit fireplace. The place was dirty, cold and unfurnished. Moth-eaten curtains covered small and crooked windows. Alfred could tell it was dark outside.

It was certainly a detached place in its own grounds — Alfred thought of countryside. Wherever it was would be remote, with no chance of a passer-by spotting light at the window. Candlelight dimly illuminated the room. He knew, without being told, that this was where the Reynolds Brothers brought all the people who crossed them, people who were never seen again.

They'd been driven for several hours straight and were now far outside London, that much was for sure. It must be the early hours. Alfred and the dressmaker girl had left Bloom's restaurant at around nine thirty.

He'd been paying the girl off and the meal had been to thank her for her work. When they got to the car Nichols, his driver and bodyguard, wasn't there. Cross had met them instead.

Because Cross worked for him — had, in fact, long been a trusted henchman of the Farrugia brothers — Alfred's guard was down. Cross had started telling some tale about why he was there instead of Nichols when a bag had been thrust over Alfred's head by someone from behind. He could hear the same thing happening to the girl, she'd cried out and rough male voices had told her to shut it.

Then there'd been the sound of a van pulling up, it smelt like the kind used to transport dead pigs to butchers' shops. They were manhandled into it — there were at least three men.

When he heard Cross's voice giving orders Alfred knew he was done for.

Cross had betrayed him, he'd been working for the Reynolds Brothers. Some pieces of the jigsaw fell into place — all of the recent bad luck in his organisation.

The Farrugia brothers had come from Malta twenty years back. Alfred's brothers were skilful and frequently violent criminals. The Maltese brothers had controlled most of the Soho's prostitution scene for nearly twenty years now.

Matthias had been the one to bring over the girls but he prided himself on having certain 'principles' — only willing participants who knew what they were getting into. He saw that the girls didn't do too badly financially and made sure that a struck-off Harley Street quack with a drink problem looked after any of their medical needs…the usual occupational hazards. Matthias always claimed he was a ladies' man who used his talents for business, not some kind of white slaver. Alfred had never understood why but it was true that women of all creeds and classes seemed captivated by Matthias.

Luis was the money man. He'd been the one who'd bought the properties that now operated as high-end brothels in Queen Street, Bond Street and Stafford Street. But he also reinvested the ill- gotten profits into enterprises that were both legal and lucrative in their own right. The Farrugia's owned restaurants and property of all kinds across the capital. Luis always said that fifty years from now they'd be London's biggest landowners and their criminality would be long forgotten. Some yet to born Farrugia might even marry royalty one day — they'd certainly be rich enough to mix in those circles. Alfred knew that Luis's business and financial skills were exceptional — as was his ruthlessness.

Elias was the muscle. He frightened Alfred the most, he knew for a fact his eldest brother had killed people in both hot and cold blood. Elias had built a team of trusted hard cases who enforced his will both within the business as well as defending it from outsiders, sometimes brutally fending off the jealous attentions of other criminal East End gangs.

Frank Cross — the cold, dead eyed cockney who believed in nothing - had been one of those men. Elias had met him after de-mob in '45. Cross had been his older brother's most trusted right-hand enforcer for nearly ten years. Alfred had never liked nor trusted him. But Alfred didn't like anyone from that world.

He didn't even like his brothers. Alfred…little Alfredo…the runt of the Farrugia litter. Physically small — puny, in fact — but he suffered a far worse handicap in the eyes of his brothers. He was soft hearted and they knew it, although he'd had to learn early in life to appear unafraid and unconcerned in the face of cruelty.

He managed one of the family's West End restaurants and had married a plain English girl called Gwen. He kept her away from his family as much as possible; he was a father of twin boys and feared the influence his macho brothers would claim on them as they got older.

Alfred didn't want them in that world; he hated the thought of anyone hurting his boys. He hated the thought of them turning out like the other Farrugias, or men like Frank Cross, even more.

Then, in the last six months, everything changed. Alfred was now the only Farrugia brother left; the unlikely and reluctant heir to the evil empire his brothers had created…which was why he was here now, at the mercy of Frank Cross.

Cross pulled up a chair, the only other piece of furniture in the room, and sat opposite Alfred. He forced himself to meet Cross's dark and expressionless eyes. He managed to stare him out with his one good eye. He'd grown up with Luis, Matthias and Elias — with brothers that nasty you have to be tough, even as the runt.

Cross smiled.

'Alfredo…little Alfredo …that's what Elias used to call you. You do know it was me what did him in? You've worked out it wasn't an accident?'

Elias had been first to go, six months ago. He'd taken a trip down to Kent on family business and never made it back to London — his Healey was wrapped round a tree and Elias had been found with his head twisted at an impossible angle. He'd been drinking and no-one else was involved; the police on the Farrugia payroll had looked into it extra carefully.

The monster of Alfred's childhood and been seen off by one too many in a Margate pub.

Except he hadn't been. It was Cross, this creature sitting opposite him and grinning — it took every ounce of Alfred's self- control to keep looking at him as the candlelight flickering against his pale skin and dark eyes.

There was a noise upstairs, a weak cry from a man, Alfred couldn't make out the words.

Naylor.

The driver hadn't betrayed Alfred, he'd been transported here along with him and the dressmaker. The men who'd accompanied Cross had the other two, presumably in upstairs rooms.

He didn't know what had happened to the girl but feared it would be brutal, he'd been dimly aware of various noises from upstairs during his own miserable hours at Cross's hands.

'Naylor's still alive, which is a miracle 'cause you're havin' an easy time compared with him…I nipped up about an hour ago, you'd passed out,' said Cross, "and that bird you were on the lash with. Here…I thought you was meant to be 'appily married man. Mind you…worse luck for her. I think my muckers have taken a shine to her."

Almost on cue a high-pitched female cry rang out upstairs, followed by some nasty laughter.

"The girl's only a dressmaker…done some work for my wife…and Naylor knows nothing …"

Cross held up his hands.

"I ain't judging little Alfredo, not me. And Naylor's a dead man, you need to know that."

"You're an animal."

Cross slapped him hard across his face, which was already hurting so badly that Alfred barely felt it.

"That's not very polite," said Cross, "not to someone who's gonna be your boss."

He let his words sink in.

"That's right Alfredo, you can come out of this alive and kicking if you use your loaf."

"My brothers …"

"Oh yes, your brothers who you love so much. Well…as you know Elias is dead and Luis was banged up last month — eligible for parole in 1985 if he's still alive. That's down to me too — all that stuff they found. And the Scotland Yard boys couldn't wait to make it stick, they're on my payroll now."

Alfred could only look at Cross. Somehow, he'd known that he'd also been responsible for Luis's downfall. It was ironic really. The amount of criminality Luis had got away with over the years and now he'd spend the next thirty years in prison because of a frame up.

"Matthias …"

"That Maltese ponce is out of the picture…I wouldn't expect to see him at any family get-togethers."

Alfred felt a hot tear run down his burning cheek.

Matthias had told him that he was taking a trip abroad a month ago, right after Luis's conviction. He'd told Alfred that the trip was to find new girls for the Queen Street house but Alfred had known that Matthias was lying low. His remaining brother had, against his wishes, put Alfred in nominal charge of all the Farrugia enterprises.

So Cross and his paymasters, the Reynolds Brothers, had got Matthias too. The Reynolds gang had wanted to work with the Farrugias to distribute their heroin in the West End. They'd also wanted a cut of the brothel businesses. They threw in some sweeteners, to make it seem like they were doing something other than muscling in. But the Farrugias weren't stupid, they knew the Reynolds were preparing to take their business with violence if they couldn't do it with a crooked deal.

They'd be capable of doing it too. The Reynolds brothers had more men, more weapons, more money and more bent politicians and coppers on their books than the Farrugias.

Alfred had always thought that no matter what you're like there's someone who's like that too…but more.

That's what the Reynolds brothers were. The even nastier alternative to the Farrugia brothers. They'd moved more quickly and with more guile than anyone had anticipated — first Elias killed, then Luis framed and now Matthias.

Alfred was the only Farrugia left and Cross and the Reynolds brothers must've thought he'd offer no resistance.

But it hadn't been that way.

Matthias had told him to let Cross deal with reprisals against Reynolds targets. But Cross had been reluctant, making all kind of excuses.

In truth, Alfred had never trusted him so he'd brought his own person in, someone who'd owed him for a long-ago good turn. Someone every bit as tough and capable as his brothers but who didn't treat him with contempt just because he wasn't a violent lunatic like Elias, a lying snake like Matthias or a cold-hearted husk of a man like Luis.

During his month in charge, on Alfred's orders, some reprisals had taken place. One of the boozers owned by Henry Reynolds himself had been burned to the ground, then two weeks later a debt collector for Tony Reynolds's protection was found with the top of his head blown off.

Alfred hated it but considered it as self-defence.

It seemed to work though, word of a truce came from the Reynolds brothers and as far as Alfred was concerned it was over.

He'd been a fool...

"Like I said, you can come out of this alive if you're sensible."

Cross held a document wallet.

"These papers sign the lot to me...it's all been drawn up legal and proper. All you need to do is sign and tell me where the pass books are to those accounts Luis has. If you do it, you'll live. But I have to tell you Marcus Edgley's on his way."

Cross looked at his watch theatrically.

"Should be here inside the hour."

In spite of his agony Alfred's heart lurched with shock. He started to shake.

Marcus 'Razor's Edge' Edgley was the Reynolds' Brothers torturer in chief. A monster who made Frank Cross look like St Francis. Rumours said that he owned a case of knives; from cleavers that could cut a man's arm off in one stroke, to scalpels fine enough to remove his skin for hours without cutting deep enough for him to bleed out.

Cross let his words sink in, then made his nastiest revelation,

"In case you think the cavalry might be on the way...Salvatore Rolfi is dead."

Alfred felt fresh tears run down his face. Cross sounded almost sympathetic.

"You showed more bottle than I'd thought, getting your own leg-breaker in — hiding him in plain sight inside the restaurant...pretty clever, bringin' someone in under the cover of doing a different sort of work, so that I wouldn't notice. I knew you never trusted me...that's why I went through your desk, I found that ledger you keep...I read the pages about 'Sal', payments for torching the pub and doing in Tony's debt collector... 'Pay Sal a thousand...Pay Sal five hundred'...all in the same month you were passing him off as a chef."

Alfred's voice was little more than a whisper, he looked like the last of his strength was ebbing away.

"What did you do to Salvatore?"

"Not me, old son…my new partners the Reynolds brothers…they lifted him last night and Marcus had a long talk with 'im. It wasn't pretty…"

Alfred was sobbing.

"He was a good man… a father and husband…he was only a chef…you're a vicious, evil…"

"Look, just sign the papers…Marcus might let you live. I might even keep you on at the restaurant…I like the idea, one of the mighty Farrugias licking my boots …"

There was a crash from upstairs.

Cross paused.

It was followed by a man's shout that turned into a short scream.

Then silence.

Cross took out a revolver and crept to the door.

"Jimmy…Georgie…what's …"

Alfred saw him stagger backwards, grasping his throat as he dropped the revolver.

A sharpened knitting needle protruded from deep inside his Adam's apple; his dark eyes were bulging, looking at the stream of blood. He started gurgling, trying to say something but Sally had picked up the revolver and blew half his face off.

Then she was in the room, crossing towards Alfred. Her dress was torn, her face bruised.

He wondered for a moment about the sharpened knitting needle. She must've had it in her hand-bag but, of course, he'd passed her off in this last month as Gwen's dressmaker. The strangest thing was she really could make the clothes.

"Naylor…?"

Sally shook her head, a look of fleeting regret on her face.

He told her in quick, panicked tones that Marcus Edgley was on his way but she silenced him, sounding cold and professional. She got the ropes off him then passed him Cross's car keys.

"Drive till you get to main road then find your way back to the smoke, lay low for a few days with Gwen and the kids. I'll be in touch. We've got to hit back hard and we've got some work to do…that's unless you still think the job's finished…do you still want to pay me off, guvnor?"

Alfred only had strength to shake his head.

"Go…now."

At the door he looked back at her.

She was checking the bullets in Cross's gun, her dark eyes scanning the room and looking for the best place to hide.

He knew their enforcer, the hardest of killers Marcus Edgley, was on his way but felt no worries for Sally.

He remembered his earlier thought; no matter who you are, there's someone just like you…except more.

*****

*The first one looked like so many of the others I'd done in over in France; more disbelief than pain on his face when I pushed that knitting needle through his eye and into his brain. The second one I did with one hard slap in his throat…textbook, like they'd trained me in S.O.E.*

*Same way I'd killed the very first time…the kid in the French woodland an hour after being parachuted in.*

*Frank Cross…well, he looked angry as well as surprised because it was a woman what'd done him in.*

*I half think that's why the government kept the role they'd given to female agents so hidden…you know, to keep us women down. Posh men …or working men…army officers, or gangsters like Frank Cross …that's one thing they all have in common…some poor cow under their thumb.*

*But it's also why S.O.E used us young women in the first place. We're not anyone's image of war heroes…and the enemy always thinks we're not tough enough when things get really nasty.*

*Which shows how much men know.*

*Alfred's gone and I wait here alone, like so many times on operations. I'm hurting and angry about the things they did upstairs.*

*I hear a car arrive outside and I smile.*

*My hand tightens around Cross's gun.*

*Before his final night is over Marcus Edgley will tell me everything I need about the Reynolds brothers.*

*And what's more he'll appreciate how talented a woman can be.*

*I'll make a bleedin' suffragette of him.*

# *Ring, Ring*

## *Alexander Frew*

It all happened so quickly.

A man was running down the street, a tall, thin man, who saw me and immediately thrust something into my hand. The instinct when someone hands you an object is to take that thing, and I felt my fingers curl around an object that was small, metallic yet glassy. The man neither hinted by look or gesture that he knew me. Instead he resumed his pace — he hadn't actually stopped moving when he thrust the thing into my hand — and soon disappeared along the street and vanished around the corner.

I did what any normal person would have done and opened my hand. There, nestling in my palm was one of the most beautiful rings I had ever seen, clearly made of platinum, with a beautiful diamond cluster. I am no expert, but I would have said that it was worth thousands of pounds. This was confirmed for me in quite a startling way when a policeman appeared, running, saw the ring on my palm and did a double take.

He was a big, sweaty man who looked a size too big for his uniform. He did not look as if running suited him at all.

'What have you got there Miss?' he asked. The police are famed for asking obvious questions, I suppose it's part of their job after all.

'It's a ring of some kind,' I answered.

'May I ask why you have this ring?'

'Certainly, it was put into my hand by a man who ran off.'

'Why was it put into your hand by a man who ran off?'

'I don't know why it was put in my hand by a man who ran off.'

'So you're denying everything?'

'I can't deny anything when I don't know what's happening.'

'Please give me that ring.'

'Certainly,' I handed the ring over. Lacking an evidence bag he wrapped it in a handkerchief and put it in his breast pocket.

'Well I'll be on my way,' I said. 'I have a busy day ahead.'

'I'm afraid you'll have to accompany me to the station Miss.'

'And what if I don't want to?'

'Then I'm afraid I'll have to arrest you under suspicion of robbery.'

'What? I never robbed anybody.'

'What is your name and address?'

'Taylor Bond, 34 High Street, Gresham.' He wrote the various details down in his notebook. For a second, while he was doing this, I contemplated legging it into the crowd, but a second officer appeared, a female who had evidently been summoned during the chase, and the pair of them marched me off to the local police station where I was to be interviewed under caution. You think something like this can't happen to you. One minute you're walking down the High Street minding your own business, the next you're in a room with a table and two chairs and a grim faced female officer facing you, feeling more frightened than you've ever felt in your life.

'So, Taylor, why did you steal the ring?'

'I didn't,' I said, 'I've never seen it before in my entire life.'

'You say that, yet you were holding the ring in your hand.'

'I know, it sounds mad, but I was walking along minding my own business when this bloke put it in my hand and ran away.'

'Do you know this man?'

'No, never saw him in my life. He just appeared from nowhere, thrust it at me and ran off.'

'So you're denying you have anything to do with the theft of this platinum jewel cluster ring?'

'Yes,' I answered. Then I shut up. As far as I was concerned there was nothing else for me to say. The female officer looked at me as if expecting something more, but I really couldn't think of what speaking would add. Indeed, I have long been of the opinion that elaborating on things when you don't need to is perhaps not the way to go, especially when you're dealing with the police.

'Can I ask you a question?' I asked finally.

'Yes,' said the female, I think my silence was making her uncomfortable.

'What actually happened?'

'I thought you could tell me,' she said.

'I can't, so what's all this about?' I could see that she was reluctant to tell me anything, but she looked at the officer who had arrested me, and who was standing behind me with his arms folded (not in the least intimidating, eh?) and he gave an imperceptible nod. I know this because I twisted around in my chair to look up at him. I am not a big woman, and quite lithe.

'Very well,' said the female officer. 'At noon, a man with a good, classy accent, went into Purves & Mason, the High Street jewellers, who stock many objects of beauty, and asked to see a platinum ring for his wife, since her birthday was the next day and it was also a special anniversary. They have security measures such as automatically locking the front door when showing such an object, but that didn't work.'

'Why?'

'The supposed customer had prepared for this by jamming the door mechanism beforehand — sticking a small piece of metal in it. The ring was displayed; he snatched it, punched the assistant, and ran off with the jewellery.'

'Right. So he was spotted by the police?'

'The sergeant here saw him running out of the store and immediately realised that something was the matter just by his attitude and behaviour. He looked in, saw the assistant slumped over the counter and immediately gave chase. That's when he saw you standing there with the ring in the palm of your hand.'

'So what happens now?' I asked.

'You tell us all about your boyfriend, or we charge you with theft.'

'I am not changing my statement,' I said. 'But I will tell you this, I want a lawyer since I didn't steal anything.' I crossed my arms and looked at the officer without any expression. I wasn't about to change my mind, I made that quite evident.

At the end of the day I wasn't charged. The lawyer established that I hadn't been near the scene of the crime, had just been walking down the street when I was handed the jewel. I did not have a motive for stealing such a thing and it had been immediately taken off me by the police. I returned home and wrote in my diary that night, what had happened. The thoughts of that day would go through my head again and again.

The police held on to the evidence as they had to do, informing the jeweller of this because they had to do so. I was told this by the female officer who escorted me home. Unfortunately the CCTV for the shop had jammed and they had no pictures of the thief for Crimewatch.

If you're reading this you're probably expecting me to say something like the thief was called Matt, that he was my boyfriend, who contacted me later with details of his con, and halved the money with me. No such thing happened because I don't have a boyfriend and I had never seen the thief before.

However, I work for an insurance company and part of my job is investigating claims. There was a missing angle here, so I sat and thought about things and did some homework of my own. Within a few days I was back at the police station. I went straight up to the desk and spoke to a puzzled looking sergeant.

'I was arrested a few days ago for supposedly stealing an extremely valuable ring. I need to speak to the investigating officer.' The sergeant stared at me for a while, he could tell from my expression that I wasn't about to go away, so he fetched the policeman who had arrested me, one Constable Shaw. I did not hesitate.

'I know what happened with that ring.'

'Tell me,' he stated.

'Can we go somewhere private?' He looked slightly worried at this but went into the interview room where I had so nearly been charged with theft before my lawyer set me free.

'It's quite a setup,' I said. 'Have the company, Purves & Mason got their ring back yet?'

'No, they haven't. It's evidence.'

'Then I want you to know that you should immediately take that ring to a chemist and have it tested.'

'Why?'

'Because it's a fake.'

'What, how would you know that?'

'Because I was always going to get that ring.'

'What?' Shaw pulled out his notebook, awaiting a confession.

'Let me explain, the man running down the street was a judge of character, he was always going to give the ring to an honest person, someone who looked prosperous, who would immediately give the cluster to the police because they would know it was stolen. It was just his luck he was spotted by the police in what he was going to do anyway.'

'But why? It doesn't make any sense.'

'Let me explain. I am insurance investigator. Do you know that many companies insure objects of high value, like platinum rings with a diamond cluster? What's more, I bet you anything the assistant who had the ring stolen was female, and reserved that very ring for her own engagement, which meant that if it was stolen her insurance would kick in.'

'You've been there and seen her,' he said accusingly.

'No I haven't, I just applied my own knowledge of how these things work. I'll tell you what she did. She 'bought' the ring with a deposit and paid it up for a few weeks, and insured it at the same time. It was left on display at her request. In the meantime she had a replica made — she works in the business, she knows how to get that done. She arranges for a relative to 'rob' her, having made sure the CCTV is off and the emergency lock doesn't work. He passes the false ring to someone like me and runs off. She waits until the ring is returned, finds out it's a dummy to her 'surprise' and claims the insurance. If I was you I would test the ring, and get a list of her male contacts, and speak to them one by one. Sergeant, you saw the so-called 'thief'. Guaranteed he's a cousin, a brother or even nephew.'

Sergeant Shaw stared at the table for a while then looked up at me.

'You saw him too,' he said, 'I'll compile the list you want, don't even need to question her, because that would make her suspicious, then we'll visit them — if you're so sure.'

'I am,' I said. 'I'll need to apply for a holiday at short notice, but we'll do this thing.' I stood up, we smiled at each other, and I suddenly realised he wasn't bad looking. Maybe I was luckier than I thought.

We arranged to meet later that day, and he went off to compile a list of the shop assistant's relatives.

It was going to be a busy few days.

# *The Hand That Feeds*
## *Kelly Lewis*

"There you go Mrs Collins, three bags of Fresh Frozen. Now, lemme see, two pounds a bag, that comes to six pounds in all."

72 year old diminutive Mrs Collins closed one eye to improve her focus and started to fish around in her purse for £1 coins in amongst the sea of loose change.

Archie Bexford, owner of *Bexford's Pet Emporium*, leaned over the scratched wooden counter top towards her. "Tell you what, love, call it a fiver for cash."

Mrs Collins, who'd never had any intention of ever paying full price when pity always got her a discount, looked up from her rummaging. "That's very kind of you. Thank you. And a big thank you from Winston as well."

Winston was her ancient Alsatian-Doberman cross. His once black and brown snout was now mostly white and grey, and the beast had worse cataracts than she did. That, and the fact it was bloody incontinent. Before he'd finally managed to get her to tie the Devil dog to the round metal bar outside the front window, she would always insist on bringing the dog into the shop. Even before she'd get the evil beast completely through the doorway it'd cock its leg and piss on the door frame. Then it would stand in the middle of the shop, twitching, dribbling urine and growling whenever something at its eye level moved or made a noise.

He'd originally had several large wire mesh cages on the floor. They housed guinea pigs, baby rabbits, that sort of thing. He'd kept them low down because they were ideal kiddie magnets. Nothing beats the power of a child who's never heard the word 'No!' Or had its parents give in and purchase the desired creature after throwing a tantrum.

The final straw, in Winston's case, had been a cage of ten chinchillas. Even numbers were good. "You see, they mate for life, so you have to have two, otherwise you're splitting a couple up, and the one left behind will simply pine away." Actually they were worse than rabbits and would habitually jump anything that got too close.

All ten had been pretty active for most of the morning after he'd put their food and water in the cage, and Winston had been attracted to the blurs of fur moving at 90 miles an hour, round and round the cage walls. Archie had gone to the large storage shed out the back, into one of the commercial chest freezers and had pulled out her usual three packs of frozen dog food. Then, on his return, as he'd waited for Mrs Collins to go through the £1 coin routine, he'd watched the dog's curiosity build, to the point where Winston had stuck his nose hard up against the wire squares to get a better smell of the creatures.

Next thing, one of the psychotic grey and white sods stops by Winston's head, sniffs at him, then bites a chunk out of the tip of Winston's nose. The buggers are like any other rodents, they'll chew on anything because their teeth don't stop growing.

Of course, Winston kicks off big time, understandable given the provocation. But with all the barking and snapping, the chinchillas go into overdrive, bouncing off the sides and corners of the cage at around Mach 1. Then *poof*! Three of them blow a ventricle, or a gasket, or whatever, and they're flat on their backs, legs in the air, having bloody heart attacks.

Well, what with the overheads, Winston had completely wiped out any hope of a profit margin.

That was when he'd decided to ban the dog from coming into the shop.

In front of him Mrs Collins made a show of dropping coins onto the counter top and waiting until Archie had counted them up and put them in the till. As Archie had told her after the last 'incident', "Once bitten, twice shy, and we don't want you making the same mistake again, do we?" Euros, Canadian 5 cents, Iranian rials — nothing was sacred, or legal tender, when it came to her inventiveness at trying to short change him.

Satisfied, he scooped up the coins and watched as she'd collected her walking stick and made her way out.

She might be hard work, but she was a loyal and, more importantly, a very regular buying customer.

Archie looked at the hexagonal mahogany and brass case clock on the wall over the boxes bird food and high fibre rabbit pellets. Quarter past nine. The Council waste disposal van would be out the back at midday as usual. If it wasn't for them then he'd be knee-deep in used bedding and animal crap. And Meltons the butchers would be at the back gates around 7pm to offload expired meat and offal — all destined for the Fresh Frozen processing plant — aka the large storage shed at the side of the house. Meltons wasn't the only butcher who saved money by passing their unsellables onto him. All for free, otherwise they'd have to pay to have it properly disposed of. That was why the dog food was only £2 a kilo. He'd spend a little time of an evening trimming and cutting it up, sealing the plastic bags with one of those industrial catering machines. Decades ago his parents used to pre-cook the stuff in an old 10 gallon bitumen cauldron, until the neighbours complained about the smell. After that it was all 'boil-in-the-bag' regardless of how many teeth your dog had left. Mind you, Mrs Collins' Winston could probably still eat the stuff frozen, then go out into the back garden and have a cat for dessert.

He checked the clock again. Time for a mid-morning cuppa and a digestive biscuit or two.

Ten minutes later, sitting in the comfortably worn easy chair in the living room, he looked over at the mantle above the fire place. The fire was a wide three bar electric, which had been bought back in the 1970s when his parents had owned the shop — around the time when the compulsory smokeless zones had been brought in. On the wooden shelf were several photographs of himself and Joanne. One on their wedding day, outside the local church, another of Joanne holding their daughter in the maternity ward. Both were no longer with him. Joanne had succumbed to ovarian cancer fifteen years before, and their little Susie had been the victim of a wife beater of a husband 18 months after that. According to the inquest she'd died instantly. Never felt a thing. Not that that was any consolation.

He dunked a biscuit several times, but when he tried to bring the wet end to his mouth it fell back into his mug.

"Bollocks."

Now he couldn't really enjoy the tea knowing there was a swampy mass at the bottom of the mug. He looked over at the calendar hanging on a picture hook on the wall. Pinned to it by a large bulldog clip was the MoT and service reminder from Pinkerton's the local garage. It was for his old Vivaro van. It had two sliding side doors, plus the back opened as well. It was perfect for transporting cages. He'd have to hose it out before taking it to the garage as the last time they'd refused to have anything to do with it because of the smell. At least the back yard had a manhole cover he could take up to let the water and droppings run straight into the sewer.

Out front the shop door opened, tripping the electric buzzer on the living room wall, breaking his reverie and stirring him into action.

"I'll just be a minute!" Then he took his mug into the back kitchen and put it in the sink. Old 'Butler' sinks were apparently 'trending' and were 'a must have' again. Maybe he should put it on the Antiques Roadshow? It was an original from when the shop had been built in the 1930s and Archie suspected if he dug into the walls he'd find the original gas pipes for the lighting.

Going back through to the shop, he'd been confronted by the twitchy form of Paul Hubbard. His head was sporadically jerking from side to side, and he kept wiping his nose with a rather dubious handkerchief.

"Archie! Arch, my man!" 5ft 7 inches, skinny as a rake, and forever wearing an old olive green parka zip-up. He'd been on methadone for decades, supplementing it with China white now and again, and as was obvious from his eyes, he'd sometimes get a taste for crystal meth.

"What can I do for you Paul?"

"It's more a case of what I can do for you. How much do you reckon these are worth?"

His hands dipped into both side pockets of his parka, came back out again, and deposited two brightly coloured birds onto the counter top. They blinked rapidly, then staggered around rather than walking, as if they were totally confused.

Archie looked up, for once genuinely amazed. "Paul, these are a pair of Lorikeets…."

But before he could ask where they'd come from, Hubbard said, "They'll be alright once they come down."

More mental confusion. "Come down from where?" Archie put a palm against the side of the counter to stop one of the birds from falling off the edge.

"I got this idea, see." Paul carried on regardless. "It was this morning. I'd been having banana toast for breakfast, and sorting out some Jamaican flower tops, separating out stalks and seeds. That's when I remembered."

When he didn't continue, Archie prompted him. "Remembered what?"

"That these birds like mashed bananas. That's what we fed them with last time we went to the petting zoo."

Again the distracted pause, until Archie said, "And?"

"And I thought, if I were to grind up the seeds, mix the powder in with the mashed banana, and then feed it to some of these," He pointed to the two Lorikeets now sitting on the counter in front of them. "They'd get blissed out, and that would make it easier to pick them up and walk off with them."

Archie looked directly at Hubbard. "Are you telling me that these two birds are high?"

Hubbard nodded. "Totally off their faces. Well, off their beaks is probably more correct."

*They're not the only ones*, Archie thought. "Okay, how much do you want for them?"

"I don't know. Would £40 sound fair?"

"It would be, provided the serial numbers have been removed."

"Serial numbers?"

"Yes, serial numbers. These aren't your average budget Australian budgies or some Chinese knock off peacocks. These are high end merchandise, so they'll have been tattooed accordingly."

Hubbard picked one up, turned it over and started squinting around its tail and between its legs. "How can you tell?"

Archie smacked Hubbard on the head, then took the half drugged bird from him. "I can tell, because I'm a professional, that's how." He picked up the second one and put both of them safely on a nearby shelf. Then, to Hubbard he said, "Okay, as they're still traceable, it'll have to be £20 the pair, best offer."

Hubbard danced from one foot to the other several times. "You couldn't make it £30, could you?" It was clear to Archie as to where the money would end up. The nearest dealer's pocket.

"C'mon Paul. I'm the one taking all the risks here. It's either that, or you take them back to where you nicked them."

Some more foot shuffling, then, "Okay, 20 it is."

Archie opened the till and handed Hubbard the note.

Ten minutes after Hubbard had left, Archie had been on the phone.

"Chedderton Zoo reception, I'm Gillian, how can I help?"

"Gillian, it's Archie Bexford from the Pet Emporium. Is Steph there?"

Moments later another female voice came on the line. "Archie, to what do we owe the pleasure?"

"Well, it's nothing to be alarmed about, but when you come to your evening roll call, you'll find you're two Lorikeets short."

There was something muffled which Archie thought sounded very much like *Shit!* Then Steph said, "I take it someone's tried to sell them to you?"

"'Fraid so. I just paid £70 for the pair. I've got them safe here. If you want to send someone from your security over to collect them?"

"I'll send Jan Denny round with the money. You haven't called the police have you?"

"No. I figured you wouldn't want the publicity if they got involved. Well, not after the Meerkats…. I'll let Jan know who sold them to me. That way you can do your own follow-up investigation. He shouldn't be hard to spot on the CCTV footage.”

“Thanks. Jan’s about the only one I trust not to try and sell the story to the local newspapers.”

An hour and two hamster sales later Jan Denny arrived.

Archie smiled at her. “You really do look the part in that uniform.”

“Thanks Archie, that’s very sweet of you. Now, I understand you have two of our escapees for me to collect.”

He went over to the shelves and picked up a pair of cardboard budgie transport boxes. He’d crossed ‘Budgie’ out and written Lorikeet in thick black felt pen. As he handed them over, Jan passed him an envelope. He took it, saying, “This all seems like some kind of ransom exchange.” She laughed as he continued, “The person you want to look out for on the videos is Paul Hubbard. You can’t miss him in that grubby parka of his.” He let a few moments of silence pass, then asked, “How’s your sister?”

There was an awkward expression on Jan’s face before she said, “As well as she can be, all things considered. It’s not like the brain damage will fix itself.” Then she smiled at the boxes in her hands. “On a good day I take her around the enclosures, so she can see the animals. There’s plenty of wheelchair access. She loves the parrots when they come down and take food from her. Usually it’s hard to tell what her mood is, but in there, with the birds, she really calms down for a while.”

“And they still haven’t found the driver who hit her?” He knew full well the police hadn’t found him — it would’ve been all over the local papers if they had — but he felt he had to ask all the same.

“No, it seems the bastard is still hiding out somewhere. You’d’ve thought one of his mates, or his family, would’ve shopped him by now. Still, I keep hoping someone will find him.”

“All we can do is hope.” Archie didn’t mention that the police had still to bring his daughter’s killer husband to justice. Misery may well love company, but there was no point in adding to Jan’s. Changing the subject, he asked, “Doing anything this weekend?”

“Not much. Yourself?”

“I’m going to pack the tent and be off down to the coast for the weekend. A little bit of solitude, and some bird watching.”

"Sounds like you've got it sorted." She turned to leave and Archie came around the counter and opened the door for her.

At midday the Council refuse lorry came and went, then the afternoon dragged on into the evening, with him shutting the shop at 4.30pm, the usual time for a Friday. By 5.30pm he'd fed and watered the various livestock, and had gone down to *Fry Me to the Moon,* a fish & chip shop two streets across, on the corner of Telford Road. Cod, chips, and a gherkin — the perfect pickle.

With the dinner things washed, dried and packed away, he cleared down the register, leaving enough in the till for Pearl Corrigan to open up with the following morning. He'd already banked the week's takings the previous day, something his father had always insisted on doing.

"That way, if they roll out of the pub pissed on a Friday night, there's bugger all for them to take if they fancy a bit of B and E."

His father had also put around the rumours that he let poisonous snakes loose of a night as well. That might be why the shop had never been burgled.

While he waited for Meltons to drop off the dodgy meat and offal, he'd spread a large tarpaulin out in the back of the van, then added an all-weather rolled up tent, a rucksack filled with several days supplies, and an oversized *Harrod's* green and gold plastic carrier bag he'd taken from the bottom of one of the chest freezers.

Packed and ready for his weekend break he opened the two wooden back gates, then went into the large shed via the side door. He turned on the fluorescent lights and checked down the long walk of shelving that had a mass of bulk goods on them. Dry dog and cat food, for those who didn't want to keep traipsing to the supermarket for sachets and half sized tins. Flea collars, squeaky toys, pet leads and some cuttlefish bones for the budgies. Furthest from the door was the pair of commercial 22 cubic foot chest freezers, occasionally humming to themselves.

At ten to seven the plain white van from Meltons came, offloaded and went, and by 8:30pm he'd cut, weighed and bagged 18 packs — all now resting in one of the freezers. Not all of it was from Meltons. Some of it had been frozen leftovers from previous evenings when the bags had come in under weight. When the pieces were frozen solid it was easier to cut them up with an old bow saw that was always hanging on the shed wall next to the two oval zinc baths. His father used to go out onto the Northfield Common area early on a Saturday morning with a pair of ferrets. He'd usually bring back a couple of still warm dead rabbits that Mum would hang by their back legs from hooks in the shed's rafters. The zinc bath caught the offal when they were gutted and skinned, the waste going down the main sewer under the manhole cover. That's where Archie had learned how to dress a carcass and handle meat without being squeamish. It had also sadly been a long time since he'd had fried rabbit for Sunday lunch.

He looked down at the butcher's block bench and the large knife in his hand.

Susie's husband, Tony Hagen, had been an electrician. Archie had been unhappy about the marriage from the start, but had kept his thoughts to himself. Well, it's what you tended to do back then. He'd also been preoccupied with Joanne's cancer. Trying to keep a brave face even when it was finally diagnosed as terminal. When she was in hospital it wasn't unusual for him to regularly cry himself to sleep.

Then one morning, 18 months after Joanne had passed away, the police had come round.

Susie had been found dead at the bottom of the stairs by her husband, supposedly coming back to the house after an all-night card game. They'd found pills in her stomach and alcohol in her blood. They'd also found bruises "that are inconsistent with a fatal fall, which appear to have happened over an extended period of time." The bastard had been careful not to hit her where it might show. "However," the Coroner had concluded, "I find it impossible to rule this as anything other than a death by misadventure, due to a lack of hard evidence to show both direct physical and mental abuse by Mr Hagen."

Of course now there were laws in place, but not back then.

He'd let things lie for about 5 months — to mid-February, when the days were short and the nights still long. There was street lighting to the front of a row of semi-detacheds, but nothing down the side alley and back gate. Plus Tony hadn't even bothered to change the locks, so the spare keys still worked.

He'd parked the van a good dozen or so cars away, then settled down to wait. Just before midnight Tony had come back by taxi — too pissed to drive — and Archie had given the bastard two hours before he'd reversed the Vivaro into the alleyway.

Once through the back kitchen door he'd let his eyes adjust to the low light.

The kitchen was a tip — old food and takeaway packages were on the counter tops — and from the lounge he could hear snoring. Tony, flat out on the couch, his head on top of an armrest. Careful not to make any noise, Archie had reached into the inside pocket of his Burberry jacket, and taken out the small wooden Rounders bat he kept under the shop counter as a deterrent. He swung the bat high, then backhanded it down hard across Tony's throat, smashing his Adam's apple and crushing his windpipe completely. For good measure he'd then put his foot onto Tony's stomach and stabbed the bat down into the damaged larynx.

Tony had died within seconds, and with the added advantage of no blood spatter or trace. And killing Tony had been so enjoyable, so cathartic, he'd had to close his eyes and force himself to slow his breathing down to a more normal rate. Didn't runners call it an endorphin rush? An addiction?

He'd then thought about just leaving the bastard's body at the bottom of the stairs, but that was perhaps a bit too obvious, so he decided it was best not to tempt Fate.

Back at the pet shop it had been easy to strip the body, and with a small block & tackle — and a bit of ingenuity — it had been just like dressing a rabbit. The advantage was that you didn't have to skin the carcass.

What could go down the sewer, within reason, went that way, or into the black bags to be collected by the Council. And after several days in one of the freezers Tony was getting mixed in with the rest of the frozen dog food — cut up into 'steaks' and marrowbone pieces. People still took it and cooked it, or fed it to their darlings raw, and he'd been sure that most of his customers who bought the stuff were just squeamish enough not to look at it too closely.

The easiest part of Tony to dispose of had been the head. He'd waited until May, then gone down to Westling on Sea and the old pier. He'd set himself up right at the very end, and spent the day crab fishing before finally cutting the line and letting the picked over head get sucked out to sea on the tide. He'd taken four of the biggest crabs to Jerry at *Fry Me to the Moon,* and Jerry had cooked and cleaned two for himself and two for Archie for free.

It had been about a year before he'd been certain he'd gotten away with it. The police had come round asking questions, but they didn't seem all that energetic at trying to get to the bottom of Tony's disappearance, which had eventually been reported by his family months afterwards.

Every time after that it had become easier and easier, especially after reading the local newspapers.

Archie went back into the kitchen and came out with a bucket of hot water, bleach, and a couple of cloths he kept under the sink. In less than a quarter of an hour everything had been washed and wiped down, and the water flushed away via the downstairs cloakroom toilet.

With everything packed for the weekend, he'd settled himself in the armchair and spent an hour listening to the radio before setting the alarm clock for 4am.

There was nothing he could do for Jan's sister. She'd been consigned to a twilight hell of a near vegetative state when the car had collided with her. Successive heart failures had led to oxygen starvation, which had resulted in her debilitating brain damage.

The bastard hadn't stopped, but had eventually turned himself in to the police two days later. By that time his blood alcohol level was almost non-existent. He'd claimed he'd been traumatised, with the local papers quoting him as saying that it was the shock that had blanked the incident completely from his memory — "like a train driver when someone jumps onto the tracks in front of their train."

Then, while on bail, he'd failed to attend the police station on a daily basis, and they'd been searching for him ever since.

At 5.40am Archie had driven out the back gates, parked in front of the shop, then had gone back and locked up. Pearl had a key to the shop door, and she really did love the animals. Then he'd started driving, heading North up the A1 rather than to the coast, before going cross country until he'd arrived at the Northumberland National Park. No SatNav or mobile phone, he'd trusted to the old way of driving, with an AA map book and a route board. Working his way into the Park, he'd left the van part way up a forestry dirt road, and had carried on, on foot, for several miles, the rucksack on his back and the *Harrord's* bag strapped to the top of it. An hour later he'd found the hiker's wooden shelter as marked on the trail map. It was weather worn but a comfort, giving walkers and backpackers protection from the rain. He rested up for a few minutes before heading back to the Vivaro — leaving behind the carrier bag on the shelter's bench seat.

Driving home, he'd gone down to the outskirts of Scarborough, and had spent a very pleasant night at a coaching inn, the proprietors glad of the out-of-season business, and the fact he paid in cash. "Too much technology can leave you stranded," he'd said to the manager. "You never know when you're likely to find yourself without signals, or defective chip and PIN readers." And you couldn't track cash like you could a credit card or a smart phone.

Back in his living room a day later, Archie settled down into his easy chair with a cup of tea and half a dozen dunking biscuits. He wondered how long it would take before a backpacker, or one of the forestry wardens, would come across the carrier bag with the head and two forearms defrosted in it.

They would obviously notify the police, who would take fingerprints. After 10 months in the freezer, wrapped up in clingfilm, they should be able to pull a good set off the hands. Once they put those on the system then they'd turn up the missing driver, and Jan would finally get some closure for her sister.

Archie sighed and put half of a tea-soaked biscuit into his mouth.

No doubt, come next Friday, Mrs Collins would be back in and grumble at him, as she usually did.

"Winston really loves to crunch up those little meaty bones you used to sometimes put in those bags. Why don't you put some more of those in for him?"

Why not indeed.

Archie picked up the local newspaper, turned to the Police Updates section and started to read.

# *The Uniform Simultaneous Death Act*

## *Carew S. Bartley*

> From the very beginning of the business, I suspected that there was some scoundrelly intrigue at the bottom of it.
>
> —Dostoevsky, *Crime and Punishment*

Mark Campbell trudged down the dingy back stairwell from his office to the Vietnamese restaurant, praying none of the previous day's callers would actually show up. Each of the numerous calls he fielded yesterday had proceeded in roughly the same manner.

Upon answering, Mark would hasten to explain that he was only answering the phone because his wonderful secretary was out with the flu. Since Mark had graduated law school last year and opened his solo practice, his 'secretary' had gamely battled twelve colds, five bouts of the flu, three difficult pregnancies, and a nasty case of dengue fever — a disease about which Mark knew nothing about, except that its invocation usually thwarted any further inquiries.

After offering their sympathies, each caller would explain they had seen in the national newspapers that he was the attorney handling dear Esther's estate, and wasn't her passing such an unexpected tragedy?

It was, he would agree. Esther A. Poe had lived ninety-eight years and been in poor health for nearly thirty of them. And what was your connection to Esther, he would ask.

Each caller would spin a yarn about great uncles and distant cousins and summer sojourns to the Municipal Borough of Richmond, to visit dear Esther. They each had letters or answering machine messages or, in one case, clairvoyant communications from Esther that would prove crucial for her executor.

Their timing was excellent, Mark would say, because tomorrow Esther's husband and their daughter were bringing Esther's will to a meeting in the restaurant banquet room beneath his second-floor London office. True, no client had ever set foot in his office — with its stained drop ceiling, scuffed desk, and squeaky chairs, it was perhaps just as well. He would add that, if it wasn't terribly inconvenient, they could come down to Richmond and help sort out the whole estate in a couple days.

At this juncture, responses diverged.

Most expressed dismay at such short notice, and grumbled about seeing what they could do. A few said they'd try to come and, rather unnervingly, the last caller had said: "Wouldn't miss it for the world."

*****

A few brown leaves crunched under the tires of Mark's Ford Zephyr as he drove the familiar route beneath reddening trees to his grandfather's West Chesterton manse that evening.

"I thought I'd struck gold when my old boss told me he was winding down his practice and referred me this estate," he said over their usual tumblers of rye. "I thought I'd just cut a couple cheques to her husband and kid and make a nice fee. But now all these calls... I barely passed the bar exam last year, and I didn't even take Trusts and Estates in law school. What if someone shows up to challenge the will or something? Would you sit in? In case I need help?"

His grandfather stared at the glowing hearth and sipped his whiskey, one ice cube clinking against the Waterford crystal. His other hand rested on the briarwood chess board between them, twiddling an ivory white pawn. "I'm glad to hear this isn't about money again." He pursed his lips, then continued, "But why do you still feel you need my help with these things? You know more about the law than I do."

The comment about money stung, but Mark pressed on. "Come on, you love this stuff. Remember a few years ago when you figured out it was Ms. Dorsett's nephew who burglarized her house? Even the police and that investigator she hired were stumped, but it only took you fifteen minutes with the guy to figure it out."

"I'm a psychiatrist, Mark, not a detective. Besides, this is a legal issue, and you're the big lawyer now."

"This isn't a legal issue, it's a people issue. Nobody knows how to people like you."

His grandfather sighed. "If you're going to be handling this case, you ought to read this." He reached across to the fireside bookshelf and extracted a thick, slightly dusty looking book. The spine read *Poe: Fiction and Poetry*. "Here," He handed it over to Mark. "Oh, and check, by the way."

Mark looked down at the board. His king was under attack from two directions. No matter what move he made, his grandfather's next move would be checkmate.

*****

Eight unhappy people were gathered around the Mekong Restaurant's banquet table when Mark took the carver style chair at the head of the table. He had prepared some opening remarks, but an elderly man in a rumpled navy blazer and pleated khaki slacks half way down the left side spoke first. "You're younger than we expected. What's your name again? And how do you know our attorney?"

Mark opened his battered briefcase and withdrew some documents. "I'm Mark Campbell. Your attorney Mister Runn was my internship mentor."

"Don't be rude, father. I'm sure Marius wouldn't have referred us to this nice young man if he didn't know what he was doing." This was from a middle-aged woman in a sensible two-piece tweed suit to the elderly man's right. Admonishment complete, she turned to Mark.

"I'm Simone Josephine Poe, Esther's daughter. And this," she indicated with a small flourish of her hand, "is my charming father, Arthur."

"All the same, Monie, this is serious business." He looked at the others gathered around the table. "And who the Hell are the rest of these vultures?"

"Only dear Esther's favourite cousins," sniffed a plump middle-aged woman from across the table. Squeezing the hand of the rail-thin man beside her, she glared at Arthur with unveiled contempt. "She and my husband Allan were related by blood, and she and I by love. We maintained a thriving correspondence for many years." She brandished a handful of crumpled letters addressed to *Lucille Poe*, jangling gaudy bracelets on her fat wrists in the process.

The letters were passed up the table and deposited in front of Mark. After a quick leafing through them, he confirmed that the postmarks and the stamps on the envelopes went back many years, and all corresponded roughly to the dates of the letters. Moreover, he noted, Esther's penmanship had obviously declined as the letters grew more recent, as one would expect of an aging hand. Mark made a mental note to report these observations to his grandfather.

A woman to Allan's right hacked a cough, then muttered, "Esther and I corresponded as well. Still do, in fact." At that revelation, all eyes turned to look at her, most looking confounded, taking in her frizzed hair, thick glasses, and patched overcoat. "She finds this whole situation deeply upsetting."

Mark recognized the woman from the flyers taped to every light pole on the High Street outside: *Madam Elmira – Love, Destiny, Fate – Palm, Tarot, Crystal.* The poster's looming, bespectacled visage always reminded him of an oculist's billboard.

Silence prompted Elmira to continue. "I'm a member of the American Edgar Allan Poe Society and a descendant — albeit three over and twice removed — of Granddaddy himself, which is as much as anyone else here can be. Esther and I communicated quite often on such matters until her health worsened. But now that she has moved beyond this world, her spirit speaks once more. She always had something of the gift, no doubt due to our sordid ancestry. Like Granddaddy was wont to say, the boundaries which divide life from death are at best shadowy and vague. Who shall say where the one ends, and where the other begins?"

The man to her right cleared his throat, fidgeting with a garish necktie. "Thank you, Elmira. Words to ponder. I guess it's my turn. I'm Joe Mornay from the Commonwealth of Virginia State Treasury, a proud part of the United States of America." He let that information, along with his accent, settle. Then he added, "In the unlikely event Mrs. Poe's property escheats to the Commonwealth, I'll be handling it."

"Escheats?" said Arthur. "As in poached by a US state government? Mr. Mornay, in what world would you hope to see a ha'penny of Esther's money?"

"Well, if she left bequests to any worthy state programs." Arthur huffed, but Mornay pressed on. "Or if there are no legitimate heirs this side of the Atlantic."

"You mean if we all dropped dead?" said an older man with a crooked nose. He looked up the table to where Mark was sitting. "I'm Lasker, by the way. I used to know Esther, a long time ago. She was always trying to get me to read." He barked a laugh, then drew a boiled egg from his worn black duster and began peeling it.

Mornay looked down, embarrassed, and said to the growing pile of eggshells, "Of course that's not what I'm saying. I hope I haven't offended anyone. There are simply boxes that must be checked and all that. Rote stuff."

Lasker waved a dismissive hand in Mornay's direction, looked at Arthur, and said, "Pass the salt." The condiment was several feet outside Arthur's reach.

"I'm sorry, just who do you —" Before Arthur could finish, the door opened. Mark's grandfather strode in and slid the salt shaker to the man with a deft sweep of his walking stick, scattering the eggshells. Ignoring the expectant faces around the table, he took the vacant seat next to Mark.

Stifling a laugh, Mark said, "Everyone, this is my grandfather, Dr. Campbell. He's a psychiatrist. He'll be consulting with me on this matter."

"I don't care if he's Dr. Doolittle!" exclaimed Arthur. "Can we please get on with this before the other half of Richmond barges in here? Here's Esther will. You'll find everything's in order." He slid a manila folder down the table to Mark. The typewritten document inside read, "To my beloved Arthur and Simone, I leave everything, including any claim I may have on the Edgar Allan Poe literary estate." Beneath were three signatures: Esther's and Arthur's scratched in black ink and Simone's in thick red.

Mark beamed as he scanned the will. "Thank you, Arthur, I'll get this down to the county court at once. Thank you all for stopping by, but..."

Lasker interrupted, his mouth full. "Can they really witness a will that leaves everything to them? Isn't that a conflict of interest?"

"No, I don't think so," said Mark. This was one of the few things he actually did remember from the bar exam. "Beneficiaries can witness the will."

"Hold on, hold on," said Lucille. "We've been reading up on this stuff. Allan read on a lawyer's website that if a will isn't handwritten by the person who died, the witnesses have to watch her sign it *and* sign it in front of her, too. How do we know they did that?"

"Of course we watched her sign it, you batty woman," said Arthur, reddening. "We brought it to her. And yes, we both signed it in her bedroom in front of her. She mentioned to everyone how helpful we were with the whole thing."

"Right," said Mark. "Of course. Now if we could..."

"Why different inks?" said Dr. Campbell.

Arthur looked on the verge of exploding, but Simone replied coolly, "I prefer my pen. I'm not an attorney, but I doubt everyone has to sign with the same pen."

Before Mark could agree, his grandfather cut him off again. "Not the same pen, no. But I did hear from a friend who had a devil of a time navigating probate that the witnesses must witness each other's signatures, too. So let me ask you, Arthur, did you watch Simone sign the will?"

Arthur flushed. "Well, I... I mean... Not..."

"No, he didn't," said Simone. Her tone was ice. "He left the room. I was alone with Mother when I signed it. But surely that doesn't matter?"

"I'm afraid it does in regard to English legislature," said Dr. Campbell. "Mark, could you look up English Legal Fundamentals, Code Title 64.2, Subtitle II, Chapter 4, Article 1, Section 403, subsection C?"

Mark lifted his briefcase, removed his copy of the Fundamentals, and thumbed through the tome. A moment later he stopped, read the relevant section, then said, "That's right," and adopting his quotations voice, "The witnesses have to sign together."

Arthur ran a hand through his thin hair. "So what happens to Esther's estate?"

"Intestacy," Mark muttered.

"*Intestines*?" Lucille said. Lasker snorted.

"No, intestacy," said Mark. "As in lacking a last will and testament. When someone dies without a will, the law dictates the order of inheritance. Normally everything goes to the surviving spouse."

Arthur smiled for the first time that morning. "Well, that settles it! Everything works out after all."

"What if Esther had other children? Not with him?" This was Elmira.

Leaning back down to the book and flipping forward a few pages, Mark said, "If the decedent has children with anyone other than the surviving spouse, the spouse only gets a third of the estate. The other two-thirds gets divided among the decedent's children."

"That's entirely irrelevant!" Arthur shouted. "We were married for almost sixty years, for God's sake!" He stood. "I'll be having a word with our attorney first thing tomorrow morning about you, Mr. Campbell, and perhaps the Solicitor's Standards Bar Registrars as well. This is no way to administer an estate." He turned back to address the whole of the table. "And shame on all of you, you vultures. You'll each get exactly what you deserve, make no mistake. Let's go, Monie." He stormed out of the banquet room, Simone following behind.

After an awkward pause, Lucille spoke. "So that's it, then? The whole estate is Arthur's now?"

"Not yet," said Dr. Campbell, twiddling a pen. "Under the Uniform Simultaneous Death Act, the estate doesn't transfer for five days. A would-be heir must survive the decedent by 120 hours or intestate succession just passes them by. It's a variation on a tontine."

"So in other words, hold off on playing in traffic if you stand to inherit?" said Lasker. "He'd sure like that, I bet." He thumbed Mornay. "Load us all up on a bus with bad brakes. Next thing you know, the US will be building an Edgar Allan Poe amusement park."

Mornay looking aghast, remained silent.

"That wouldn't work anyway," said Mark. "Under the slayer rule, intestate succession passes by the murderer, too."

"Mr. Lasker is right though about one thing, though," said Elmira. "Death stalks this family. Always has. I think he was a fan of Granddaddy's."

*****

A loud knock at the door the next morning startled Mark as he was brewing a pot of tea. A uniformed police officer and a plainclothes detective stood on his porch. "Mr. Campbell, you're the attorney handling Esther Poe's estate, correct?"

"Yes, yes, I am. What's going on?"

"When was the last time you saw her widower, Arthur?"

Mark blanched. "I just saw Arthur yesterday afternoon at my office. We met to discuss Esther's estate."

"That's what we thought. Mr. Campbell, Arthur was found dead last night in a booth at the Blue Beefeater steakhouse in Castleford street. We haven't gotten the toxicology report back yet, but he smelled like alcohol and cyanide. No one saw who he was with, but the bartender said he sent their table montiados, or something. It must have been a strong cocktail to mask the cyanide."

"We found these papers in his blazer pocket," said the uniformed officer, handing Mark two photocopies. "They mean anything to you?" One was a copy of the invalid will Arthur had brought to the meeting yesterday. The other read:

1. P2-K4 P-QB3 2. B-QB4 QP2-Q4 3. P4xP4/Q5 BPxP3/4Q 4. QB4-N5+ Kt(1N)-QB3   5. KKt1-KB3 QB-KKt5   6. 0-0 QRP2-R3   7. QBxQN5/6ch QNP2xB2/B3 8. P(R)-R3 B(KKt5)-R4 9. QP-Q4 KP-K3 10. QB1-K3 Q1-N3 11. P(N2)-QN3 BP-B4 12. QPxBP/B QBxPQB/QB 13. BxQB3/5B QxKB3/QB   14. N(1N)-Q2 N(N)-K2   15. Q(Q1)-K1 QBxKt4/B   16. QN2xB2/B3 QxPQB4   17. Q(1)-K5 0-0   18. QN3-Q4 Q(B7)-QB4   19. R(R)-B1 Q-QR6   20. R(QB1)-QB3 Q6xRP6/7QR   21. KR-KN3 KN2-N3 22. Q(K)-KN5 RP2-KR3 23. Q(5KN)-Kt4 PQR3-R4

24. N(Q)-QB6 R(B1)-K1   25. Kt(6QB)-K5 QxP7/6Kt   26. RxQ/QN QNxQKt/4K 27. Q(4KN)-Kt3 P(R)-QR5  28. KR3-QR3 Kt(4)-QB5 29. R(QR)-B3 RP5-QR6   30. KR1-QR1 P(R)-QR7   31. Q(KKt3)-QB7 R(K1)-QN1        32.  R(B3)-KB3  R(N)-QKt8+        33.   RxKR/QN1 RP7xKR/(Q)+ 34. K(1KN)-KR2 Q8-QKt1 35. QxQ/Kt+ WIN

The detective looked at Mark as he puzzled over the document. "Can you think of anyone who would have reason to hurt Arthur?"

*Oh yes*, Mark thought.

*****

The party assembled in the Mekong banquet room was even more dour than before. Mark had ordered lunch, but the steaming bowls went mostly untouched. Only Lasker shovelled the rice and noodles into his mouth, along with the two boiled eggs from his jacket pocket.

Arthur's chair at the table was empty. Next to it, Simone had dark circles under her puffy eyes.

Mark cleared his throat. "I thought I ought to deliver this news in person. For those who haven't heard, Arthur has died." No gasps from the table; obviously bad news travelled fast. "Simone, I think I speak for everyone when I say we're all profoundly sorry for your loss."

"Thank you. Arthur and I went our separate ways after the meeting yesterday, but I'm working with the police to determine where he went and who he was with. I'll find out who did this to my father, make no mistake. Regarding the whole inheritance mess, he left everything to me in his will, so the Poe estate will pass from him to me. The rest of you can scatter back to whatever holes you crawled out of."

"But what about the uniformed simian acting thing?" asked Lucille, her voice climbing an octave. "Didn't Dr. Campbell say nothing is really settled until five days after dear Esther's passing? Are we in danger, too?"

"Father didn't think the estate should go into intestacy at all," Simone said coldly, standing up. "I'm going to have our lawyer look at Mother's will. Don't hold your breaths for any scrap of it." She left, and the others made to follow.

Dr. Campbell held up a hand. "Lucille, Allan? Might I have a quick word?" The couple glanced at each other again, then remaining seated until the rest of the group had gone.

"Why are you both here?" Dr. Campbell asked.

Lucille looked confused. "To claim our rightful portion of dear Esther's estate, of course!"

"That's the problem," said Dr. Campbell. "Your rightful portion is nothing."

"Oh, all that legal mumbo jumbo," Lucille said, jangling her bracelets with a dismissive wave. "We've got proof Esther wanted us to inherit."

Dr. Campbell looked at her gravely. "All you've got is proof of your own greed. Your letters are fake."

"They're in Esther's own handwriting!" shrilled Lucille, one fat finger tapping the bottom of a letter. "That's her signature!"

Dr. Campbell picked up one of the envelopes, then looked at Allan. "Do you collect stamps, Mr. Poe?"

Allan's gaze was fixed on the table. Lucille flushed. "So what if he does? Loads of old codgers do."

"The stamps on these letters go back decades, as they should. Their edges are even distressed, as if an amateur tore them from a sheet. But something's wrong. When people purchase stamps, they often have leftover stamps at the end of the year. As time goes by, people collect and use a hodgepodge of outdated stamps. But your letters from Esther all bear stamps issued the year the letters were sent. That suggests the stamps on your letters were drawn not from an old woman's kitchen drawer, but from a collector's album."

Allan's eyes were closed as he drew shaky breaths. Lucille's eyes watered as she fanned herself with a tinkling hand.

"My intent is not to embarrass you," said Dr. Campbell. "Something more sinister is happening here. Where did you get Esther's handwriting, her signature?"

Lucille hesitated, then spoke through wet heaves. "When we got into town, we called around to the hotels in Richmond until we discovered Arthur had a suite at the Haverford Hotel. We went there with an elaborate plan involving Allan and a hotel porter's uniform, but luckily Arthur was already in the hotel bar drinking gin. I charmed him while

Allan slipped his room key off the bar, snuck into his suite, and photographed every scrap of paper he could find, including letters from Esther. Show them, Allan." Allan pulled some crumpled black and white photos from his back pocket and handed them to Dr. Campbell.

"But we all met early the next morning," Mark said. "How did you have time to copy so many letters?"

Lucille dabbed at her eyes, heaves diminished to sniffles. "We both worked on them through the night. I started from the beginning, Allan started from the end, and we worked toward the middle. Allan tried his best, but the old dog's got terrible penmanship."

"Who was winning?" asked Dr. Campbell, examining one of the photos.

Lucille frowned. "Winning what?"

"This chess match." Dr. Campbell tapped the photo. In the background was a chess board on the dining table, but the pieces were out of focus. "Who was winning?"

Lucille looked at him like he'd asked her the capital of Zimbabwe. Allan mumbled something inaudible. Dr. Campbell leaned forward. "What, Mr. Poe?"

"I don't play," Allan mumbled.

*****

An hour later, Mark and his grandfather were ensconced in leather armchairs in the Haverford Hotel's main foyer. A thick oriental rug covered the marble floor. Exotic ferns basked in sunlight slanting through a glass canopy three stories above. Simone emerged from behind a column and walked over to them. "Whatever you wanted to discuss, let's make it quick," she said.

"We just spoke with Lucille and her husband," said Dr. Campbell. "You may want to sit down."

He leaned forward and in a low, confidential tone, explained the couple's scheme. Simone had sunk into an armchair and now was shaking her head in disgust.

"Well, thank you for ferreting them out," she said. "Despite my bravado at our last meeting, the truth is I haven't been able to stop looking over my shoulder."

Dr. Campbell put a knobby hand over Simone's cold fingers. "You've been through a lot, my dear. If you ever need someone to talk it over with, my door is always open. Mark and I have had many a good conversation over whiskey and chess."

Simone smiled wanly. "I hate whiskey, and I hate chess."

"Oh? When did you last play?"

Simone shrugged. "I don't know, it's been ages."

"That's a pity. We had hoped you could help us with something. The police came by after they found Arthur. They asked us if we knew anything about this note they found in his coat." Dr. Campbell produced the note bearing the strange sequence. "I assume you received a copy as well. Did it mean anything to you?"

"No," said Simone. "And I already told the police that, too."

"I expected as much. Before your time. Well, at the time Arthur and I were learning to play chess, the chess world had yet to transition to the modern algebraic notation system with which you might be more familiar." He produced a heavy rollerball pen from his jacket and below the sequence wrote:

1. P2-K4 P-QB3 = 1. e4 c6

Simone stared at the note, jaw clenched.

Dr. Campbell continued. "Arthur clearly played shortly before his death, apparently as white, but the match perplexed me. Black played a textbook Caro-Kann defence, but then blundered his queen on move twenty-five. Arthur should've won. But somehow Black hung on and forced Arthur to lose his queen on move thirty-two. How could Arthur have played chess since before the modern notation system was invented and still not have learned to protect his queen?"

Simone said nothing, so Dr. Campbell went on. "Then I saw a photo Allan took in Arthur's suite which showed a chess match in progress, and I realized Arthur probably wrote the note right before his death, which might explain the amateurish mistakes. But who would Arthur have invited to his suite that night to play chess? He didn't seem to be in a socializing mood. So I'm going to ask you this again, Simone, but this time I want you to tell me the truth. When did you last play chess?"

Simone was silent for a moment longer, blue eyes drilling into Dr. Campbell's, then the ice cracked. "Last night. Listen, when it became clear Mother didn't have much time left, Father and I disagreed over how to handle the estate. He wanted to keep the money in a savings account like Esther always had. I told him we needed to *invest*. Truth be told, I needed the dividends. He refused to entertain the idea and interrogated me about my spending. Things got uglier than I think either of us intended. That's why we witnessed the will separately."

She let out a long, shaky breath. "So the evening of his death, Father came by my suite. He said he wanted to play chess, but really we talked about Mother. Her passing shook him deeply. Seeing these people show up to strip the meat off her bones was too much for him. Mr. Campbell, I've come to believe that the closer you are to someone, the less you really look at them. Maybe you think you already know them, and maybe that's usually true. But that night I looked at my father, I mean really looked at him, as you would a stranger, and I saw a grey old man, too weary to hold up his own face. My father as I knew him was gone."

Simone had been looking out across the hotel lobby as she spoke, her gaze frosted over, but now she returned her attention to Dr. Campbell. "I asked him about something that had been bothering me: Why had someone asked what would happen with the estate if Mother had other children?"

She looked at her hands resting in her lap. "He told me, 'Everyone has secrets, Monie. Your mother was no exception. She and I were married for a long time, but not our whole lives. In fact, she was already in her mid-thirties when we met. Before we married, she told me she'd been engaged to an older man, Allister Griswold, and that she'd had a son with him named Edwin. She said Allister was wicked until the day the alcohol finally took him, and the boy wasn't much better. When Edwin was fifteen, soon after his father died, he ran away. She and I met not long after. Over the years she watched the newspapers, especially the obituaries, but she never heard of him again. She was heartbroken.'"

Simone's eyes were glittering now. "When they found Father

slumped in that booth, I decided to see what I could dig up on Edwin. Come up to my room. I've got something to show you."

*****

The penthouse suite was sumptuous, certainly nicer than any hotel room Mark had ever set foot in. He looked around while Simone set about arranging various printed pages and newspaper clippings on a walnut dining table.

"I went to the library to look through the microfiche archives and found these." She indicated the printouts, photocopies of old editions of the *Richmond Gazette*. The first contained a brief obituary:

> Allister Griswold, 41, died peacefully in his home last Sunday. He is survived by his wife, Esther Griswold, and his son, Edwin Griswold.

Simone moved this one to the side and spread out the rest of the papers. Headlines announced:

*Local Boy Wins Henry Wincampton Chess Tournament*

*Richmond Youth Triumphs in Local Chess Tournament*

and

*British Prodigy Takes Top Chess Prize in Buenos Aires.*

Beneath the last headline was a black and white photograph of a smiling boy shaking hands with his opponent over a chess board. The caption read:

> Edwin Griswold, 14, takes first place in the Youth Division at the World Chess Championship in Buenos Aires, Argentina.

*****

At noon the next day, Mark, his grandfather, Lucille, Allan, Elmira, Joe, and Lasker sat around a pine table in the back room of the Fishcoteque — a fish & chip shop in the centre of Richmond. Mark had spent many slow afternoons here with other hard-working attorneys, enjoying the smell of hot food and tobacco. Local sports memorabilia and paraphernalia covered the wood-panelled walls. Today, a handmade sign reading *RVA Pieces: Richmond's Premier Chess Club* was propped on a nearby table. Patrons laughed and drank beer while concentrating on portable chess sets.

Mark spoke. "Thank you all for answering my call once again. It pains me to tell you that—"

"Where's Simone?" said Lucille. "We can't do whatever this is without her."

"Unfortunately, we've no choice," Mark said. "That's why I asked you here. Simone has been arrested. Apparently she lied when she said she hadn't seen her father since the afternoon, because someone tipped off the police that they saw them together just hours before he was killed."

"*What?*" exclaimed Lasker.

"My God," said Lucille, and Allan put out a hand to steady her.

"Karmic justice," muttered Elmira, her eyes closed, her smile serene.

"That's wonderful news!" said Mornay. When everyone turned to him, he reddened. "I mean, it's wonderful they're bringing her father's killer to justice. There's a good chance the estate escheats to the Commonwealth after all, slayer rule and all that."

"That would certainly be a boon for your great Commonwealth," said Lasker. "Who's up for drinks? I'm parched."

Joe and Elmira begged off, Joe offering awkward goodbyes, Elmira with a tranquil smile still lingering on her lips.

Lasker hardly glanced at their departure as he sized up the chess players around the pub, a lion scanning for the limping gazelle.

"Wonder if there's anyone here who's any good."

"My grandfather's pretty good," Mark said.

"No, no, only the occasional game," said Dr. Campbell.

"Come on," said Lasker. "A quid a move. Thirty quid says I beat you in thirty moves. I'll even let you go first. Grab that board over on the empty table, the rest here won't mind."

They all buzzed about Simone's arrest as the two men set up the pieces: Dr. Campbell was white, Lasker black. Dr. Campbell drew a small notebook from his jacket. "Sometimes I like recording my games. You don't mind, do you?"

"Whatever. Let's play."

Mark watched the notebook page fill as the game began.

1. e4 c6  2. Bc4 d5  3. exd5 cxd5

His grandfather paused, hand on cheek. "Stuck already?" asked Lasker, then to a passing waitress: "Hey honey, do you happen to have a jar of pickled eggs up by the counter?"

She grimaced. "Yes."

Lasker half leered back. "Well bring me a couple, they help me concentrate on my game."

4. Bb5+ Nc6  5. Nf3 Bg4  6. O-O a6

Lasker made every move without hesitating. "You know your Caro-Kann lines, I'll give you that. Maybe you were being too modest. Maybe you were trying to hustle me…"

7. Bxc6+ bxc6  8. h3 Bh5  9. d4 …

The two vinegar-loaded boiled eggs sat untouched on the paper plate next to Lasker — the sharp smell of acetic acid pungent in the air. As Lasker was studying the board, his eyes narrowed.

9. … e6  10. Be3 Qb6  11. b3 c5  12. dxc5 …

Lasker looked up at Dr. Campbell and Mark. His face burned. All pretense had evaporated. "You memorized these moves. What's this all about, you bastard?"

"Bastard," Dr. Campbell repeated, looking at him with pity. "Yes, I've memorized this game. But it's not cheating if you know the game too. We both know it ends poorly for White."

"I don't know who… But how did you… I thought Simone was…"

"Still here." Simone leaned into the doorway. Lasker and the others were dumbstruck.

"Simone, would you play black?" asked Dr. Campbell, getting up from the table. "I don't think Lasker's going to continue."

"Happily." She sat. "Are you done with these?" she asked Lasker, indicating the pickled eggs. Without waiting for an answer, she picked one up, bit it in half, and swallowed it down without chewing.

12. … Bxc5  13. Bxc5 Qxc5  14. Nbd2 Ne7

"I know it was you who tipped off the police that I was with Father the night he was murdered," Simone said to him. "No one else could have known."

15. Qe1 Bxf3  16. Nxf3 Qxc2  17. Qe5 O-O

"You didn't think anyone could place you with my father that night, but you didn't know about his little notebook, did you? It seems that sometimes, when he was playing someone he really wanted to beat, he would secretly recorded the game under the table so he could study it later to prepare for their next game."

She moved Lasker's pieces for him.

"He always used to say, 'Remember, Monie, knowledge is power, but secret knowledge is unbeatable.'"

18. Nd4 Qc5  19. Rac1 Qa3  20. Rc3 Qxa2

"I guess that was true, wasn't it? You knew something he didn't: there would be no next game. How'd you lure him to the restaurant that night? Promises? Threats?"

Lasker glared daggers at her.

21. Rg3 Ng6  22. Qg5 h6  23. Qg4 a5  24. Nc6 Rfe8

"Do you remember this moment, move twenty-five? When you lost your queen? Was that a ploy to distract my father so he wouldn't notice you slip a pill in his drink?"

25. Ne5 Qxb3  26. Rxb3 Nxe5  27. Qg3 a4

"It should've been an easy win for him after that. After all, he was up a queen. But he couldn't capitalize."

28. Ra3 Nc4  29. Rc3 a3  30. Ra1 a2  31. Qc7 Reb8

"Did you notice his focus slipping?"

32. Rf3 Rb1+

"Muscles failing?"

33. Rxb1 axb1=Q+

"You knew it wouldn't be long, so you just kept circling, waiting for him to collapse."

34. Kh2 Qb8

"Until finally he did."

35. QxB8+ WIN.

Dr. Campbell laid down the white king. "Losing his queen was the last recorded move for White. As for the final entry for Black, I had never seen someone record the end of a game that way. When I first examined the note, I assumed it was Arthur's personal shorthand for resignation, for surrender. But it wasn't. It was a gambit from the grave." He picked up his pen and wrote two more letters. Now the final entry read:

35. QxB8+ EDWIN.

Everyone stared at the page. "The false name was too cute by half," said Dr. Campbell. "Emanuel Lasker's reign as the World Chess Champion ended before I was born, but my grandfather taught me to play with his book."

Simone was livid. "Tell me something, *Edwin.* When you talked to my father, did you explain why you ran away and abandoned my mother, *your* mother? Did my father tell you she spent the rest of her life watching the papers for you? How could you disappear for fifty years, just to swoop down to her deathbed? Why were you even reading the obituaries? You know, after that first meeting, Father said to me, 'People think vultures only find carrion with their eyes, Monie, but that's not true. They can smell it, too.' I guess you used your nose."

"You think you know our mother?" Edwin spat. "You don't. And you don't know me either. You heard all about me from Arthur, didn't you? He spouted that same bullshit, all about my mother actually missing me, at the restaurant."

Mark frowned. "How did you know it was bullshit?"

Edwin glanced at Mark, moistening his lips. "I just knew Esther didn't give a damn about me, and neither did Arthur or Simone."

Now Simone was frowning. "What are you talking about? Father said Mother pined for you, and they never even told me about you."

Edwin laughed. "*Pined?* She was glad to be rid of me. I knew what she'd done, and she knew I hated her for it."

"What she'd done? To whom?"

"To Dad. To me. To our family. After what she did to him, after he was gone, I ran away. I knew it was only a matter of time before she'd do the same thing to me."

"After he was gone? Father said Allister died of alcoholism."

"He probably would have, if she had left him to his own devices. But that could take decades. Not quick enough for her. The Richmond aristocracy who had made their fortunes before the Wars always looked down their noses at our family. She agreed to marry Dad because his family had a few government connections she could leverage. She had big dreams: country clubs, debutante balls, the whole country squire special. But when it became obvious his passions lay in the tavern rather than the House of Commons, she and the rest of the clan decided marriage was out of the question."

He sighed. "Then I came into the picture, and breaking off the engagement quietly was out of the question, too. That only left one solution. One night, I saw her make him a drink, a whiskey sour with egg white froth, his favourite. She never did that. The next morning, he was still in his armchair. I thought he'd passed out there like usual, but when I shook him, his arm was cold, and he didn't wake up. The police never did an autopsy. He was a notorious drunk. And she couldn't stand to look at me after that. She said I reminded her of Dad, and that it made her sad. I don't think that was quite true. I think I reminded her of what she'd done, and what I could do to her and the family if I ever told anyone. Now that she's dead, her money belongs to me. It's the least she can do."

Simone was shaking her head. "She never said a word about any of that to me, nor to Father. My God. All those years."

"I didn't believe Arthur when he told me she tried to find me," Edwin said, "but I guess he was telling what he thought was the truth. She really had you both fooled, that bitch."

Mark frowned again, pursing his lips. "I still don't understand why you're so sure Esther still secretly hated you, her only son, after fifty years... Unless..." He looked wide-eyed at his grandfather. "What drinks did that police detective say their table ordered at the restaurant the night Arthur died?"

"Montiados," said Dr. Campbell slowly.

"Right," said Mark. "At the time I thought that sounded strange. I know my way around a bar, and I'd never heard of a montiado. Have you, Edwin?"

Edwin licked his lips again and said nothing.

"My grandfather gave me a collection of Edgar Allan Poe's fiction and poetry when this case started, and I've been making my way through it ever since. Guess which story I read last night. I'll give you a hint: an insulted man entices a fortunate friend to his death with the promise of a rare sherry."

His grandfather was grinning. "The Cask of Amontillado."

"That's the one," Mark said. "Arthur didn't drink a 'montiado,' he drank *amontillado*. But you would never have ordered that, Edwin. You said yourself Esther was always trying to get you to read. And Arthur probably wouldn't have ordered it either. Lucille, didn't you say Arthur was drinking gin at the hotel bar when you and Allan stole his room key?"

"Yes, he was!" exclaimed Lucille. "And he had several more bottles in his room!"

"Exactly," said Mark, rising to his feet. "Edwin, before you poisoned Arthur, someone had already been poisoning you, against Esther and her new family. You weren't alone with Arthur at the restaurant that night, were you? Someone else was there, probably to make sure the job was done right. A devotee of Poe who would've seen the 'karmic justice' in having you mix the cyanide into amontillado to mask the flavour."

Dr. Campbell stood up, leaning on his cane. "You'll have to answer for what you've done, Edwin, but you're not the only one. Let's go, Mark."

*****

Mark and his grandfather parked on Main Street in front of the Aquarian Bookshop. Mark pretended to browse shelves filled with crystals, incense, and tarot cards. Dr. Campbell approached the pierced and tattooed waif at the counter.

"Excuse me, miss. My grandson and I are looking for a medium, Elmira. We heard she sometimes uses the room above this shop. Have you seen her?"

The girl's eyes widened. "No, no, she's not here."

Suddenly from the back of the store there was a cascade of shattering.

Mark rushed to the back and pushed open a metal door into a dingy stairwell, his grandfather close behind. His shoes crunched on a sea of crystal shards. A cardboard box filled with more crystals propped open an exit door. At the top of the stairs stood Elmira, hands still outstretched. Her eyes bulged from behind her thick glasses when she saw Mark. He could almost hear her mental gears whirring, then something clicked into place and her expression settled into equanimity.

"Mark, Dr. Campbell. Come upstairs, and please mind the glass. I can be so clumsy. My mind is always elsewhere."

Mark and his grandfather exchanged a glance, then picked their way up the stairs. "I hope those crystals weren't valuable," Dr. Campbell said.

"They were only tools," said Elmira. "Sometimes tools break."

Dark velvet curtains caressed Mark's arms and neck like cobwebs causing him to shiver as he entered Elmira's room. The only light sputtered from rows of stumpy candles, illuminating stacks of musty books, many with "Poe" on the spine. The smell of incense was stifling. Following Elmira's lead, Mark and his grandfather seated themselves around a small circular table draped in more velvet.

"We're here to ask you about Arthur's death," said Dr. Campbell.

"A tragedy," said Elmira.

"Drop the act," Mark said. "We know you were at the restaurant the night he died. Why?"

Elmira began idly stroking a crystal shard she had collected from the landing. Its jagged edge twinkled in the candlelight. "Edwin came to me when he read of Esther's passing. He was troubled. He told me what his mother had done to his father. He told me he had hated her, that he had feared what she might do to him, an inconvenient bastard, that he ran away. He had heard she remarried and had another child, but he knew little of them. He wanted to know what she thought of him, what Arthur and Simone thought of him, but with her passing, he could no longer speak to her. So he came to me."

"What did you tell him?" Mark asked.

"First I told him our family's history. Granddaddy was abandoned too, you know, by his father in life and then his mother by her death. These things repeat, you know. Then I told him how Esther despised him and feared him, and how she imparted those feelings to her new husband and their new daughter. How the three of them laughed at his expense, secure in their family and fortune."

"Those were lies," said Mark. "I'm guessing you told him the fortune ought to be his, too."

"Of course not," said Elmira, her voice growing discordant, shrill. "That's what he told me. Anything Edwin may have done rests with him, not me."

"A jury may not agree with such a generous assessment of your culpability," said Dr. Campbell. "After you showed up at the first meeting, we checked into you. Your landlord says you are months behind on rent. I'm sure siphoning a hefty percentage of the Poe estate from Edwin would have solved a lot of your problems."

Mark cut in. "The only sound you heard when you rubbed those crystals to 'commune with Esther' was the whirr of an ATM. Psychics, mediums, fortune-tellers, you're all scavengers. You prey on the vulnerable, and you don't stop until you've sucked the marrow from their bones."

"There won't be a jury," said Elmira. Her expression was haughty now, her tone ugly.

Just then the shop door downstairs banged open. Mark heard beads from the screen scattering across the floor. Men were shouting. Red and blue lights flashed through the dark curtains.

Elmira ignored the din. "Granddaddy said the boundaries between life and death are shadowy and vague, but he was wrong. When he asked who can say where one ends and the other begins, I told him we all can." She dug the crystal shard into her left wrist and tore downward. A stream of hot red blood flowed down her sallow fingers and trickled to the floor, staining the faded rug an even darker brown.

*****

The group which gathered in the Mekong Restaurant's banquet room the next day now numbered only three, but this time the only food left untouched was a bowl of fish ball soup at the head of the table. According to Simone, it had been Arthur's favourite Vietnamese dish. Without the two of them, she had said, eyes resolutely dry, she might be the one going to prison instead of Edwin, and Arthur wouldn't have received the justice he deserved. Anything she could ever do for them, she would. Now she had gone, and Mark was staring absently at Arthur's empty chair.

"One day that'll be me, Mark," said his grandfather. "I won't always be around to help you." Mark looked at him, really looked at him, for the first time in a long time. His face was more tired than Mark had ever seen. Deep lines furrowed his forehead and eyes. But then Mark thought about where the creases had come from: big laughs, wry smirks, and kind smiles. It was a face well lived in.

"That's not true," Mark said, resting a hand on his arm. "When I need to say the right thing, I'll think about what you'd say. When I need to do the right thing, I'll think about what you'd do. You'll always be around to help me."

His grandfather smiled and patted his hand, then laughed as he rose to his feet. "Besides, I'm not dead yet, am I? You may have solved this case, but I can still beat you in chess. Only when that ceases to be the case do you have permission to put me in the ground."

"Deal," said Mark, getting up as well. "Hey, would you come up to my office? I know it's not much now, but with the money from Simone I think I can finally afford some decent furniture, maybe even hire a secretary."

"Sure," his grandfather said as they exited the restaurant and turned toward Mark's adjacent door. "In fact, I'm still one step ahead of you. I hope you don't mind me getting the renovation started." On the glass door, freshly lettered in white vinyl, were the words "Mark Campbell, Esq."

# *Murder at St. Bott's*
## *Madeleine McDonald*

"Drink up, Pam, old girl. It's medicinal."

The elderly gentleman returned the hip flask to the pocket of his battered Barbour jacket and watched his companion blink in surprise as she obediently swallowed her tea. She shook her head slightly to clear it.

"Snifter of brandy," he explained. "You're in shock, and I don't blame you. Luckily, I went fishing at first light this morning, and I always take a flask with me. He patted his capacious pockets.

"Thank you, Peter. I don't normally drink in the daytime, but in this case…" Her voice trailed off. Although colour returned to her cheeks, her features remained rigid with distaste. "Without wishing to sound unChristian—"

Peter snorted. "Be as unChristian as you like. She's an appalling woman. What was the bishop thinking?"

"I know he's in favour of this happy clappy nonsense, but that's no reason to inflict it on St Botolph's."

"Agreed." Peter warmed to his favourite theme. "If the Church of England is to survive in this heathen world, some of us must take a stand. Horatius keeping the bridge and all that." He paused, for Pam looked puzzled. That was the trouble with women, they were dear souls but most of them lacked a proper education. In his heart of hearts, Peter still deplored the appointment of women priests, but he had to tread carefully among his fellow churchwardens, all female, all of whom displayed a regrettable enthusiasm for that particular revolution. He rephrased his opinion. "The church has stood for 2000 years. There's no point indulging every passing fad."

*****

Earlier that day, the meeting to welcome the new vicar of St Botolph's had been a disaster. Despite the sunshine outside, the interior of the church was chilly, and the half dozen elderly churchwardens had shifted uncomfortably on the hard oak pews for almost an hour. Only Rachel Matthew, a newly retired teacher, appeared outwardly unconcerned. She busied herself doing a Sudoku puzzle on her phone, but since logic was her forte and she never made mistakes, she finally pocketed the phone with a shrug of annoyance at the delay.

The door flew open. "G'day, everyone." The speaker was tall and athletic, with purple streaks in her cropped hair. She wore black trousers and, instead of a dog collar, a plain, black polo-neck top. The only sign of her calling was a heavy silver cross that bounced on her broad, lean bosom as she strode in. "Sorry I'm late. I got stuck behind a humungous tractor, and your English roads won't let me overtake. I tried leaning on the horn, but the drongo wouldn't pull over."

There was a stunned silence, before Pamela pulled herself together. "Well, you're here now. Nice to meet you, vicar. I'm Pamela Hart."

The newcomer waved a greeting to all instead of taking Pamela's outstretched hand. She moved a pile of embroidered kneelers, plumped down on the end of a pew and stretched her legs out. In the light from a stained glass window, her hair turned blood red. "Let's get one thing straight, right off. Don't call me vicar. I mean, it's sort of sweet and English and old-fashioned, but the name's Toni, as in Antoinette. You can call me Reverend Toni."

Under his breath, Peter muttered, "Good Lord, deliver us."

Reverend Toni steamrollered on. "The new vicar of St Bott's, at your service."

"St Botolph's," came a frosty correction.

"Well, who was he? Some medieval hermit guy, I've read. St Bott's sounds more modern. Catchy." The Australian accent made the last word sound like ketchup.

Pamela found her voice again. "Vicar" — she laid emphasis on the title — "I understand you've been at St Jude's since you arrived in England. I think you will find that here at St Botolph's we do things differently."

"St Botolph's dates back to the 12th century. Well, parts of it do. Our green man carvings are mentioned in Pevsner." That was Miriam Ashford, her voice stiff with pride. She had written the leaflet for visitors, available at the entrance for 50p. Unfortunately too many visitors failed to put 50p in the box, and the dog-eared leaflets were left at the entrance again.

"You've lost me there. Green man? Pevver?" Reverend Toni flung her hands wide. Her cross bounced in sympathy.

"And that just proves our point." Unlike Miriam, Peter was tetchy. "No disrespect to St Jude's, but it's a square box plonked on the edge of a modern housing estate. And they have plastic chairs."

"Whatever. My priority is bums on seats, whether the seats are plastic or wood. The bishop has sent me here because I gee'd up St Jude's parish. If we're going to Spread the Word, we need bums on seats. OK?"

She cut short the murmurs of protest. "Look, I don't want to hurry you guys, but that tractor held me up, and I've got to be back at St Jude's for six o'clock. We'll have a proper get-to-know-you next time."

She strode to the door, blood red streaks of hair turning purple again, and heels clacking on the stone floor. Just before she reached it, she almost tripped on an uneven slab, leaned down and hoicked up a trouser leg to reveal black boots with stiletto heels. "Bugger me!" the shocked churchwardens heard, "I've torn the hem." The heavy oak door thudded shut behind her.

*****

"I hope she falls over and breaks a leg. Fancy a vicar wearing ridiculous heels like that."

The tearoom was empty now. Peter had topped up their cups with a brandy snifter a couple more times, which loosened their tongues. However, when they bade each other goodbye they were no nearer a plan of campaign to oust the appalling Antoinette.

"The others won't be much help," Peter concluded. "Miriam is a mouse, and Rachel is always staring at her phone. It will be up to you and me, Pamela."

Even the thought that the Reverend Toni would be with them for only six months, since she was in England on some kind of international exchange scheme, was no consolation.

*****

Miriam was next in the line of fire. One morning, it being her turn to sweep and dust, she unlocked the door only to be confronted by a large easel bearing a poster for new Bible classes. Round the edge were pinned leaflets advertising family holidays at a local camp site. The little pile of dog-eared information leaflets had vanished.

"No worries, Mimi." Reverend Toni had breezed in behind her. "It's all on the website now."

"A website!" Miriam blinked back tears. "I spent hours on those leaflets. I double-checked everything in the parish records."

"What is your problem, Mimi?" Seeing Miriam's distress, she continued in gentler tones. "Look, I know how important all this ancient history is to you. Your little green men, and your Norman arches, and your rood screen, and whatever whatever. History has its place, I agree, so long as it doesn't get in the way of real life. I made sure you got a special page on the website."

Miriam ignored the olive branch and Reverend Toni huffed. "Don't you see, Miriam. It's vital we bring the church into the 21$^{st}$ century. Make it part of the community." She unpinned a leaflet and thrust it at Miriam. "I'm sure you know our new converts Mr and Mrs Fowler from Lane End Farm. If we put business their way, they will make a small donation to St Bott's for every family who shows one of these leaflets when they book a holiday." She beamed. "It's a win win situation."

*****

"Moneychangers in the temple," Peter exploded, when Miriam reported the latest outrage. Without Toni, the churchwardens convened in the local tearoom for warmth and comfort. "It was bad enough when she introduced those hymns that sound like nursery rhymes." The others nodded in sympathy, for the vicar had sacked the organist, dear old Mr Rutland, and replaced him with recorded music of her own choosing.

*****

Matters came to a head a month later. Regrettably, St Botolph's former parish hall, next door to the church, had been sold two decades earlier to raise much needed funds for the restoration of the church itself. A young couple had turned it into a residence with period features.

Since then the dwindling and cash-strapped congregation had been obliged to rent the Methodist church hall for various organised activities a couple of times a week. Neither congregation liked the arrangement, for the old distrust between church and chapel lingered. Needs must, however, and Peter Stone had – with some difficulty – negotiated a reduction on the usual hourly fee for use of the Methodist hall.

This being an official meeting, vicar and churchwardens met in the church.

Peter opened the hostilities. "Let me get this straight. You want to buy yoga mats out of the funds earmarked for the restoration of the spire. Vicar, that is illegal. Let me assure you, the restoration fund is ring-fenced. It is kept in a separate building society account."

"I sense a lot of negativity in your reply. Mr Stone, I'm sure you do a great job as treasurer, but there must be a way for St Bott's to afford repairs to the spire *and* yoga mats."

Rachel finished a Sudoku puzzle and made a contribution to the conversation. "What's wrong with the lino in the Methodist hall? It's in good condition."

"And it's easy to clean," Miriam Ashford sniffed. "We make sure to tidy up after all our activities, you know. We don't want *them* criticising us."

"Yes, but we don't want people to get cold, do we? Tums and Bums for Busy Mums has been a great success at St Jude's. We push the chairs back, put some music on, and the younger mums do the exercises, and a couple of the older ones look after the ankle-biters. Now, no offence meant, how about some of you grandmas volunteer for kiddie-minding?

"Certainly not. At St Botolph's we worship with dignity," Miriam squawked.

"The whole scheme is outrageous," Peter spluttered. "I shall write to the bishop."

"Go ahead, Mr Stone. You'll find the bishop agrees with me. I signed up four new families thanks to Tums and Bums."

The churchwardens could only stare in dismay.

Reverend Toni shuffled her papers. "Now, next item on the agenda, the harvest festival. It's a chance to reach out to the community and increase our footfall. Instead of fruit and flowers, same old, same old, I found a box of these cute little windmills on sticks in the garden centre." In a metallic clatter, she hefted a box from the pew beside her and dumped it on the floor. "They spoke to me. Windmills. Wind. And what do we have on our doorstep? A wind farm."

"Those monstrosities."

"Saving the planet, that'll pull in the greenies. And guess what, I've found out the wind farm was an airfield back in the war. Wartime memories; that'll pull in the oldies. We can decorate the church with flags. The Aussie flag too, don't forget.

"As if we could."

"I will ignore that remark, Mr Stone. Moving on, we can hand out these cute windmills to the ankle biters. See." Her finger sent one of the windmills spinning. "It's so important for the church to catch 'em young."

"I've had enough. That is not a toy. It is a garden ornament. Quite unsuitable for small children."

"Mrs Hart, Pamela, stop. No, everyone, stop. You can't leave. We haven't finished the agenda. Stop. I say!" Reverend Toni blocked the aisle, windmill to the fore, a lone Horatia keeping the bridge against the Etruscan horde. As she took a step towards them, her heel caught on a stone slab. She stumbled, almost losing her balance.

A hand seized the windmill. The metal spike found its target.

"Bugger me!" were Reverend Toni's last words on this earth.

*****

The police could make neither head nor tail of what had happened, apart from the fact that the Reverend Antoinette Hedley lay dead, skewered through the heart with the metal spike of a windmill. She lay in a pool of blood amid a scattering of similar garden ornaments. There were no usable fingerprints on the spike, because the paramedics had touched it when attempting to staunch the wound.

Yet the first witness to be interviewed, a Mrs Pamela Hart, readily admitted her guilt.

"I did it, and I'm not sorry." Her face glowed with the fervour of the early Christian martyrs. "Officer, Divine Providence placed the weapon in my hands. One does not reject Divine Providence. I shall plead guilty and take my punishment."

The trouble was that each and every one of the witnesses present then claimed responsibility for the act. Some in calm, measured tones. Some with an edge of impatience.

None of the churchwardens buckled under pressure. Forty eight hours later, the inspector in charge decided that the best solution was to declare the vicar's death a tragic accident. He allowed himself the satisfaction of arresting all the churchwardens for wasting police time.

# *The Big Dig*

## *Edward Lodi*

Arlene Winters received few visitors. When she heard a car pull into the driveway she left her knitting on the recliner by the flame effect gas fire and went to the living room window. Parting the curtains, she peered out and was delighted to see two figures emerge from a black Ford Mondeo.

"Plainclothes police, Whiskers," she said, excited.

As the occupants got out, Arlene saw that the passenger was a well-dressed black woman, and her partner-driver was a much taller Asian man, who was carrying a briefcase. After making sure the car was locked, they both strode up the driveway, then paused for several seconds at the front door, as if composing themselves. Arlene waited for their knock, paused for several seconds so as not to seem too eager, then answered the door.

"Mrs. Winters?" the woman asked.

In her mid-thirties, she was about five feet one, shorter even than Arlene, who stood five feet two in her stocking feet. She was too petite to be a police officer, Arlene thought. But then, what did she know about such matters? Her tall companion, perhaps a decade younger, had the build of someone who worked out regularly. Not someone you'd like to mess with in a confrontation—not that Arlene had any intention of doing such a thing. Well, not at her age.

Arlene cleared her throat, then said, "Yes, I'm Arlene Winters."

The woman flashed a badge. "Inspector Pinkney. This is Sergeant Ahn. We're with the Metropolitan Police. May we come in?"

"Why, yes." Arlene stepped aside so they could enter. "I've got the fire going. It may be April, but it feels like March." She pointed to a sofa facing the fireplace. "Make yourselves comfortable."

Pinkney and Ahn remained standing.

Arlene set her knitting aside and sank into the well-worn leather recliner — once her husband's favourite chair, it now belonged exclusively to her. "Are you collecting for the Policeman's Fund? I thought I gave already, but maybe that was last year."

Inspector Pinkney smiled. "Thank you for your contribution, Mrs. Winters, but we're here on a different matter. We want to look at your back garden."

Arlene's face took on a puzzled expression. "Why on earth do you want to do that? There's nothing to see. It's overgrown with weeds, briars, Deadly Nightshade — all sorts of unpleasant things. I think I saw a giant hogweed close to the back fence." She paused, thoughtful, then, "Or maybe it's Japanese Knotweed..." She shrugged her shoulders dismissively. "The only one who uses it is Whiskers."

"Whiskers?" Ahn asked.

"My cat." She pointed to an overweight Persian Blue, regally stretched out before the hearth. "I let him out at night. He likes to hunt, though of course he can't go far because of the fence."

"If you don't mind we'd still like to see the back garden," Pinkney said.

Arlene got up from the recliner. "Follow me. Whoa, not you, Whiskers!"

She led the officers through the kitchen to the back door, which she unlatched and swung open. She left the screen door in place. "I don't want Whiskers scooting out," she explained. "I'd have to comb him afterwards for burrs and ticks."

While Mrs. Winters stood guard behind them, a slightly impatient Pinkney opened the mesh door and, followed by Ahn, stepped outside.

"Keep an eye out for ticks," Arlene yelled after them. "And the briars, they'll trip you up given half a chance." She stood in the doorway and watched as they crossed the small clearing at the foot of the backdoor steps and contemplated the tangle of vegetation that confronted them.

"Bigger than I expected," she heard Inspector Pinkney remark.

"This isn't going to be easy," Ahn agreed.

They returned to the house. Once inside, Inspector Pinkney said to

Arlene, "We have a few questions we'd like to ask."

"How exciting!" Arlene exclaimed. "I've never been interrogated by the police. Are you hauling me off to New Scotland Yard, or wherever it is these days?"

Pinkney smiled. "Your living room will do. And this is not an interrogation, Mrs. Winters. Just a few questions. We'll only take a moment of your time."

This time she and Ahn sat on the sofa. Arlene offered to brew a pot of tea but they declined. As Ahn opened his briefcase and took out a pencil and pad of paper Arlene went to the fireplace, bent down slightly, and adjusted the gas so the flames barely flickered above the imitation pieces of coal. Finally satisfied, and disregarding Whiskers' stare of indignation, she sank into her recliner.

"Mrs. Winters, how long have you lived at this address?" Inspector Pinkney asked.

"About thirty years. No, tell a lie. Thirty-one, to be exact."

Ahn raised his eyebrows and glanced at his boss.

"What was the back garden like when you moved in?" Pinkney asked.

Arlene shrugged. "Just an ordinary back garden I suppose. A bit of grass, concrete path down to the bottom. Cement washing line down there as well…."

"What condition was it in? Overgrown like now?"

"Well, it was winter when Jack and I put the deposit down on the house. Everything was covered with snow. Jack used to look after it, but after a while he seemed to lose interest." She glanced at a framed photograph on the mantelpiece of a bearded man in his late fifties. "That's his picture."

"Where's Jack now?"

Arlene frowned. "He left me a couple of months ago — for a younger woman."

"I'm sorry to hear that, Mrs. Winters." After a tactful pause she asked: "Do you know his current address? We may want to contact him."

"I don't know where he's gone off to. Hell, I hope."

Inspector Pinkney nodded her understanding, then asked: "Can you describe what the yard looked like before? When the snow melted?"

"It was so long ago, Inspector. I really don't recall. We were a very traditional couple. My place was always in the home. Jack did all the DIY repairs and the gardening."

"Can you remember whether there was any sign of recent digging?"

Arlene brought her hand up to her mouth. "Goodness! Is there a body buried out back? Why else would you be asking such questions?"

"We don't know for sure, but it's possible," Inspector Pinkney admitted.

"What makes you think so? When Jack and I bought the place we were told that the previous owners were two elderly sisters. When one died the other moved into a rest home." Arlene tilted her head slightly to one side. "Surely they weren't like the old ladies in *Arsenic and Old Lace*? Poisoning people and burying them in the cellar? Or in the back garden?"

Sergeant Ahn allowed a chuckle to escape.

Instead of answering, Inspector Pinkney rubbed the side of her nose as if contemplating her next move. Finally she said: "Mrs. Winters, I'm going to confide in you. But only if you promise not to reveal to anyone what I'm about to tell you."

"Goodness," Arlene exclaimed, clasping her hands together. "A secret! Of course you have my word. Anyhow, who would I confide in, other than Whiskers?"

At his name, the cat paused licking one of its paws, looked contemptuously at its audience, then went back to washing itself.

"Three days ago we received a letter in the mail," Pinkney explained. She turned to Ahn. "Sarge."

Ahn removed a paper from his brief case and brought it over to Arlene. "This is a photocopy," he said.

Hands trembling, Arlene read the typewritten script:

> Thirty-two years ago I committed the perfect crime. I killed my wife.
>
> I got away with murder.

Why did I kill my wife? That is my concern, not yours.

So, what is the purpose of this letter? To confess, and in confessing assuage a guilty conscience? To repent of my sins? To seek forgiveness? To throw myself at the mercy of the courts?

Hardly. My conscience is clear. I have no regrets for what I did. I would gladly kill again, and again, *ad infinitum* should the need arise.

I have been diagnosed with a fatal disease. I don't have long to live. At most a year. To amuse myself before I die, to occupy my time, I want to play a game, a game of cat and mouse.

The rules of the game are simple: I reveal to you the location of my wife's remains. You, through forensic evidence, attempt to discover my identity.

I don't think you'll be able to do so. But who knows? I may be wrong.

*The body of my wife lies somewhere in the back yard of the house at 176 Wood St.*

I'm sorry that I cannot more precisely pinpoint the location. After all, it's been thirty-two years since I did away with the thorn in my side and buried her on a moonless night, with only a flashlight to guide me.

I can tell you this: the digging was rough. The ground was so hard and riddled with stones that I needed a pickax as well as a shovel.

This is the last you will hear from me. Have fun!

Signed: Catch Me If You Can.

Arlene read the letter twice, then handed it back to Ahn. "I don't know," she mused. "Don't you think someone's playing a prank?"

"That's possible, of course," Pinkney said. "But my gut tells me it's genuine. Obviously the writer is educated. Not many people these days use Latin phrases."

"There are educated fools," Arlene pointed out.

"True," Pinkney agreed. "But tell me: is the ground out back 'hard and riddled with stones'?"

Arlene pursed her lips. "Jack always said the soil was boney."

Pinkney and Ahn exchanged glances. "Boney?"

"It's an expression he always used to use, meaning the soil has a lot of stones in it."

"Oh," Pinkney said, disappointed. "So he didn't find any actual bones?"

"If he did, he never told me."

"Even so, from what you say, the ground in your back yard is how our friend Catch Me If You Can described it." She sat thinking, then said: "Is that offer of tea still valid?"

"Why yes," Arlene said, delighted. "I'll get it going right now. This is exciting. Whiskers and I hardly ever have visitors." She rose from the recliner. "Whiskers, stay put. It's not mealtime yet."

The cat gave her another glare, then purposefully rolled onto his side, so his belly was close to the fire.

To pass the time while Arlene was busy in the kitchen brewing tea Ahn went to the hearth, bent down and held out a hand to stroke Whiskers. The Persian repaid his ministrations with bristled fur and a hiss. Ahn beat a hasty retreat back to the relative safety of the sofa.

Arlene returned shortly with a pot of tea, milk and sugar, cups and saucers, and an assortment of biscuits neatly arranged on a plate. "They're homemade," she informed Ahn when she saw the Sergeant eyeing them. "I'm doing some for the local W.I."

"Delicious," he said as, polishing off an oatmeal-and-raisin, he reached for a chocolate-chip.

"Very nice," the Inspector agreed, taking a bite. Setting the unfinished biscuit aside she said: "Mrs. Winters, I won't beat around the bush. We'd like to dig up your back garden."

"Dig it up?" Arlene appeared taken aback. "But you can't do that! It's where Whiskers hunts. He needs the exercise. Look how fat he is."

The cat didn't even deign to look at her, just inhaled, then deliberately exhaled noisily in a disgusted huff.

Pinkney tried again. "We can't just ignore the letter."

"Well, I think it's a hoax. It looks like it was composed on a computer, so I imagine it's difficult if not impossible to trace. I assume there weren't any fingerprints."

"Unfortunately there weren't. But—"

"No," Arlene said emphatically. "If you want to dig up my property then you'll have to obtain a warrant. Or whatever it's called."

Inspector Pinkney spent the next ten minutes trying to win Arlene over. But her attempts proved futile. Arlene remained adamant. No one was going to do any digging, least of all in her back garden.

Pinkney tried a different tact: "I'll be honest with you, Mrs. Winters. I tried to obtain a warrant and failed. 'Insufficient cause.'" She paused. "However…the Town has certain funds. I've been authorized to offer a limited amount of landscaping to repair the damage once we've finished digging. Nothing fancy of course: a few shrubs, perennials, some flagstones for a new pathway. Re-turf everything as well."

"Grass? Over my dead body! Oops." Arlene brought her hand to her mouth. "A poor choice of words. But you catch my drift, I'm sure. I don't have the time or the energy to pamper a lawn. Besides, Whiskers needs bare ground in order to do his business."

"No grass then. A few extra shrubs instead. Mrs. Winters, do we have a deal? I'm sure you don't want to go to bed at night thinking some unfortunate woman may be buried beneath your window."

"Give me a moment to think." Then, "Where are my manners — more tea? Inspector? Sarge?"

By the time she'd finishing pouring, Arlene had come to a decision. "I'll agree," she said, "so long as you promise to cart away any big stones before planting gets underway.

Pen and ink amendments made to the official document, Pinkney and Ahn obtained a signature and left shortly afterwards. Arlene watched through parted curtains as the Ford Mondeo backed out of her driveway and headed off.

"I told you my plan would work, Whiskers. They took the bait."

*****

And so it came to pass that two weeks from that very day, after the mini-digger, wheelbarrows, and what seemed like an army of Police Officers with spades and the like had done their worst, the landscapers had arrived. They set about cleaning up the chaos left by the Metropolitan Police, and once everything was made whole again they had also taken their departure, leaving Whiskers to suspiciously investigate the newly furbished yard in which he could once again hunt and 'do his business.'

As Arlene stood at her back door admiring the shrubs and perennials, fresh from the nursery and already beginning to bloom, Inspector Pinkney and Sergeant Ahn were back at the station sharing a pepper-and-onion pizza and discussing the case. No skeletal remains had been found.

Pinkney frowned. "Dammit Sarge, she played us for a pair of suckers."

Ahn wiped tomato sauce from the corners of his mouth with a paper napkin. "How do you mean, boss? It wasn't her idea to dig up the yard in the first place. She was dead set against it."

"Oh was she? Think about it, Sarge. Like 'Catch Me If You Can,' she comes across as educated. She could have written that letter herself."

"True, but—"

"And she knew the soil was 'boney.'"

"That in itself doesn't prove anything."

"Then what about this? She mentioned that she hardly ever gets visitors. So how did she happen to have two dozen homemade cookies on hand? For the Women's Institute? Did you notice she didn't eat any herself? She was expecting us!"

"But why would she pull a prank like that. To make us look like fools?"

Pinkney shook her head. "No. She did it to save herself the three or four thousand pounds it would've cost her to landscape her back yard."

Ahn, eying up the last slice of pizza, stopped in mid-reach. "And here I am thinking she's a sweet old lady."

⁂

It is unfortunate that the two homicide detectives were not privy to the conversation—albeit one-sided—that Arlene Winters had later that evening with her cat over a glass of sherry.

"Just think, Whiskers. Now I can bring Jack up from the cellar. You'll have to help me find a nice spot out back where I can tuck him in. The soil is soft now and easy to dig, and he'll be safe there. No one will ever think to dig up the garden a second time."

# *Everything Money Can Buy*
## *Michaele Jordan*

"Why!?! How can you ask?" demanded Regina, tossing back her head with its beautifully coifed golden curls so forcefully her diamond earrings bounced and flashed. "Because I'm a decent person, of course! I can't abide animal cruelty!"

"My apologies, Ma'am," gasped Howie in a tremulous whisper, cowed by her fury, but even so, unable to risk a glance down at the lush maroon leather sofa on which they sat and around the room to the ivory Buddha adorning the mantel and the chinchilla coat tossed over a chair.

She caught his glance and her mouth tightened. For a moment he thought she was going to hit him with her riding crop (which, like her riding boots, was leather). But she controlled herself. She paused to breathe deeply, to lay the whip down and to remove her riding jacket. The blouse beneath was watered silk.

"I live in the real world," she admitted, albeit somewhat coldly. "I make some compromises. I eat meat. I wear leather." She glanced toward the coat, "I even wear fur." She sighed and slumped. "God help me, I do love fur." Then she raised her head defiantly. "But I purchase everything—my meat, my eggs and milk, my leather—from cruelty-free farms." She glared at Howie. "And I have personally visited these farms to verify they are genuinely cruelty free."

"Cruelty free slaughter houses?" Howie was so startled by the concept that he forgot to cower. He was also distracted from his fear by a pretty little Latina in a maid uniform, who darted out from the bedroom to kneel before Regina and start unbuttoning her jodhpurs.

Regina ignored the servant, but Howie stared so hard that he almost missed Regina's reply. "You've probably never heard of those. They're rare. The animals are lulled to sleep and killed quickly while still unconscious. I don't suppose there are more than a half dozen in the country. The Japanese are far more sensitive in such matters."

"Really?" The pants were unbuttoned and Regina lifted a foot so the maid could tug off the boot and slide the jodhpurs free. "I thought the Japanese prided themselves on …Well, toughness, blade skills, all that martial stuff." The maid set the jodhpurs aside and half rose to unbutton the silk blouse.

"They are martial ARTISTS," explained Regina. "They pride themselves on the exquisite refinement of their blade work. Also on their superb Kobe beef—the best in the world. Their master chefs believe that fear hormones can affect the taste of the meat. So they provide their beasts with a fear free, pain free end."

Rising, she shrugged out of the blouse and, dressed only in lacy under-things, turned toward the bedroom door. "Stay for lunch. We have much to discuss after my bath." As she walked toward the door, the maid ran up behind her to unclasp the bra, which fell free. Then she was gone, leaving Howie to gaze after her, and the maid to pick up the scattered clothing. He did gaze a long time. She had the loveliest body he'd ever seen in person, even if she was just as inaccessible as a movie star.

*****

"It shouldn't be all that complicated," said Regina, gesturing in the air with her fork (real silver, not stainless steel). She paused to sip from the Waterford crystal glass holding her iced tea, and the little Latina appeared magically at her elbow to refill the glass as soon as she put it down. "You already know a lot of the people in the field, right?" Regina slid the fork back into her spinach and Gorgonzola quiche.

The quiche filled its ramekin so perfectly that Howie couldn't see the pattern on the china, but the salad bowl beside it was Wedgewood Hibiscus. Howie knew it was Wedgewood Hibiscus because his sister had drooled over one just like it for an hour when he took her to register for wedding china. Not that she'd registered for it. Nobody she knew could have afforded to give her Wedgewood Hibiscus.

"Actually, I don't know anybody in the field. I'm not sure there even is such a field." A voice at the back of Howie's mind was begging him to play along with Regina. She was so very rich. She was willing to pay so very much. He still hadn't paid off his vet school loans. But he knew he wasn't a good enough liar to pull it off. "I've never heard of a snow leopard ranch."

"Well, of course not. There isn't one—yet. That's what I'm saying. I want you to start one. I've even got the land already. About twenty-five thousand acres on the Knoydart peninsula. You think that's enough? I figure if we provide food, we can reduce the necessary range. Anyway, all you have to do is to get hold of a couple of breeding pairs, and make sure they're settled in comfortably. I read somewhere they've been successfully bred in captivity, so after that, you can just let nature take its course."

"But they're endangered! I can't just scoop up a couple of breeding pairs!"

Regina rolled her eyes. "Honestly, why is it, poor people have no imagination? You can get anything you want if you just throw a little money at it. Talk to the zoos. Talk to the black market. Go to the Himalayas and dicker with the natives. Trust me, if you can get diamonds off the beach in South Africa…." she flicked her earrings, "You can get snow leopards."

She made it sound so easy. Funny thing was, she was so sure of herself, it was hypnotic. He was halfway to believing that he really could do it, with her money behind him. She had enough money to do anything. He shook his head. It was still crazy. "But it would take years! And it wouldn't just cost a fortune. It would cost ten fortunes. Couldn't you just buy a fur coat?" He couldn't believe the words he heard coming out of his mouth. He hated the fur trade.

She leapt to her feet with a hiss. "Buy a coat? Made from a skin stripped from a glorious creature more beautiful than man? A noble beast trapped and hunted and tormented to a cruel and ignominious end? Leaving no offspring for posterity? I'd sooner buy a coat of human skin, much sooner."

He slid off his chair and huddled at her feet, hiccupping under her ferocious glare. "I'm sorry, Ma'am, so sorry. I didn't mean it. Please forgive me."

She took a deep breath. "No. You didn't mean it. I know you didn't—I checked your Facebook page." She squatted down beside him and patted his shoulder. "I'm sorry I lost my temper. Please get up." She put an arm around him and helped him up. "Have some dessert. It's crème brûlée, your favorite." She actually picked up a spoon and fed him a bite of the dessert that had appeared while he was huddling on the floor. "You're not just a vet. You're a devoted animal rights activist. You're even a vegetarian—I admire that. We should be allies, friends."

He couldn't imagine how she knew crème brûlée was his favorite. He didn't usually talk about food on Facebook. But the spoonful of custard in his mouth was so good, that he couldn't help himself. He took another bite, and then another. It was all he could do not to gobble it up like a child. And all the while he was eating, she was murmuring to him about animal rights and protecting endangered species and private wildlife sanctuaries, like an irresistible siren song. Or maybe more like a lullaby, since he suddenly and unexpectedly fell asleep with his head in the empty Wedgewood Hibiscus dessert bowl.

*****

He woke up on a plane. It was, he dimly realized, a very luxurious plane furnished like a living room, with deep plush couches and chairs, and a large polished table in the centre. He shook his head. Bad idea. His head was full of sand. He looked out the window and that was not a great idea either. Miles and miles of flat grey stratus clouds. He opened his mouth, meaning to demand answers to a hundred questions: where he was, how he had gotten there, where they were headed, and what was going on. What actually came out of his mouth was, "Wha…?"

"Oh, good, you're awake," chirped Regina. She was seated in front of a laptop, pecking at the keys. She had abandoned her chinchilla coat for a mink hoodie. Howie wanted to gag at the sight of the garment. How many animals had died—no matter how painlessly—for a stupid hoodie? "Have some coffee," she said. "We're almost there, and you're probably groggy."

"How did you kn—" he started, and then realized it was obvious how she knew. She'd drugged the dessert. He wasn't agreeing to her crazy plan fast enough to suit her, so she'd hi-jacked him. Thought she was so rich she was above the law. Joke was on her, though. She wasn't above the law. He pulled his phone out of his pocket. He was calling a cop. Right now. Except...Except he couldn't get a signal. He glanced nervously at the clouds outside the window. "I mean, where...?"

She turned to him with a smile, and then the smile faded and her eyebrows went up. "Wow, you look awful. You really need that coffee." She snapped her fingers, and the little maid popped in from another room with a mug. "Get yourself together," she told Howie sternly. "We should be landing in Lhasa in about fifteen minutes, and you need to be functional."

"Lhasa!?!" He choked on the rich Kona coffee, already laced with extra cream. "Lhasa, Tibet?"

An eye roll. "No, Lhasa, Massachusetts."

"But you can't!?!"

She looked at him in general bewilderment. "What do you mean? Of course we can. We're nearly there. The weather's perfect. Smooth sailing all the way."

"But you kidnapped me! And I don't even have a passport!"

Another eye roll. "Oh, come on. You wanted it. You know you did."

"What!?!"

"What guy doesn't fantasize about suddenly careening off on an adventure with a gorgeous woman like me?" She pecked at a few keys, nodded, and closed the laptop. "So get dressed."

"Dressed? But...?" There was no point protesting. Regina had already opened the door to the cockpit, and disappeared through it. The maid had reappeared, holding a large box, which she offered him. "I won't!" he snarled, and crossed his arms defiantly. The maid nearly went into shock. She hunched up her shoulders and glanced toward the cockpit door with a terrified expression, then thrust the box toward him again with all her strength. When he backed away she started to hyperventilate and tears came into her eyes. Hiccupping, she pushed the box at him, frantically, again and again, until he relented and took it from her. As soon as his fingers closed around it, she ran into the galley. He could hear the latch click behind her

There was a uniform of some kind in the box, but not out of stock. Both the tailoring and the material suggested custom tailoring. Even the shirt was silk. It all fit perfectly. Howie wondered vaguely how Regina had found out his sizes. He was absolutely sure he'd never mentioned them on Facebook. He also wondered how, even with money, she'd gotten it onto the plane in time. Had she been planning the kidnapping in advance? Or did she keep dozens of spare uniforms on hand, so one would always be ready on a moment's notice?

No matter. The uniform was there. He put it on and, as long as he was still alone in the room, he decided to snoop a little. He opened every drawer, finding nothing more than pens, notepads and computer cables. But the contents of the cabinets were a lot more interesting

They were full of money. Boxes and boxes of money. Judging by the size of the stacks, and the denominations shown on the individual packets, there had to something like a million dollars in twenties, fifties and hundreds. And that was just the American dollars. There was a box of Bahamian dollars, too (although nothing like a million). There were large boxes of British pounds and Euros and Japanese yen, and smaller boxes of half a dozen currencies he didn't recognize.

On the floor by the chair next to the laptop, was a handsome, well-made carry-on. When he opened it, all he could see at first glance was a make-up case and a folded raincoat. For a moment, he supposed it was a regular overnight bag, but the raincoat looked strangely inexpensive for anything belonging to Regina.

It wasn't like her to carry her own luggage, either. Sure enough, under the coat, the bag was full of money, a variety of different coloured bills, all decorated with a picture of some Chinese guy, and inscribed with Asian lettering. Tibetan money?

There was also a much smaller stack of money in the side pocket. So she could get some out without showing how much she was carrying, he guessed. He stared at the money until the earth moved. It was actually just the wheels bouncing off the runway as the plane shuddered its way down onto the earth, but somehow it felt more significant.

"You're a U.N. inspector," Regina whispered as they stood at the top of the stairs that had been wheeled up to the door. "Just look stern and say nothing. Pretend you don't speak English. If somebody insists on trying to talk to you, say something in German."

"My German's pretty rusty," he answered, looking out over the airport. It was a very small airport, although Lhasa, in the distance, looked like a good-sized city. "I haven't used it since college."

"None of them speak enough German to notice," she said, stepping grandly down as if she were entering a ballroom. Howie followed slowly, trying to look stern. The maid followed with a briefcase. A well-dressed civilian and a handful of uniformed officials were waiting at the foot of the steps. The maid handed her briefcase to the civilian—the interpreter, Howie supposed—who bowed to Regina, before opening the case, reviewing the documents, and turning to dicker with the officials.

They spoke earnestly and at length. There was much waving of hands, passing of documents back and forth, and gesturing toward Regina and Howie. Regina looked bored. Howie continued to gaze loftily into the distance. The city looked surprisingly flat and the mountains were a long way off. He'd expected the mountains to be closer.

The tone of the gabble grew strained. One of the officials was not happy about something in the papers. But whatever it was, he was nervous about challenging the party. They couldn't be at the main airport, Howie decided. There would have been a lot more officials at the main airport, and at least some of them would have been Chinese Communist Party Representatives. Chinese Communists would not be impressed by Regina's money, and utterly unafraid of challenging anyone.

At last the interpreter turned to Regina and murmured something…Explanatory? Apologetic? Howie couldn't hear him. Whatever it was, Regina rolled her eyes, and reached into the side pocket of her travel case. Some hot pink bills appeared, and just as rapidly disappeared. Everybody, especially the unhappy official, smiled and bowed—even Regina inclined her head. Howie nodded, too. So much for Communist immunity to money.

It turned out the interpreter wasn't an interpreter. "I am your tour guide," he announced bowing. "My name is Metok, and it will be my pleasure to assist you in every way, and take care of all the permits and paperwork. But in return, I must request you stay with me, and do not try to go anywhere alone. It is illegal for foreigners to wander about without an escort, and you might get hurt if you were caught and I was not there to intervene." Tucking the briefcase under one arm, he escorted them around the side of the main building.

A car was waiting, a dark blue Bentley Bentayga. A small, dark man beamed at them from the driver's seat. "Gyormey, your driver," said Metok. "I'm afraid he does not speak English, but he is a most excellent driver." Metok opened the side door for Regina, then came around to open the other door for Howie. The interior was paneled in wood. The seats were suede. Howie wondered if Regina had persuaded Bentley Motors to set up a cruelty-free tanning factory in London so her car could have leather seats.

*****

The ride was the smoothest Howie had ever known. But they drove for less than an hour. They stopped at a village, tucked under a rock heap on a barren, snow dusted plain in the middle of nowhere. Rock heap or no, the mountains still looked a long way off. The village was small and poor, hosting a dozen buildings which, even under curly Chinese roofs, looked more ramshackle than exotic.

There was a helicopter. Metok helped Regina, Howie and the maid climb up and into the open door. The villagers all looked tired and patient, but just in case, Gyormey stood guard with a rifle. Howie had to admit to himself it was very exciting. Metok paused outside the helicopter, and presented a thick wad of cash to the village headman, who beamed and bowed. Gyormey climbed into the pilot's seat. Apparently he really was a most excellent driver.

Forty-five minutes later, they lit down on a ledge cut into the side of a slope too steep for a real road, and there was no more pretending the mountains were far away. There was a village, smaller even than the previous one, but better kept and more prosperous looking—until you realized there was no electricity.

The guests were ushered into the largest of the local buildings, which proved to be a shrine, and served buttered tea. Howie looked around. The walls were sumptuously decorated with paintings and embroidered hangings, all brilliantly coloured renditions of Buddhist devotional motifs. Metok turned to Regina and smiled and nodded. "Please say something, so I may pretend to translate."

"Of course," she agreed. "I suppose you'll want to start with our thanks for this peculiar tea. Perhaps you can work that around to asking them to share a few of our provisions? I'm simply starved, and almost afraid to ask what kind of slop passes for food here. How long do you think it will take before we can talk business?"

"Please mention also," interrupted Howie, "how impressed we are by the art work. It is magnificent. And very ancient, I think?" Regina turned to look at him as if he'd grown a second head. Metok bowed and started talking. Food and drink appeared, none of it slop (unless you counted the buttered tea, which Howie found surprisingly tasty). The head monk thanked Howie for his kind words, and they actually achieved something like a real conversation, albeit a short one.

Eventually they got around to business. The villagers all grew very serious. "We are all very worried about our snow leopards," the headman told them. "We hold the management of the preserve as a sacred trust. The cats have prospered under our care. We would never consider parting with any of them, if we were not afraid for their safety."

Regina smiled and nodded. *She doesn't believe a word of it*, realized Howie. *She just thinks they'll do anything for money, as usual.* But he believed it. These good people were responsible for management of the preserve, and they were worried about their beloved cats.

"There's a poacher out there," growled the headman. "Some city bastard—may he rot in a thousand hells—thinks he can make a few yuan off the blood of our snow leopards. We know this—we've seen his tracks. We think we know where he is hiding. But it's an extremely inaccessible spot and he has an excellent rifle, far better than any of ours. And every minute he stays free, our cats remain in danger. Just last week he killed a beautiful young she-cat, and left her cubs to starve."

"Monster!" burst out Howie, and then ducked his head in embarrassment. He had meant to stay out of the discussion. Regina would not be pleased by his interference.

But the villagers turned to him in full understanding, with no need for Metok's translation. "Yes," they all murmured together, bowing. "A monster."

"So you want guns?" asked Regina. "To protect your cats?"

The headman turned back to her. "Your friend tells us you have offered us yuan, many yuan, for the privilege of helping to protect our cats." He smiled. "And we are not stupid. We will take your yuan. But, yes, we are very interested in vengeance on this preta demon."

"Is vengeance permitted?" asked Howie, in spite of Regina's glare. He knew a little about Buddhism.

The monk smiled sadly. "No. But there is a place on the wheel for everything. The cats have karma, too, which calls to us. And much that is done in the defence of an innocent can be cleansed."

"How many guns?" said Regina. "How many yuan?'

Howie hunched his shoulders and lowered his head. He wanted no more part of this painful discussion. The dickering went on around him, but he declined to hear it. Only when he felt a hand on his shoulder, did he lift his head. The monk was looking at him with great tenderness. "You grieve?" Metok must have leaned in to whisper a translation, but Howie felt like he'd understood the monk's words directly.

"There aren't enough yuan to pay for the suffering of those poor motherless cubs."

The monk smiled. "I think you are the one." And before Howie could ask what that meant, the monk waved a hand. "Bring them out."

The door burst open and a small gang of women and teenagers stumbled into the hall, dragging a huge basket behind them. Tumbling around in the basket were a half dozen miracles of beauty and grace. Snow leopard cubs!

All the long way to Tibet, despite all Regina's big talk, Howie had never truly believed he would ever see a snow leopard. Not really, not close enough to look in the eye—except their eyes were mostly still closed, the darlings! He'd never dreamed he'd have a chance to stroke that fabulous fur. His heart rose up in his throat, half choking him, and he climbed into the basket. In an instant the cubs were all over him, sniffing him, licking him, chewing on his sleeve, and he couldn't open his eyes because they were too beautiful to bear.

Behind him, he heard the headman say, "We will have to provide you with more females. If they all mate with their own brothers and sisters, the line will grow sickly in only a few generations. But you are fortunate. We have several females of thirteen or fourteen, too old to compete in the wild. Left on the mountain, they would not last more than a year or two. But if they were cared for, they would be good for at least three or four more litters, and might well live as much as ten more years. We will arrange to send them to you as soon as we can capture them."

"We'll need males for them to mate with," pointed out Regina.

"You wouldn't really need males. The sperm would be sufficient. We would be happy to sell you sperm."

"Are you really in a position to acquire sperm? No disrespect intended, but you don't even have electricity."

"Not now, no. But one of the things we mean to do with the money you're offering is buy a generator. And one of our boys is in Lhasa right now, studying to be a scientist doctor."

Howie stopped listening and went back to kissing the cub in his arms, who was trying to suckle one the buttons on his uniform. The monk climbed into the basket with him and offered him a yak skin wine bag. Except it didn't have wine in it. It had yak milk. The cub abandoned

Howie's button for the milk, and another cub climbed into his lap to see what was what. Fortunately, the monk was able to provide another wine skin. "This is what money is for," said Howie. "Horrible as she is, Regina made this happen. So she's right. Money has value."

"这是非常好的 你和他们分享业力" answered the monk. They understood each other perfectly. Behind them, a crate of guns appeared, and was opened. The guns were examined and money changed hands. More food and drink appeared. Regina kept one of the rifles, and gave the villagers a demonstration of her sharpshooting, to much applause. Howie and the monk cuddled the beautiful kittens.

Eventually, it was time to go. Howie had to give the darling cubs a tiny dose of sedative, and they were transferred from the big shallow, open basket to two tall, narrow baskets that Howie could keep on the seat next to him on the helicopter. It meant the poor maid had to crawl into the luggage carrier, but everybody—including the maid—agreed that the comfort and safety of the cubs was the most important issue. Since the maid was in the luggage compartment, Regina kept her rifle with her, propping it against her shoulder.

What with all the traveling and bad Tibetan food, Regina was tired and fractious all the way back. She complained about the noise but, seeing as they were in a helicopter, there was nothing anybody could do about it. She complained about the smell. The helicopter did smell somewhat of machine oil and sweat, but there was nothing anybody could do about that either. She opened the window so she could practice taking potshots at the ground, but within seconds, the Himalayan winds had rendered the cabin unbearable. So she shut the window again, and started complaining she was cold.

"God, it's freezing in here," she snarled. "Maria, pass me my coat." There was a very long pause while everybody but Regina reflected that Maria was not in a position to pass anything to anybody, having been stuffed into the back like a suitcase. "Maria?" snarled Regina. "What's taking you so long?"

A faint whisper emerged from the back. But the helicopter was still loud. So Maria had to scream her apology at the top of her lungs. "I'm so sorry, Ma'am. I'm afraid I left your coat in the car." The information came as no surprise to anybody but Regina, as there'd been considerable discussion at the time about what could or could not be fitted into the helicopter.

"What?" shrieked Regina. "You useless piece of shit! You're nothing more than a disgusting wetback skank! I should have left you peddling ass in Tijuana." She turned over on her side, wrapped her arms around her rifle and pretended to go to sleep. No further attempts at conversation were made.

They arrived at the other village. Howie lowered the baskets one at a time into Gyormey's waiting arms, and jumped down after them to check on the wellbeing of their precious contents. That done, he climbed back up and helped Metok extricate Maria. The luggage carrier hadn't actually been outside the cabin, but it was a lot closer to the external wall and a lot further from the heater than the passenger seating. The poor girl was frozen and shaky.

"I might not have agreed if I'd known what I was getting into," she admitted, with a pathetic attempt at a laugh.

Howie thought to himself that he shouldn't have agreed either. Except…If she hadn't been in the luggage carrier, what would he have done with the kittens? Could Regina have been persuaded to leave her behind and send the chopper back for her? "I'm sorry. You were very brave," he told Maria. But no sooner did they have her safely on the ground, then she jumped up and started toward the car. "Wait!" he called. "You need to rest."

"Can't," she said over her shoulder. "Miss Regina won't have forgotten she told me to get her coat. She'll expect me to have it for her. She'll want coffee, too."

He stayed with her. "How can you possibly get her coffee out here?"

She smiled. "That car is really posh. It's got a fridge and a microwave."

Behind them, Regina snarled. "If you're all quite finished unpacking the luggage, could somebody give me a hand?" She was still sitting in the helicopter, having made no move to get down by herself. Metok and

Howie rushed over. Instead of taking Howie's hands, she thrust her rifle into his arms, and allowed Metok to assist her down instead. Howie sighed. He was out of favor already. Once installed on the ground, Regina stretched hugely and turned her head toward the car. "Maria? Any chance of coffee?"

"Coming right up, Ma'am," answered Maria, backing out of the car. Regina smiled. Maria looked comically laden, with Regina's magnificent chinchilla over one arm, only barely leaving enough of her hand free to coordinate with the other hand in pouring coffee out of a thermos. She moved toward Regina as quickly as the uneven ground permitted, focusing all her attention on not spilling the coffee.

It was the same rich, pungent Kona that she'd served on the plane, and the penetrating scent brought a smile to Howie's face, even though he was several feet away. Metok, too, sniffed hugely and sighed happily at smell of it. Regina reached out her hands to receive the cup.

The ground was rough and frozen. Maria was still unsteady after her ordeal, and paying a lot more attention to her hands than to her feet. So Maria tripped. She fell face forward onto Regina. The coffee spilled everywhere. All over Maria. All over Regina. All over the chinchilla coat.

There was a horrific, frozen moment while everyone waited for the sky to open. Then Regina roared. There was no other word for the noise she made. She flung Maria off and, as the girl stumbled backwards, she slung the carry-on bag around like a weapon, screaming, "You stupid slut—look what you've done." The bag caught Maria across the head and knocked her to the ground. Regina rushed forward and started kicking her, still screaming incoherently.

Howie didn't remember how it happened. He didn't even remember that he had the rifle, and he certainly didn't remember that his grandfather had made him learn how to shoot when he was a boy. Shouldn't he at least remember hearing a bang?

But no. There was just Regina screaming and kicking one instant, and then Regina lying motionless on the ground with a huge hole in the back of her nasty mink hoodie. *Did I do that*? he wondered. He picked up the carry-on bag, and turned it over in his hands. It didn't look like a weapon. It had pink and lavender flowers on it.

After a while, Metok helped Maria up and put her in the car. He led Howie over to the car, too. Gyormey brought over the baskets of unconscious snow leopard cubs. He smiled, and nodded, as he pressed one the baskets into Howie's numb hands. Howie looked up at him and he smiled and nodded again, before setting the other basket between Howie's feet.

Metok stayed by Maria until she managed to stop crying. When she wiped her eyes at last, he smiled gently. "You can't seriously be sorry she's gone, can you? The way she treated you?"

"But…." Maria shook her head and tried again. "But…." She couldn't seem to think what came next.

"But nothing," said Metok. "Your mistress went out one day. She was in such a good mood she gave you the day off. When you came in to work the next day, she was still gone, but you thought nothing of it. Why would you? She travels a lot. She doesn't always tell you where she's going. So you just keep going in to work every day, until somebody in her family or her company starts to worry. Then it will be their problem."

Howie lifted his head. "You want us to pretend nothing happened?"

"Why not? Nothing did happen." Metok opened up the briefcase, and pulled out several documents. "See? The paperwork is very clear. How could anything have happened? She never left London — or the UK come to that — and she certainly never came to Tibet. She was never here and, of course, neither were you. You just picked up these wonderful snow leopard cubs at the airport—these poor little cubs, orphaned when their mother died of illness, and sent away for fear they carried disease. It's all right here in the paperwork." Metok looked earnestly into his eyes. "Please try to pull yourself together. Somebody has to look out for the snow leopard cubs."

Under his fingers, one of the cubs stirred and shifted slightly, snuggling its little nose into the palm of his hand. Howie's heart turned over. "Yes," he agreed. "Somebody has to take care of the kittens. Maria, too."

Metok smiled. "Maria, too."

He closed the door, and climbed into the front seat next to Gyormey, who started the car. They drove back to the airport in silence. Metok chattered at the airport officials in Chinese, and the steps were rolled up to the plane. Just before he boarded, Howie picked up the flowered carry-on. It was still pretty heavy. "Just in case, there are more orphaned kittens before they catch the poacher," he said, handing the bag to Metok. "Or if somebody thinks they remember something peculiar. Whatever."

Metok peeked inside and his eyes lit up. "You sure you don't need this?"

Howie smiled. "Naw, plenty more where that came from." He reflected on the cupboards full of money on the plane. Money enough for a whole lot of animal sanctuaries.

Yes, it was certainly amazing just what good money could do.

# *Murder at Elephant & Castle*
## *J. Aquino*

The two women stood outside the Elephant and Castle station shivering, rubbing their hands together even though they were wearing gloves, which identified them to the few Londoners who were about that January evening as Americans. Actually, the women were happy if people thought they were tourists rather than suspect that they were spies.

"What was it that Charles II said about England—that it has the best climate and the worst weather in the world?" Jenny asked Lynn in order to pass the time while also searching the area with just her eyes.

"That's a distinction without a difference isn't it," her friend said as her teeth chattered. "And, as king, he probably didn't stand outside in the cold much without a retinue of 50 surrounding him so he could suck up their body heat, hence the origin of the term."

"Come on," Jenny turned her around and slowly ran her hands up her partner's back and arms while at the same time maxing out her peripheral vision, looking all around. The few people nearby saw two women friends dressed in black jackets, turtlenecks, and slacks keeping each other warm and, as far as Jenny was concerned, they could think what they wanted, especially because it was true.

"What's the matter with Poliakoff?" Lynn continued. "Can't he encrypt the names and email them to us or come by our London office and drop them off like most people?"

"He's a diplomat not used to having his life and that of his second wife Anna in danger. The list fell into his lap, and he ends up betraying his country. Said he'd been hacked and that he was afraid he wouldn't get up the stairs of our building before he was picked off. But here, he's coming back from work like always and hands the list off to us."

"Yeah," Lynn answered, her breath vapour obscuring her face. "But then, why is he half an hour late?"

"Yeah," Jenny nodded, conceding the point. "Come on."

Crossing the street, Jenny said, "If we were in the states, we'd make a call and have access to security camera at the station on our phones. But since Lester insisted on our not notifying the authorities we're here, fearful that any  moles in the London office here would inform on Poliakoff to his superiors, we have to play Sherlock Holmes."

She flagged a passing black cab, and they both jumped into the rear seats. The driver was bearded, mop-haired, and in his 30s, with the name of Harvey according to the driver display card on his dashboard. "Here's the deal, Harvey," Jenny announced while shoving 20 euros through the opening. "We're looking for a friend who may be lost. We need you to drive really slow, and, if I see people to ask, I'll bang on the window, and you stop because I'm going to jump out. Ok?"

Harvey smiled at her accent and took the money. "Bangin', lady. Beast." Jenny smiled and shook her head to Lynn at the slang as the hackney began to move.

It was just after 11:00. The traffic was light, and the sidewalks remained empty until they passed a pub with a few coatless young men and women gabbing outside. Jenny banged her hand and jumped out, ran over, asked, and ran back. "Nothing." She looked ahead and saw a fellow built like a midwestern quarterback moving swiftly. Jenny ordered Harvey, "I'm running ahead. Follow and wait for me."

Her tall, lithe frame threw a wraith-like shadow up Waterloo Road. As she approached the man, she heard a click and saw his right hand glimmer in the lamp light. He whirled to his right, she grabbed his hand at the wrist and slammed him against the wall of a shuttered building, her right hand jammed against his throat. "Me money's in my back pocket," his bloated face wheezed. "Don't kill me!"

Jenny sighed, yanked the knife from his hand, and released her grip. "Sorry," she muttered, backing away, and dropping the switchblade at his feet. "But, incidentally, did you see a white middle-aged man, balding, black hair, your height, not as well built, around here?"

"Yeah," the quarterback said, still gasping for breath. "Looked like he was drunk, I think. He's plough his way along like he was going through mud, and then he'd stop and lean against the wall or—" he pointed at a street sign in the cement, "over there."

"Thanks," Jenny pushed another 20 into his shirt pocket. She signalled Harvey without looking to come along and raced to the sign. Coming back to the cab, she showed Lynn the blood on her hand. "It's all over the sign. I think we'd better go faster." She turned her head at the cries of sirens. "Come on, Harvey, straight ahead and floor it."

"Beast," he answered without turning around.

Lynn looked at Jenny quizzically. "It means 'cool,'" her partner whispered.

Harvey rammed the cab up Waterloo Road until they were blocked and met with a bombardment of pulsating red lights from atop vehicles of various colours, crisscrossing across ornamental friezes of the station's entrance. Jenny jammed another 20 in the glass opening and slid with Lynn into the crowd to get as close as they could. They were able to make out the body of a man sprawled in front of the route destination sign that had a crimson smear from where he had tried to hold himself up before dropping to the pavement. Even though his face was turned away, Jenny could tell it was Poliakoff from his shape and the monk's ball spot on his head.

Lynn touched Jenny's arm and pointed to a red-haired woman in a nurse's uniform who appeared to be giving a statement to a police officer. The two slim brunettes squeezed their way through and worked around the evolving mass of onlookers and soldiers, sailors, and RAF on their ways to bases in Salisbury, Aldershot, Chatham, Woolwich Portsmouth, Plymouth, and Farnborough. Lynn started to move closer to the officer and nurse, but with a gesture Jenny kept her back, mouthing the word, "Beast." They both placed amplifiers in their ears and programmed them with a touch to filter out the surrounding din.

"I saw this man pressed against the wall and went to ask if he was all right," the agitated nurse explained. Jenny placed her accent as Midlands. "And then I could see the blood on the map and on his face and torso, and he fell. It looked like a stab wound, possibly piercing the large intestine. I knelt beside him, and he tried to speak. I got closer and he—he—,' she hesitated.

"What did he say?" the officer asked.

The Midlands nurse blushed at first and then answered with an exasperated bark. "He said he wanted to have sex with me!'

"He said he wanted to have sex with you?" the officer repeated as a question.

"Louder, officer. Not everyone could hear you." She was embarrassed and turned to go, but Lynn was in her face, handing her a card. 'Excuse me, I know this is not an appropriate time. But my company is doing a documentary on murders in this area. We are willing to pay a considerable stipend for just an hour or two of your time if you would come by our offices tomorrow morning."

In the cab on the way back to the agency's London office, Lynn broke the silence, "He died saying he wanted to have sex with her?"

"Admittedly, not the best of last words. However, Poliakoff has a history of cheating on his first wife, even though his excuse was that she was bed-ridden and he had needs. But is it possible that as he was dying all he thought about was his needs."

As soon as they walked into the office suite, Marcia Burke, their British liaison, formal but very efficient, told them Lester was on line one wanting an update, Mrs. Poliakoff on line two demanding to know the whereabouts of her husband, and Nurse Ellen Braxton asking for an appointment. "You were supposed to be in and out," Marcia reproached them. She was wearing an Audrey Hepburn-black cocktail dress, having been called back from a party at a fashionable address. "You're here three hours, and all hell breaks loose."

Jenny didn't miss a beat. "I'll take line one, Lynn, you take two, and Marcia, would you please ask Nurse Ellen to come at eight-thirty. And, for the record, we've actually been here four hours, including the arrival at Heathrow."

After she finished the call with Lester, she told Lynn that he had instructed them to provide Monica with a general briefing. The three of them sat in the conference room and Jenny worked to be direct, succinct, and general. "Poliakoff had been teaching at the University of Winchester on a special work visa as a visiting professor of music. He moved there with his second wife and lived just outside the city for five years. It was then, in conjunction with his government's request, that he applied for and was granted a diplomatic passport. He was working in the embassy in the UK when he discovered a computer error that generated a file merging the names of moles in governments of the UK, the U.S., and a number of EU countries with names for invitations to the premiere's upcoming speech on party unity. Poliakoff did not have access to the list of moles, but it was obvious what it was. He first made a copy of the file on a flash drive and then notified his supervisor of the computer error. Her boss corrected the mistake before the invitations were sent out and placed a letter of commendation in Poliakoff's file. I'd met him once in Budapest three years ago, and he felt that he owed me something for saving his brother's life there. He'd also grown tired of working for a totalitarian regime, and so he contacted me."

By eight o'clock, as dawn was breaking over London town, after the early morning spent on the briefing, transatlantic phone calls, and emailed reports, Monica was taking a nap in her office, and Jenny and Lynn were alone in the conference room, their shoes off, their bare feet on the table. "So," Jenny began, "Lester wants us on the 6:00 flight this evening whether we have the names or not. Anna Poliakoff is identifying the body in the morgue even as we speak. The Waterloo police are investigating Poliakoff's death as a mugging gone wrong. And so," she sighed while stretching her arms over her head, "what do we got?"

"Nothing," Lynn concluded. "We were on time, so he must have been early, was spotted, and was stabbed. The killer may have the names. We may want to catch an earlier plane."

"Meebe," Jenny nodded glumly. She repeated what Lynn had said. "He came early, was spotted and was killed. But he didn't die instantly, did he? He staggers down Waterloo Road and doesn't stop at the pub along the way for help." She sat up suddenly with a jerk. "Instead, he walks one mile to Waterloo Station. He *had* to get to Waterloo Station! Why?"

Lynn sat quickly up too. "He wasn't in a condition to get a train. He knew that he was dying—"

"—so he made one, last superhuman effort to get to the station—"

"—to send a message!" Lynn all but shouted triumphantly.

Jenny shared Lynn's excitement, but soon the glow in her eyes dimmed. "And when he had the chance to give the message, he tells the nurse he wants to have sex with her."

"Yeah," said Lynn, equally and just as suddenly bummed. "You know, maybe it's like when the actor John Barrymore was dying and giving his last confession to a priest. He said, 'Father, I've had carnal thoughts.' And the priest asked, 'For whom?' And Barrymore pointed to the elderly nurse in the room and said, 'For her.' Well," Lynn leaned back in her chair again, "at least Poliakoff died with a happy thought." They could hear the door opening outside. "That's probably Nurse Ellen. As for us," Lynn continued, "without additional resources, we are—what's British slang for being up the creek without a paddle?"

"I dunno. 'It's a shambles,' I think." The excitement suddenly returned to Jenny's eyes. "Wait a minute! British slang!" She jumped to her feet and ripped open the door, revealing Monica and Nurse Ellen talking in the foyer. "Would you please come in," she invited the nurse. Lynn closed the door after her and in Monica's face as Jenny pulled five 20 euro bills from her slacks and handed them to the nurse. "For your time and an answer to just one question. You said the man's last words were that he wanted to have sex with you. Were those his exact last words? Exact?"

The nurse fumbled for an answer, embarrassed. "Well, no—not exactly. He used an expression for it. He said, 'oh-vo-dee-o-doe.'"

The two women shook their heads slightly, indicating they did not understand.

Nurse Ellen stammered, as if she were struggling to explain why the grass is green to a child. "You know! Someone will say, 'He's looking for the old oh-vo-dee-o-doe.' Or, she gave in and did the oh-vo-dee-o-doe.'"

"So, it means having sex."

"Exactly," the nurse sighed with a mixture of triumph and exasperation.

"Thank you, Ellen," Jenny opened the door for the woman to leave.

"But aren't you going to ask me questions for your documentary?"

"That's all we need, really,' Lynn prattled as she walked the nurse to the door. "It's going to be a short documentary. But it's also part of a police investigation, so we ask you not to discuss this with anyone. Just leave. We'll have the police contact you for an official statement about the man's exact words." Lynn shut the door behind her and waited to hear the office suite door close.

"Let's assume he wasn't asking for sex," Jenny proposed. "What else does 'oh-vo-dee-o-doe' mean?' She began to pace, repeating, "Oh-vo-dee-o-doe, oh-vo-dee-o-doe."

Lynn started to say it too but found herself singing, "Oh-vo-dee-o-doe-doe-doe-doe." With an enlightened grin, she whispered, "The lyrics for 'Winchester Cathedral!'"

Jenny slapped her forehead as if to say, "of course."

Lynn pressed on, "Suppose he had the names ready to pass off to us but gets there early and spots them spotting him. He rips up the paper, but he knows he placed a backup in a secret spot for safety. He tries to get away, is stabbed, staggers the mile to Waterloo Station, and dies while trying to point at a spot on the route map, leaving a streak of blood there. He tried to do x-marks-the-spot for us. He tried to point to the Winchester Station stop. When someone comes up to him, he has no breath, and the thought of the cathedral makes him remember a song from his youth. So, he pushes out these five syllables as his message. "

Jenny yanked the door open and shouted, "Monica! Can you catch a train from Waterloo Station to Winchester Cathedral?"

Monica, roused from sleep, rushed into the room at the bellow, still wearing her cocktail dress. "Yes. Yes, you can. And I think there's a direct train. Shall I get you a schedule?"

"No, thanks. At least, not yet. Back in a 'sec," she shut the door.

"But where?" Jenny wondered aloud, turning back into the room. "Where in Winchester Cathedral could it be?" she asked. "It's a huge place! Over a mile long, or something. I was there a few years back during its renovations. It could be anywhere. We know he taught music education and performance before he was given the embassy assignment. Hey, Mrs. Poliakoff might know," Jenny mused. "Maybe they were married there. Perhaps there's a spot in the cathedral he was fond of, or a place in Winchester that has extra meaning to the couple. A special spot." Opening the door again, she asked, "Monica, would you call the morgue and get Mrs. Poliakoff over here—."

"She's gone," Monica cut her off.

"Gone? How do you—?"

"They phoned and said she created a bit of a scene there, which isn't unusual for a grieving widow," Monica noted sympathetically. "But they said she asked for his clothes and all but ripped them apart, searching for something. She was almost hysterical when she couldn't find it. Ran out in tears, poor thing."

Jenny and Lynn stared at each other for a moment. Jenny finally grinned and declared, "She's after the list too. She's not the woeful widow, Monica. Anna Poliakoff has been ordered to get the names back so that we don't get them. She's working for them!"

Looking lost but game, Monica came in and sat down with the two agents, the duet suddenly becoming a trio with an alto added. "But wouldn't she think the police had searched through his clothes and found whatever it is?"

Jenny realized that Monica likely had no idea what they were talking about, and, smiling, patted her hand. "Thanks for playing, Monica. And you're actually not bad at this. It's a good point. But maybe there was a secret compartment in his pants or shoes. But whatever it was, the paper wasn't there."

Lynn leaned in. "And I'll tell you something else. I was never comfortable with the idea that a professional would take Poliakoff out with a knife in the belly on a public street. A single shot with a silencer is more like it rather than risking a struggle or unexpected strength from the target. But a wife could get close, even if the husband was suspecting her, even if he was resisting her. And she could have set him up by calling him at work and lying that Jenny had called and asked him to be early"

Monica's eyes widened with the exciting experience of deduction. "So, she's the killer."

"We think so, Monica," Jenny confided. "We just have to wrap it up. Thanks for your assistance. Come on," she took her arm to help her up. "I'll phone Lester, and, with his approval, you can call people you know at the Waterloo Police and set in motion a good old-fashioned woman-hunt. I'll bet you a euro that when Lynn and I leave this building, Mrs. Poliakoff will follow us because we've figured out where the list is. She has to follow us because it's her job and because her life will be on the line."

"Tell me first," Monica persisted, glowing with excitement, "how did you find out where the list is hidden."

"We're still under orders to be on the 6:00 plane, so we have to hustle. I'll tell you later. Let's make those calls."

At 1:05, the train for Winchester began its journey from Waterloo Station slowly, as if teasing the traveller with anticipation of a destination just an hour away with a pace more in tune with the body's natural rhythms, no towering structures, and an intimacy at odds with the mad, wild rush of London city. Jenny and Lynn were sitting in first-class leather seats facing two empty ones with a table between. The engine was pepping along and beginning to pick up speed. Jenny broke the silence. "Nice of Monica to arrange for us to travel so comfortably." Lynn nodded. Her partner turned slightly to look behind her at four rows of passenger-less seats. "Nice of her to arrange this private compartment."

Lynn nodded again, solemnly. "She's very efficient." The door whisked open, and, rather than a conductor asking for tickets, Monica and a raven-haired woman wearing dark glasses entered and quickly sat down in the chairs opposite them. Monica was looking particularly sharp in a tweed suit with skirt and brown boots. A tan scarf was draped around her neck, and its ends partially hid the automatic in her right hand. "And dangerous," Lynn finished.

"Oh, Monica, Monica!" Jenny exclaimed in over-wrought anguish! "And we were getting on so well together! Should you be pointing that gun at us, Monica, with a train full of Waterloo police?"

Monica whipped the gun from under the scarf and pointed it directly at Jenny. "There are no police here. I never made the call. What you heard was me calling my answering machine and altering the people who screen my calls to meet us at Winchester. You'll either tell me now or the survivor will lead us to where the list is when we arrive and our people will recover it."

"That's amazing," Jenny said unamazed. She nodded at the woman across from her. "And who is this young lady?"

"It's Anna Poliakoff!" Monica proclaimed to the empty seats in the rear.

"She doesn't look like her picture. Not at all." Jenny turned to Lynn, who nodded sagely.

The woman removed her black wig and dark glasses, revealing comely blonde hair and a face 20 years younger than her late husband's. "That's her!" Jenny turned to Lynn and the vacant chairs. "Like in her picture! I can't believe it," she said soberly.

Monica eyes narrowed as if sensing something amiss. But she continued with her planned revelation. "We had to change her appearance because you broadcasted her face all over the country."

"Well, that's because you threw her under the bus! Oh, wait! How do you say that here?" Jenny thought and quickly found the correct wording. "Had her take the flak." Anna eyed Monica uncertainly. "Mrs. Poliakoff, she told us you had searched through your husband's clothes frantically looking for the names to lead us to think you were the mole and that you killed your husband, when in fact Monica is the mole and you and she killed your husband together."

"You are bluffing. You have no evidence!" Monica snapped, ignoring Anna's yanking of her arm to demand an answer to Jenny's accusation.

"Mebbe," Jenny conceded. "Except," she raised one finger, "you may recall, while we included you in some of our conference room discussions, we closed the door for certain portions, such as when we discovered Poliakoff's clues. And we wondered, who wears a cocktail dress all morning when she has a business suit hanging behind her office door? You wore it to establish your alibi, just in case. It was also an easy change in case the blood spattered on your clothes when you were torturing Poliakoff with the knife for the names. And it did. Men don't know that, for all the pretence women put on about taking time to prettify ourselves, a cocktail dress with little or no underwear takes no time at all. I smelled two perfume scents on your dress last night, Joy and My Sin, and My Sin is what Anna is wearing now. I saw two strands of blonde hair on your black dress—"

"Enough!" Monica barked, tiring of Jenny's airing her shortcomings. She aimed the gun between Jenny's eyes. "Just tell us where the names are!"

Lynn abruptly appeared scared. "Wait! Don't! I'll tell you where the names are! But first—now would be a good time," she said calmly into her shoulder. "Testing one, two, three, four."

At once, the train was flooded with armed members of the Waterloo Police coming in from the front and back doors. Lynn leaned forward and yanked away Monica's gun. "We knew that you hadn't called the police, but we recorded what you said, phoned them, and played it back, making it an official request from someone they knew. Our people have already been to the cathedral and have found the names, which, by the way, include yours as the mole in our agency's UK office. And, in cooperation with the local police, they are arresting your people as they cross into Winchester."

Monica dropped back into her leather chair. "All right," she hissed. "But just tell me—what was the clue that led you to where the names were?"

"May I?" Jenny asked Lynn impishly.

"Of course," her friend bowed theatrically.

Jenny placed her elbows on the table and leaned forward, not toward Monica, but toward Anna. "He loved you. No, he adored you. But you married him on orders to watch him, to keep him in line. And when he betrayed his country, you betrayed him. His last words were quoting a 50-year-old song, a one-hit wonder by Geoff Stevens as sung by the New Vaudeville Band about a man who finds his love has left him and blames the cathedral bells for not stopping her."

"'Winchester Cathedral,'" Monica all but whispered. 'The list was in the bells."

"Bell," Jenny corrected her. "Please quote the lyrics correctly. One bell, the oldest, the 8th flat, dating from 1621. It took just five minutes for our people to find the list tied around the clapper, wrapped there by your husband, Mrs. Poliakoff, when he was in Winchester day before yesterday. Was that the night he was late for dinner?"

"Yes," was all she said, staring ahead motionless and lost.

"And the thing of it is, Anna, is that she seduced you, and she didn't love you either."

"What happens now?" Monica asked wearily.

Behind Jenny's cold stare were images in her mind of the gentle Poliakoff's bloody body on the sidewalk and of hundreds if not thousands of lives lost by the treachery of moles like Monica. "Just be grateful there's no death penalty in England." She handed the nearest Officer Monica's gun. "You both will be taken off the train at Wimbledon station by the Waterloo police and turned over by them to the Wimbledon police who will surrender you to representatives of MI5, who have been summoned there just for you. It's either protocol or the British version of 'hot potato,' an American game," she explained to the officers. "Thanks again for playing, Monica. But there will be no parting gifts." She instructed the police, "Please take them out, and don't treat them kindly."

Soon, Jenny and Lynn were once again alone in a first-class compartment with luxury seats. "Well, that's that," Lynn concluded. "The objective's accomplished, the murderers are apprehended, and an international incident avoided. Should we get off in Wimbledon and catch the train to Paddington to get to Heathrow for the 6:00 plane to the states?"

Jenny made a face as if tasting something sour. "After 12 hours of non-stop excitement, my adrenaline is up, and I don't feel like leaving the country quietly. I'm in the mood for something pleasant but daring." She turned to Lynn like a mischievous schoolgirl. "It's 3:15. Let's stay on the train, get off in Winchester, buy flowers, visit the cathedral, pay homage to Jane Austen's grave,  leave the flowers, pop over to the Old Vine for a quick pint, take the next train on the Paddington line ,and go to Heathrow, just in time to make the 6:00 plane."

Lynn looked at the wide-eyed grin of her partner's beautiful face and just shook her head. "Well, I had thought of a quiet dinner at Heathrow toasting our success. But as for your idea—it is indeed a pleasant and daring plan." She placed her head on Jenny's shoulder and closed her eyes. "Wake me when we get to Winchester."

# A Student Deferment
## David Rich

"There's a tear in your umbrella. Not much good with a tear is it?"

Enright straightened his umbrella so the short woman would no longer be able to see the tear.

"I put it there on purpose," he said. "So I know if it's still raining."

She smiled at him. "And I suppose you put a hole in your shoe to check for a puddle." The light turned green and he hurried across to Victoria Station. Water leaked onto his shoulder. Enright had not bothered to consult the forecast but a rough channel crossing suited him. The spectre of passengers recently wretched might make the customs officials sympathetic. Enright considered himself expert at pretending he had been sick. Like an actor summoning tears to give the appearance of misery, he pictured scenes from his four years in the Royal Navy, much of it spent shivering in the North Sea. I should have started my spying then, he thought. I would have some security by now. He chuckled at that thought. A bald man with a moustache looked at him with disdain. Enright closed his umbrella and tossed it into the bin and entered the station.

Enright checked the board. His train was scheduled for platform twelve in thirty two minutes. Though he had been through the station hundreds of times, Enright made a show of looking around for the track like a worried tourist. The thin man wearing the grey hounds tooth hat had followed him into the station. Enright first noticed him near Trafalgar Square. A pretty young woman whose open coat revealed her red mini skirt and tight blue angora sweater marched past the hounds tooth man and captured Enright's gaze until she disappeared onto a platform. She was a dab of colour in a world so thick with grey that Enright wondered if the skylights were letting the grey in or out. The colours on the cigarette and clothing adverts seemed to dissipate a few feet out, overwhelmed by the haze. Perhaps clouds seem clear from the inside, thought Enright, and wondered for a moment if he could sell an article about points of view.

But if this deal went through he would not have to write any pathetic, straining articles for some time, long enough to finish a book, even two if he was at his best. He had never been a top journalist, but he could put words on paper fast enough when he had to. Now he was selling pictures and smiled at the knowledge that, indeed, each one was worth much more than a thousand words.

At the kiosk the tea lady smiled at him and showed a chipped front tooth. She looked tired. Enright asked for a cup of tea. "Are the cheese rolls fresh?" he said.

"You'll have to pay to find out, won't you love?" She was Welsh. She winked at him and showed her chipped tooth again. She slid the cup toward him and then reached into the covered dish for the roll. "Two and six."

Enright fished out the coins unhappily. The pound devaluation was already showing up in the smallest ways. Another sign of the inevitable decline of the West. Enright could write that article without pausing to think: the brink of chaos, leading to fascism, war, hunger. But he could write the counter argument with equal ease and sophisticated superficiality: a better life for all, competition will out, boost for England in the end. Enright needed money, and the article, either side of it, paid little more than the cost of a good dinner. The undeveloped photos in his pocket were worth one thousand quid. Enright squeezed the cheese roll and crumbs flaked off the hard, stale bread.

The tea lady said, "Wait until you get to France and see what it costs."

"How do you know that's where I'm going?"

"Got to do something with my spare time, don't I. I watch the people. See that girl in the white coat and white hat? Weekend in Brighton for her with her boyfriend I bet."

"Lucky man," Enright said softly. He watched the girl's firm thighs flex as she strode toward the platform. A tall young man with dark curly hair and a wispy beard walked toward the woman staring at her openly. The woman stared back at him. In the three years since his wife had finally left him, Enright had been with one woman, a barmaid who got herself drunk and stayed sober enough to make sure Enright was not the same man she had bedded the night before. Miniskirts: another sign of the end, a taunt directed at the poor: look but don't touch. And calling it the sexual revolution was a purposeful sneer. You still needed money to get near those women. They could not be had for a cheese roll. Someone had to buy those boots. It was the counter revolution. But Enright had grown tired of writing pieces which ignored human nature.

The tall young man stopped beside Enright at the kiosk. He bought a Kit-Kat bar and put it in his backpack next to his camera. "For later. Is that cheese roll fresh?" He was an American.

The tea lady said, "You'll have to buy it to find out."

"And then it's too late," said Enright.

"Thanks." The American fiddled with his backpack, taking out the camera, a Pentax. He removed the film inside and opened a box and expertly threaded another roll.

Enright lit a cigarette. When the American had gone, the tea lady said, "Yanks. I like 'em. Can't help it." She shrugged.

"What about that one? With the checkered hat. Where's he going?" Enright said to the tea lady.

"Copper, ini't he? They don't go overseas."

She did have a good eye. "What about me? What do I do?"

She looked him in the eye. Another customer arrived and leaned toward her but she kept her gaze on Enright. "You'll never tell, not the truth anyhow, now wouldya?"

Enright took a last bite of his cheese roll and smiled at the tea lady. "I'm Peter Sellers. In disguise for a new film." He winked at her. As he left he thought: now I'm down to charming tea ladies.

He followed the girl in white, the one with the firm thighs, down the platform. She entered the fourth car, first class. Enright had sprung for first class himself. He believed the customs men treated the first class passengers with greater deference. He wanted to look fresh and ready for the Russians, as well. This was a job interview; Enright looked on it as a new phase of his career. First class was a solid investment. From the front car he walked back through the first class cars. The seat next to the woman in white was open. She glanced at Enright with her face set, expressionless and unwelcoming. He sat across the aisle from her.

A moment later the American came up the aisle from behind Enright. He stopped, looked at the empty seat next to the woman in white and said, "Thanks for saving that for me."

"I didn't," she said.

"But you weren't saving it for anyone else, were you?"

She laughed. Enright saw her smile for the first time, white, and a gap between her front teeth. Before the American sat down, he took off his fleece lined coat; it looked new. Enright could feel the American's ease like a rebuke. The low murmur of his voice wafted across the aisle interrupted by the girl's purring replies and laughter.

Enright thought, I could make sounds like those if I knew I had the money to back them up. But when he tried to imagine exactly what the American was saying, he could not be more specific than telling the woman that she was beautiful and that her thighs were haunting him. The stories he might tell all veered toward bitterness: an unappreciative boss, his wife's duplicity, the insolence of ambitious colleagues. He had stories of victories, too, but they were small and time made them sound hollow even to Enright.

He would not be able to brag of this triumph. It had all come so easily, a phone call from Phillips who once owned a club in Soho but lost it. "I have something," Phillips said. "Bit out of my line, but it fits a story you worked on." Phillips's line was blackmail. He had two or three young prostitutes and a flat in Belgravia where he could hide and photograph the johns. He sold the photos to them over dinner in an Indian restaurant in Beauchamp Place.

This time the john was an MP, Marley, Labour, from a district in Birmingham. Secretary of State for Work and Pensions, but slated for greater heights. Enright had interviewed him a year ago and questioned his commitment to party principles. Enright arrived late to Phillips's flat and only saw Marley getting dressed and the prostitute lounging under the sheets. Phillips handed over the roll of film and said Enright could decide best how to use it, but he would hate to see good material like this go to waste. Enright asked how much Phillips wanted but Phillips said he would be happy with a small cut of whatever Enright got for them.

The first enquiry Enright made resulted in a reproach from the editor. He wanted nothing to do with what amounted to blackmail. "It isn't news, Enright. Dog bites man. Bring me photos of an MP refusing a prostitute. Unless you have a Christine Keeler here. Do you?"

Enright dreaded the work involved in discovering the prostitute's past and connections. Phillips would demand to have the film roll back if Enright asked him for information. Enright stopped for a drink to plan his next call. Go straight to the point, he thought, not all the way, no names, but something less vague. He decided to contact the editor of a conservative magazine and mention that an opposition party leader was involved. He left the pub and used a call box down the street.

The editor wanted to hear it over the phone. Enright fumbled, admitted he had not seen the photos. The editor hinted he thought Enright might be setting him up. "I have no illusions about you, Enright," he said.

Back at the pub, film burning a hole in his pocket, the bell rang and Enright ordered another double whiskey from the barmaid.

A man two seats along the wall said, "Same for me. In fact, I'll have two of those. Him, too." He turned to Enright. "On me. One of those days. Dinner tonight with the wife's sister and her son. Takes all day to prepare." He was in his sixties, jowly and red faced and jovial.

The man was fascinated by the state of journalism in the western world. He knew Enright's work, praised his reputation, remembered details from his piece on Willy Brandt and DeGaulle. He counted editors all across Europe as friends. "What are you working on now?"

The next afternoon Enright went to a flat in Kensington to meet the publisher of a German magazine. The publisher was intent on making a splash with the debut issue. He offered Enright one thousand pounds, if the pictures were clear. Enright was ready to turn them over on the spot, but the publisher asked that he deliver then to the office in Berlin, undeveloped.

"I wouldn't want to risk having anyone else getting a first glimpse. You understand," he said.

Enright did understand. "Where is the office in Berlin?'

"Not far from the Friedrichstrasse station," said the publisher and slipped an envelope with a one hundred pound advance into Enright's hand. "Take the train. It's the best way."

Enright understood: you did not need vows or promises or declarations to take a step, just a drunken tumble, a caress, a casual cruelty or crude dismissal. Or an envelope slid across a table top. There would be no objections about newsworthiness or relevance or inquiries about the prostitute's other clients. There would be no publication. There was no magazine.

The strained voice of the conductor announcing Dover in ten minutes pulled Enright back onto the train. He felt in his pocket for the film, and pulled his hand out self-consciously. When the conductor passed their row, the woman whispered to the American and they both turned to Enright. He was caught staring at them, but the American's smile held him and kept him from turning away.

"Excuse me, do you know if they serve drinks on the ferry?"

*****

The American introduced himself as Carson. The woman was Katya, a German. She could barely put two words in English together. She seemed to understand most of the conversation, though Enright thought she might be pretending. He bought the first round in the barroom crowded with Belgian football fans celebrating a victory over England. The Belgians pushed them toward the outside edge of the room. A bench padded in worn blue cloth ran along the wall. Carson set his backpack down and tossed his coat over it.

"I've never been to Germany," Carson said. "Katya is going to show me around. Aren't you?" Katya flashed the gap in her teeth.

"Berlin?"

"Yes," said Carson. "She has relatives in the east and we can visit them. That sounds so cool."

"I'm going to Berlin, as well. Always take the train. I enjoy the gradual immersion. Like a hot bath."

Katya took her cue from Carson and chuckled along. Enright began planning other lies to cover the first, adventures from previous train trips. But the boat bobbed and with each crest and each trough Enright could feel customs inspectors bringing him into focus. The man with the houndstooth hat entered the room and battled his way through the Belgians to the bar. Enright started to put his hand in his pocket to feel the film and stopped. He was sure the man was from MI5. He was sure the man would have the customs officials search him.

He tried focusing on the story Carson was telling about his life as a graduate student of Anthropology. "My specialty is primitive myths. I made a trip with Levi Strauss. Know him?  We paddled up the Orinoco, as peaceful and beautiful as any trip on earth. Toucans and parrots, marmosets, caiman. Unspoiled. Then we heard a small tap, tap, tap. Our canoes started taking on water. Slowly, so slowly that we denied it was meaningful. But soon it reached our ankles…."

Enright could not concentrate. The Belgians were all shouting, except for those who were singing. Carson's story went on. Indians, it seems, had shot darts into the canoes. He is a bigger liar than I am, thought Enright. There was more.

"Why London," Enright said. "No primitive tribes there. Why not just go to the jungle?"

"I need my student deferment," Carson said. "Otherwise I go to another jungle." He smiled. "And I would never have met Katya."

She seemed to understand that and she got on her toes to kiss his cheek. Her arms held his shoulders and that motion hiked her skirt up. Carson smiled at Enright like a boy who filched the extra chocolates.

Two Belgians moved aggressively, without warning, toward Carson, like the caiman in his story.

"American?" The fatter Belgian said in a high, smoky voice.

"Yes," Carson said. "American." He showed no fear or self-consciousness. "Vietnam, no?"

"Noooo," said Carson.

The Belgians looked at each other wide eyed and turned as one to Carson and shouted, "Whiskey!"

As the Belgians guided Carson toward the bar, he looked back at Enright apologetically. Another Belgian pulled Katya along. Enright shrugged and sat down. The noise seemed to dim, travel above him. He could not see Carson. He could not see the man in the houndstooth hat. Enright sighed as if relieved of a burden. Two middle aged women huddled in close conference on his right. An old man dozed, pint in hand, to his left.

Carson's backpack sat next to Enright's right hand. He reached into his pocket and fingered the film. Then he palmed it and slipped it inside the small pocket of the backpack. I'll retrieve it after customs, he thought. He'll never know. He'll doze from all the liquor. It's a long trip to Berlin. There will be plenty of time. Enright looked at the back pack and reconsidered. The cry went up, dampened, as if from a stadium blocks away, "Vietnam, no?"

"Noooo."

"Whiskey!"

The urge to take the film back, to rescind his decision gripped Enright. He could barely swallow his drink. He dared not glance toward the backpack. If I stand up, he thought, that will stop me. He stood and looked toward the bar but did not see Carson with the Belgians. Enright gulped the rest of his drink. He looked toward the door. There he saw Carson talking with the man in the hounds tooth hat.

*****

As they debarked, Carson said, "I think he's following you." Enright bothered to play dumb. "That's why I was talking to him. He denied it, of course. He said his name is Riley. But I doubt it. Do you know him?"

"Why would he follow me?"

They waited in Calais, bags on the long table, for the customs men to give them the nod. Katya smiled at the bald headed customs man, but that just seemed to make him delay her. When he lifted a bra from her case, she grabbed it and gestured angrily and swore in German. The man with the thick moustache waved Carson through.

Enright knew he was in the clear but he worried anyway. They could plant anything, and certainly did at times. He had no idea how that decision was made. It irritated him that he could not present himself in a way that made the inspectors let him pass. They let Riley pass with a nod. When everything from Enright's valise was on the table he said, "If you're looking for something specific, maybe I can help you." The customs man sneered and walked away.

*****

The pavement outside the Gare du Nord looked clean, rinsed by the rain. The night was clear and Paris smelled of bread and cigarettes and roasted chestnuts. Carson slowed down to admire a shop window. When Riley came along, Carson said, "There's plenty of time for a meal. Why don't you join us?"

They chose a bistro near Gare de l'est. Riley seemed less like a cop now that Enright could hear him talk. He knew his way around Paris and regarded the city with a sardonic affection. Enright told a story about the time he interviewed Bridgit Bardot who only wanted to talk about her dog's sex life. "Now I can't think of her without thinking of dogs stuck together."

Carson wanted to know about Enright's career. "Are you working on a story now?  In Berlin?"

"I am," said Enright. "Unfortunately, I can't talk about it. My sources are very sensitive."

"You're lying. I think you're lying.

"Are you a spy, Enright?  Katya thinks you are. Don't you, Katya?"

Katya sipped her wine and looked out the window.

Carson went on. "What do you think, Riley?"

Riley said, "They say the best spies are the ones who are most obvious. Think of Philby."

"I think you're just hanging out with us for cover," Carson said to Enright.

"I thought you were doing the same, using me." Enright held up his glass as if to toast.

Carson laughed. He sipped his wine and became serious. "That's the beauty of the game, isn't it. No one tells the truth. Everyone has to guess all the time. That means there's room for an outsider to step between the lines and profit."

"Profit?"

"I study primitive tribes and their customs and I think the spy services operate very much like those tribes. They have arcane rules of warfare that only insiders can grasp, shifting priorities, peculiar alliances. They even use the equivalent of blow darts."

Riley broke into a short silence. "You might be right in one case in a thousand, but that leaves plenty of people caught in between and not getting out."

Carson held up his glass. "To the one in a thousand."

Enright was buoyed by Carson's attitude which complemented his own disgust with the arrogance he had encountered whenever he dealt with the bureaucrats connected to the secret services. Riley seemed benign, even pleasant. The wine, the delicious food, Carson's rebellious energy and Katya's lovely thighs combined to dissolve London's grey gauze from Enright's consciousness. He reached for the check. Carson grabbed it away from him and insisted. Enright hid his relief by offering to buy a round of brandies. I want to make sure he sleeps, Enright thought. But he was not worried anymore. Everything was moving along in the right direction.

Even the train was better, more comfortable and less austere than Enright had anticipated. Soldiers filled the third class cars. A few officers came forward. Enright placed his bag on the rack next to Carson's backpack and sat across the aisle from Carson and Katya. Riley had excused himself and gone into another car.

Enright thought of the article he might sell to a travel magazine, maybe the Sunday Times, about train travel to Berlin, French style: the luxury, the alternative to the Orient Express, the drama. He looked around for officers to interview. Better to invent the interviews, he thought. I don't want any of these soldiers watching what I do. He closed his eyes and tried to break down some of the unspoken rules of this cold war clandestine world. He drifted out and fought his way back to consciousness. Carson's dinner conversation filled the space between waking and sleeping: play the middle, hover above the fray, exploit tribal warfare and voodoo; ignore the rules, rather than guess at them poorly. No more working as a partisan shill. He forced his eyes open. Katya was snuggled against Carson, his arm draped around her, resting between her breast and her hip. She had slipped off her white boots and curled her feet up on the seat. The pangs of resentment and envy stabbed Enright for a moment, but he smiled: Carson had given him a gift – insight – and with it came the promise of a life with a stream of mini-skirted Katyas.

He stood and without looking around, reached over the sleeping couple and removed the film from the pocket of the backpack where he had placed it. He palmed it and slipped it into his coat pocket. He thought: perhaps I am good at this. He sat down again, taking one more longing look at Katya, then drifted back into wonderland and his vaguely bright future.

Greppos invaded the train at Marienbord. The first announcement came in German. Enright could understand enough of it: they were entering the German Democratic Republic and no one will be allowed off the train until it reached Friedrichstrasse station in Berlin. That information was repeated in French and English. It occurred to Enright that East Germany was a safe zone for him now. Danger lurked in England.

Carson startled him out of his meditation on exile. "How long is it usually before we get going again? The border guards look nasty."

Enright remembered his lie. "About thirty minutes. But you never know with these boys. They might decide to show their muscle."

Two Greppos, young and sullen, AK-47s slung over their shoulders, made their way down the aisle, gesturing wordlessly for the passports. They were already expert at staring threateningly at the passengers. This shift is probably punishment, thought Enright. Maybe they were suspected of Western Weaknesses.

By the time they reached Brandenburg the sun had risen and begun waking the passengers. Katya pulled on her boots and went forward to use the toilet. A moment later, Carson opened his eyes and stretched. "Where are you staying in Berlin?"

Enright had not booked a room for fear his movements could be traced. "The Kempinski," he said. "What about you?" It was the only hotel Enright could name.

"Is it nice? Maybe I'll try that, too," Carson said. Katya rejoined them.

"I have to meet someone first thing on arrival," Enright said. "I'll look you up when I get in."

Friedrichstrasse train station was larger than Victoria Station and busier. It seemed that everyone getting off the train was going to West Berlin except for Enright, who explained that he was meeting his source in the shops below the station. To go west they had to walk to platform B where they could catch a U-Bahn train.

Carson stopped to take a photo. "Ah, the jungle. Look at it, Enright. It even has a canopy. And all the natives going their ways, every one of them trained in the dangers, everyone hoping not to be singled out before he returns to his own side. I could spend a lifetime documenting their habits. But… I think there might be more interesting approaches. See you soon, Enright. Don't step in any traps."

Soldiers stood by every few feet wearing different uniforms from the Greppos but holding the same rifles the Greppos had. Some Stasi men were easy to identify, hands in pockets, boldly staring at whatever passengers caught their attention. The signs confused Enright. He did not know U-Bahn from S-Bahn. He stopped to make sure Riley was not following him, then turned down a long crowded hallway.

He felt a tap on his shoulder and turned angrily. One of the men he had identified as Stasi faced him. The man smiled. "Mr. Enright? I think you would rather go this way. It will be much faster. You can call me Willi."

"Yes, but what's your name?" Enright said and smiled.

Willi smiled back. "Please give me your passport and I will see to everything."

The office was on the fourth floor of an old stone building on Dorotheenstrasse, just a ten minute walk from the station. The door was smoked glass, unmarked and there was no plaque on the wall identifying the occupants. Willi opened the door courteously and said, "I will wait here to escort you back."

The first room held only two chairs and a small table between them. Enright was about to knock on the door to the inner office but it opened first and young woman said, "May I have the film, please?"

A wave of suspicion hit Enright. He leaned forward, trying to peek inside the next office. The woman put a hand on his chest. "How do I know…." Enright said.

"You will be paid when we have developed the photos. It is the way this is done."

Enright had resolved not to go along with the way things are done. He felt like a prisoner. Willi was guarding the door and Enright did not know the way back to the West anyway. He wished someone would enter the room, someone he could attempt to charm, or complain to. I would be better off if I did not understand the rules. Better off if I made my own. It's the money, again, the money. I just want that and to get out.

Enright missed Carson's casual cynicism and tried to repeat the tropes as he had begun to do on the train. As an hour passed, the questions Enright had eluded shuffled in and he fended them off with rationalizations: who was he betraying; was cooperating with the enemy the same as betraying your country; did the level of harm matter? After all, this politician was not England. And the West was about money. They admitted as much. But it was not betrayal, Enright, realized with a shudder, that was haunting him; it was commitment. He had chosen a side at last. And the commitment was not something gained because his only early ambition had been to hang above the fray, disinterested, even indifferent.

When the door opened, a tall, dignified man in a three piece suit beckoned Enright to the inner office. Spread on the table were photos: Victoria Station, inside and out, from various angles; the National Gallery; Trafalgar Square; Riley in his hat; Katya; Enright biting into his cheese roll.

*****

Carson was smiling when he answered the door to his suite at the Kempinski. "So you are a spy after all, Enright. But I knew that as soon as I found the film. And Riley was following you all along. Tribes. Jungle wars."

"I need the photos, please."

Carson moved aside and waved Enright in. The living room was vast, five times, at least, the size of Enright's bedsitter. It was decorated in gold and silver and the light streaming in the huge windows made the wall paper seem worth mining.

"You let me hump the photos. I own them."

"That sounds like Vietnam talk," said Riley.

"Please. I promised them," said Enright.

"How much are you getting?"

Enright did not want to talk in front of Riley.

"It's okay. Riley, if that's his name, seems to know a lot. I've offered him the photos for twenty five hundred quid. I'll see you get your share. He's MI5 after all, something, one of them. A real spy. Could be Stasi for all I know."

"Please, Carson. They're serious."

Carson squinted at Enright and then smiled. "Enright, you don't even know what you've got, do you? Come here."

Carson taunted Riley with a smile and pulled two photos from a large envelope. He placed them on the sideboard and moved out of the way so Enright could approach.

The first photo showed the prostitute in close up on the bed. The sheets had been pulled down and they were splotched with her blood. She had been beaten. The side of her head was just a dark mass of blood.

The second photo showed Marley, the politician, in the foreground without his shirt and the prostitute behind him on the sullied sheets.

Fear flared through Enright's body like an infection unleashed. He fought to hide it and knew he failed. Though he could see the two men plainly, the room felt draped in blackness so thick that he dared not move.

"Just forget you saw the photos, Enright," Riley said. "Force yourself."

"She was alive when I was there, when he handed me the film."

Riley turned away.

"I told you, walk between the sides and ignore the rules." Carson said. "You're too obedient, Enright. It'll get you in trouble." He turned to Riley. "Twenty five hundred and the cost of this suite."

Riley said, "I'll pay the twenty five. But you have to accompany Enright to deliver the pictures. He has to have a reason to show why he didn't have them. Otherwise they'll suspect tampering or a set up."

"You want me to deliver the pictures?"

"Do you accept?"

"Why not?"

Riley left. The hour Enright spent in the East German office was bathed in regret but the time spent waiting for Riley in the suite was a bottomless sea of confusion. "I don't get it. Who is he?  I can't piece this together. Maybe we should get out of here."

"MI5 or MI6 I suppose. He wants you to sell the pictures to the Russians or Germans or whoever it is. I don't know why, and it doesn't matter."

Carson's charm seemed to have evaporated. He sounded like a simpleton. Both Riley and Carson advocated wilful ignorance, but from Riley it sounded like wisdom and from Carson like foolishness. Enright almost chuckled: the decision was clear, only his perception of it remained to be determined.

Carson showered and changed. Enright paced. I should be walking out of Germany. I should be disappearing. Forget the money. I could write this up as an adventure. But Riley returned with Carson's money. "I'll wait here, if that's alright with you," he said.

Carson's first stop was the front desk where he had deposited the developed photos in the safe. They walked along Kurfurstendamm toward Tiergarten.

"You keep the money the Germans give you and I'll kick in another five hundred," Carson said.

"Maybe you shouldn't take all that money to the east."

"I'm a rich American to them. Forget the rules, Enright. Who are these people?  They're the same ones sending my friends to die in Vietnam. The only way to fight them is find the gaps, change the game on them. They're the old guard, Enright. The past. Do you really think the world would be a worse place if they stopped playing altogether? We're going to make out very well on this."

A blur of white caught Enright's eye across the street. Katya. Carson insisted they follow her. "She can't come with us," Enright said.

"But after we get back I'm going to want to know where she is. We'll have to celebrate."

They followed her into a small hotel just yards from the U – Bahn station. Katya looked back and saw them just as they came into the bar. Carson called out to her. She flashed the gap in her teeth and waved for them to follow her and she passed through the bar. Carson followed. Enright looked to the bartender for some sort of reprimand but he busied himself wiping the wine glasses.

Katya waved for them to follow her down a dim staircase. "Come. I'm meeting ein Freund," she said.

"We only have a few minutes," Carson said. "Slow down." But he followed her and Enright went along.

Katya disappeared into a room at the bottom of the stairs.

By the time Enright entered two men were holding Carson by his arms. Enright turned to face a large, stone faced man wearing an overcoat. Riley entered from a door at the rear of the room. Carson spoke first to Katya, asking what was going on. She shrugged as if she could not understand, but this time her smile seemed taunting.

Riley ordered the men to take the photos and the money from Carson. "Do keep quiet, Carson. No one will hear you." Carson was no longer an entertaining travel companion; he was a nuisance, a bore.

Carson spit at Riley but missed. "I'll tell the world who you are. I'll end you. You're a roach and I'm gonna shine a light on you, Riley, or whatever your name is. What do you have?  Is it a law that says you can act like this?  A policy?  I doubt it. It's a notion you had. You sensed you could get away with it and intimidate anyone who challenged you by calling it secret and important. You're just an overindulged little boy. I'll shine a light on you."

Riley nodded and one of the men let go of Carson's arm. The man hit Carson in the gut and when Carson doubled over, the man smashed his elbow into Carson's jaw. A tooth fell onto the floor.

"No one can hear you now, Carson," Riley said. "No one will believe you later. You were mugged, or you tried to chat up the wrong woman. We'll let you decide the story. But do not mention these photos. Not ever. We will find you."

Riley led Enright out of the room and they stood, with Katya, on the landing at the bottom of the staircase. Carson's shouts came through as a slight humming sound.

"One in a thousand. I tried to explain that to him," Riley said.

Enright said, "You changed the roll of film even before Carson did. I've been played from the start."

"That's alright, Enright. You've done fine so far without understanding a thing. Perhaps you'll figure it out, perhaps you won't. It doesn't matter. You have a role to play so listen carefully." Riley handed him the envelope of photos, "You will say you were delayed because you decided to develop the pictures. You didn't want any mistakes this time. And you will ask for more money. Now you see how valuable they are. Ask for fifteen hundred pounds. Be insistent. Don't worry, they won't hurt you. Make the best deal you can."

Enright nodded along. He looked toward the closed door, as if hoping for sounds, but there were none. He looked up the staircase.

"Follow Katya. She'll lead you to the correct station. Cheer up, Enright. There were many candidates and you were chosen. And you've impressed me. Stashing the film to get through customs – well, you were unlucky. Lesson learned, I hope. You're a spy now. You're in the game."

Enright stood still. "But the girl, the prostitute… is she dead?"

"Don't put yourself in the middle, Enright. It doesn't pay."

Katya walked up stairs without waiting for more, white boots, short white skirt, white jacket, and Enright followed her.

# Incognito

## Kelly Zimmer

*"Believe me, my young friend, there is nothing, absolutely nothing, half so much worth doing as simply messing about in boats."*

*- Kenneth Grahame, The Wind in the Willows*

I stood in the galley, pressed my fists on my hips, and called to my husband. "There's a finger in the weedhatch."

Alex frowned at the canal charts spread over his lap. He was only a few feet away in the narrowboat's lounge, half reclined in his chair, but too engrossed in his beloved maps to comprehend me.

"Did you hear me? There's a blooming finger in the blooming weedhatch!"

His features creased in confusion. "Did you cut it on the propeller? I told you to wear gloves whilst clearing out the weeds."

I raised both hands and wiggled all ten intact digits at him. "It's not my finger, you goof. There's a man's finger in the weedhatch."

Alex pushed to his feet, sending his charts spilling to the carpet. "What man? Who's on the boat?"

I ordered my eyes not to roll. For over twenty years, Alex, bless him, taught French to teenage girls at a posh boarding school. He suspected strange men lurked everywhere, eager to debauch his charges. I'd worked in the registrar's office at the same school and often reminded him his students were seriously bright and spiteful young women who could look after themselves.

I took a breath. "There's no one else on the boat, darling. There is, however, a man's severed finger in the weedhatch."

His brows drew together. "How'd it get there?"

"I don't know. You need to come fetch it out and call the police."

"Do you think they're looking for it?"

"Not yet, but its owner may be."

The befuddled grimace finally faded as he caught up with me. His full lips pressed into a determined line, Alex strode off toward the stern, where a heavy steel panel on the deck gave access to the propeller.

I followed, grabbing a pair of gloves and a plastic sandwich bag from the galley along the way.

When I reached him, Alex was squatted over the hatch, his chin lowered almost to his chest. Without looking at me, he reached for the gloves and bag. "There's a ring. If it has an engraving, it may help the police identify him."

Alex pulled on the gloves, then dipped his hand into the mess of trash and weeds. He pinched the pale, bloodless digit between his thumb and forefinger and scowled. "It looks like a wedding ring."

I shuddered. "It's on tight."

"Swollen with canal water." Alex dropped the finger in the plastic bag. "The police will want to know where we picked it up. When did you last clean the weeds out?"

"End of the day yesterday. It must have got sucked in somewhere between Dunchurch Pools and here."

He rose from his squat. "I'll call the police." He passed the bag to me. "What should we do with this?"

I chewed my lip. "Freezer for now, I guess. You want a cuppa?"

"Oh, absolutely." Alex stripped off the gloves and stomped off to find his mobile.

*****

An hour later, a pair of young uniformed officers arrived at our black-and-gold trimmed narrowboat, *The Incognito*. They introduced themselves as Officers Anjali Bajwha and Ray Dunlawton.

I led them inside to the galley and seated us at the dinette. It had been a fine day for cruising, but as evening closed in, clouds were gathering and the late spring air had turned coolish. I'd whipped up a pot of tea and laid out biscuits to take off the chill.

Officer Bajwha smoothed her black hair behind her ears and nodded at the bag in the centre of our dinette table. "It must have been a shock finding that."

I poured the tea. "I couldn't quite believe what I was seeing. When I told my husband there was a finger in the weedhatch, he thought it was mine."

She gave me a sympathetic smile. "I'm glad it wasn't. Have you removed any other contents from that hatch?"

Alex squirmed on the bench next to me. "You think there are other bits and bobs of him in there?"

The officer's smile faded. "Hopefully, there's something that might give us a clue to where the finger entered the boat. A scene of crime tech is on the way."

I sent a longing glance out the galley's porthole, across the towpath, and up the low rise to the pub. "Do we have to stay onboard while you poke around? Wouldn't it be easier if Alex and I got out of your way?"

Officer Dunlawton shook his head. "The tech might have questions. We won't be long, I promise."

A few moments later, something buzzed on Officer Bajwha's person. She pulled a mobile phone from her vest pocket and read the screen. "Carrie's here." She scooted off the dinette's bench and sidled to the bow, returning in under a minute accompanied by a petite woman in a blue paper suit. Ginger curls escaped from the edges of the hood. She held a grey box that looked like it weighed as much as she did.

Dunlawton stood. "Mr. and Mrs. Foley, this is our crime scene tech, Carrie Bowles."

Alex extended his hand across the table. "Vi and Alex, please."

Ms. Bowles nodded at the plastic bag. "Is that the, uh, remains?"

"Yes," I said. "I hope you'll be carrying it away."

"I will. Where was it found?"

"The weedhatch." I rose to show her the way.

Ms. Bowles motioned for me to stay seated. "And what is a weedhatch?"

"Just a door in the floor at the stern," Alex said. "Gives you access to the area around the propeller to clean out any debris that gets sucked up. Grass, weeds, bits of fishing line."

The tech's grey eyes clouded. "Was the finger wedged in the propeller?"

"It was wrapped up among a tangle of weeds." I made a rolling motion with my hands. "Like it got sucked in then whisked around with the grass and stuff."

"Interesting. Would you show me this hatch, please?" she asked Officer Dunlawton.

He led her to the back of the boat, leaving Officer Bajwha on babysitting duty.

She smiled at us from across our dinette table. "Are you on holiday?"

Though we'd expected the question, my husband and I exchanged a glance.

"We're retired," I said. "We're always on holiday."

"Retired? You seem so young."

I slid a plate of Hobnobs toward her. "You're too kind."

She reached a hand toward the biscuits, then pulled it back. "I should have a look at your identification. For the record."

Alex pulled his wallet from a hip pocket. "Will a driving license do?"

"Perfectly." She retrieved a small notebook from her vest and jotted down his details, frowning as she did so. When she'd finished, she turned to me. "Mrs. Foley?"

Three steps took me to my tan leather recliner, specially made for the tight space of a narrowboat. I retrieved my wallet and returned to the bench next to my husband.

"Here you go, Officer." I passed her the license.

She rubbed at the corner of her mouth. "This birthdate is correct? You're fifty?"

"Forty-nine. I'll catch up with my husband in July."

Alex chuckled. Bajwha did not.

"You seem uncomfortable," Alex said. "Is this your first encounter with a severed finger?"

"Sadly, no. I've attended many automobile accidents." She seemed to gather herself. "It's just that I expect retirees to be like my gram—white-haired, struggling to get by on a pension. Not middle-aged folks like you, flitting about on a narrowboat. What are you retired from?"

"Teaching," Alex said. "Vi worked in administration. We put in twenty years. Saved a bit." Alex tilted his head slightly. "You're wondering how we could afford this boat, aren't you? Trying to make detective?"

Officer Bajwha lowered her eyes and smiled sheepishly. "Sorry."

I forced myself to sound shocked. Not quite offended, but getting there. "You don't think we cut off someone's finger, do you?"

"No. Not at all." The poor woman was thoroughly flustered. "Sorry. I don't know why I asked." She paused. "Sorry. It's a lovely boat."

Alex straightened in his seat. He was stupidly proud of *The Incognito* and welcomed any opportunity to talk about her. "Fifty-eight-footer. Sleeps four, but not comfortably. We bought her off a neighbour who'd gotten in over his head. He'd dropped a fair bit of change into her, adding custom this and that. A divorce cost the poor fellow, so he gave us a nice price."

"Sorry," she said again. "I didn't mean to pry, but you two are rather young, and—"

Bustling at the business-end of the boat drew the officer's attention from our financial situation.

"That was fast," I said.

The tech swung her grey box onto the dinette table. "Not much to see."

"When will you determine who the finger belongs to?" I asked.

"Hard to say. We'll look at the ring first."

"And I'll check hospitals and casualty wards for anyone reporting a missing finger," Officer Dunlawton said.

"What about you?" I asked Officer Bajwha. "Will you check into missing persons?"

She blinked twice, rapidly. "You think there's more of him out in the canal?"

I raised my eyes to the nervous young officer across the table. "You never know. Couldn't hurt to see if anyone's gone missing within the last day or so. The detective assigned to the case would appreciate your initiative, I'm sure."

Her dark eyes sparkled in the lamplight. Alex was right. She did indeed hope to make detective one day.

The rumble of distant thunder ended our chat.

"We'd better get moving. Thanks for the tea and biscuits," Dunlawton said.

From the towpath, Alex and I waved goodbye to the team as they climbed into their vehicles. The uniformed officers had left their patrol car at the top of the rise, just off the road into town. In the evening gloom, I could just make out the roof of tech's van parked further down the lane.

"What do you think?" Alex asked.

"I think we can do something with this, but I'm knackered. Do you fancy dinner at the pub?"

"Oh, absolutely."

We grabbed umbrellas, crossed the towpath, then climbed the rise until it met the road.

The Goat and Tiger pub was a quarter mile ahead, past an estate agent that was closed and a hair salon with one customer still in the chair. Inside, the G&T sported the expected old-timey touches: exposed timber beams, dark wood, and a fireplace. The menu, however, was thoroughly modern.

I ordered a veggie burger with avocado. Alex went with crispy chicken wings and sticky Korean sauce.

When our food arrived, we ordered another round of drinks. Ale for Alex, and a gin and slimline for me.

"You were teasing that girl," Alex said.

"Did you see the way she looked at our driving licenses? She thinks we're criminals."

Alex snorted.

"Tax cheats at the very least. I wanted to shake her up a bit. How'd I do?"

He smoothed his hair from his forehead. His limp golden brown locks were now shot with silver, which made him even more handsome. My greys were dyed a chestnut brown and overdue for a touchup. I wondered if I could work in an appointment at the salon while we were docked.

"Should we call Maddie?" I asked.

"We just left her place, Violet."

"I mean about the finger."

He checked his watch. "It's past ten, and she's nursing a three-month-old. I'd hate to wake her if she was catching some sleep. Besides, we're here to work, remember?"

We ordered coffee and talked about our current project a bit. Alex had just called for the bill when Officer Bajwha entered the pub dripping wet and still in her uniform. After a glance around the room, she approached us with long, confident steps.

I admired this sudden show of self-assurance and revised my opinion of her upward. "Good evening, Officer. Are you looking for us?"

"I hope you don't mind, Mrs. Foley. When you weren't at the boat, I assumed you'd come here for dinner. May I sit down?"

"Call me Vi, please. Would you like a drink?"

"No, but I have a question for you." She pulled out her phone. "Actually, I want to show you something." After a few pokes and swipes, she turned the screen our way.

I studied the photo on her phone. It was a headshot of a man about my age, with a round face and dark eyes. "Is that who the finger belongs to?"

"Do you recognize him?" she asked.

I leaned in closer. The picture had been taken on holiday. There was a palm tree and a stretch of blue-green water in the background. I turned to Alex. "I don't. What about you, darling?"

"No. Who is he?"

"His name is Roger Thornton." She angled the phone's screen from me to Alex. "He's an estate agent specializing in warehouse and office space. He owns several high-end properties in and around London."

Lines creased my husband's forehead. "There was a student at St.

Cat's." He paused and raised his eyes to Officer Bajwha. "That's the school I taught at. It has to be over ten years ago. Her name was Matilda Thornton, Tilly. I seem to remember her father did something in the building business."

"Did you ever meet her father?" Bajwha asked.

Alex shrugged. "I may have. St. Cat's is a boarding school. I knew the girls well, but the parents weren't around much. It's the type of place well-heeled folk dump their offspring while they make millions and vacation in places like Puerto Banus and Thailand."

She frowned and returned her phone to her pocket.

I suspected I knew the reason for the frown, but asked anyway. "What's wrong, Officer?"

"Mr. Thornton's body was found further along the canal about an hour ago. He's missing a finger on his left hand."

My heart skipped a beat. "Any idea how?"

"The post-mortem is scheduled for tomorrow afternoon. We'll know more then. You're certain you didn't know Mr. Thornton, didn't see him along the canal?"

"We keep ourselves to ourselves when we cruise," Alex said. "He'd have to ram his boat into ours to get my attention."

"But you admit you knew the dead man?"

My husband stretched his arms across the back of the upholstered wooden bench and studied her. "You're saying this man was Tilly Thornton's dad?"

"Yes. The deceased has a daughter named Matilda," Bajwha confirmed.

"I wouldn't say I knew him. He was just the father of one of the girls I taught." Alex raised one brow and grinned. "And if I had killed the man, why would I report finding a piece of him?"

"I don't think you killed Thornton. It's just that." She took a deep breath. "This is going to sound foolish, but you knew the dead man, and." She swallowed. "Sorry, but I feel you two are hiding something."

Alex and I bust out in laughter. This woman had good instincts. She'd make an excellent detective inspector one day.

"My husband and I were at St. Cat's for over twenty years. We met thousands of girls. They all had parents and most have their own families by now. It's not inconceivable we might cross paths with someone connected to the school. Granted, finding one of their body parts is a bit out of the ordinary."

Bajwha shifted in her seat. "Sorry. But. Well. It's just my boss will want all the t's crossed."

I welcomed the change in direction. "A detective's been assigned already? I'm surprised they're not here questioning us instead of you."

Bajwha moved her attention to the menu board. "Detective Inspector Brannon is indisposed this evening." Her words tumbled out in a mechanical tone, as if from long practice.

Alex saw an opening. He nodded to me ever so slightly.

"Is this detective inspector prone to drinking too much too early in the day?" I asked gently.

She blinked, tried to smile, but gave up. "I'll catch him up in the morning, but he'll want to speak to you. I'm sorry to have to ask you this, but can you stay on in town until he's interviewed you?"

*As if we'd miss the opportunity.* "We'd already staying on, dear. Tomorrow's laundry day and I hate using that tiny machine on *The Incognito.* I'll visit the launderette in the morning. In the meantime, if you like, Alex and I could get in touch with our contacts at the school, see what they know about Roger Thornton."

Bajwha glanced around the rapidly emptying pub. She dropped her voice to a whisper. "I wouldn't mind having the case wrapped up in a bow for him."

"By him, you mean your detective inspector?" I asked.

She nodded.

"You're saying you want to close the case before he can take credit for solving it?"

Her smile finally broke through. "That would be nice for a change."

"Call us in the morning," Alex said. "We'll let you know if we learn anything of interest."

Officer Bajwha said goodnight and left us.

After settling the bill, Alex and I returned to the boat. We swung our interlocked hands between us as we walked through the rain.

"What do you say? Should we help the young officer?" I asked. "Can our job wait another day?"

"Why should we want to do that? We're already behind."

*Why did it matter so much to me?* We had work to do, and Alex hated distractions. "I see a bit of my younger self in Anjali. When we started out all those years ago, I was pretty timid. Too shy to put myself out there." I paused our walk and turned to face him. "Then you came along and made me step outside my comfort zone. Without that boost, I'd still be an office done." I kissed the tip of his nose. "You convinced me I was meant for something more."

"We make a good team." His lopsided grin, the one that never failed to melt my heart, appeared. "We'll be short on sleep tonight."

"Won't be the first time." I resumed our walk. "Do you think she knows?"

"I doubt it. She's probably already looked us up, saw we have no criminal records, and confirmed our work history at St. Cat's. Everything lines up with what we told her. Why focus on us?"

"You're right. Let's keep her focused on someone else."

*****

Our research tools aren't what the police have access to, but they're better than most. By two in the morning, we'd identified at least three people with reasons to kill Thornton.

We knocked off for a few hours' sleep. I was still in bed when I called Officer Bajwha at seven.

"Good morning, Anjali. May I call you Anjali?"

"Ah, yes. No. It doesn't matter. What can I do for you?" Her voice was groggy with sleep.

"My husband and I have collected background information on the dead man from the canal. If you'd like to stop by the boat to go over the material, I'll have coffee and eggy bread."

"Ah, um. Now?"

I added an enticing sparkle to my voice. "I make a mean mango compote to go with the eggy bread."

"I'll be there in half an hour."

It took her closer to forty minutes, which was fine. It gave Alex an opportunity to follow up on a few details about our suspects.

When the officer arrived, her long black hair was still damp from the shower and she wore a blue jumper over jeans. She settled onto the dinette bench across from my husband. "Sorry, I don't have much time. It's my day off, but I'm meeting with Detective Inspector Brannon at eleven to review the Thornton case."

I poured her coffee. "Why doesn't Alex get right to it then while I serve up breakfast?"

My husband downed the dregs of his second cup and flipped opened a manila folder holding about two dozen sheets of paper. The results of our burning the midnight oil.

"Roger Elliott Thornton. Forty-nine-years old. Finance graduate. Went into property investment early in his career. Besides brokering large deals for commercial and industrial property, he's amassed a respectable portfolio of his own."

He slid three stapled pages across the dinette table to Anjali.

"Several months ago, Thornton got into a dispute with the estate agent handling his most recent acquisition, a small warehouse close to the A1 in Central London." Alex turned to the third page and tapped a photo of a man in a dark suit. "This fellow threatened to take Thornton to court. However, the pair ran into each other at a restaurant in Soho and got into a public brawl. The other agent was charged with causing a public disturbance. To make the charge go away, he apologized to Thornton and dropped the lawsuit."

Anjali cut into the eggy bread I'd set before her. "The dispute's settled then."

I leaned over her shoulder. "Coincidentally, the fellow's renting a vacation home on the North Oxford Canal this week."

The officer's fork paused at her open mouth. "Where on the canal?"

"I'm sure you'll ask, Officer." Alex said. "His mobile number is under his photo."

She nodded, took a bite of her eggy bread, and chewed thoughtfully.

Alex pulled another sheet from the stack. A headshot of a lovely young blonde woman graced the top of the page. "My former student, Tilly Thornton, and her dad have been estranged for several years. Recently, Tilly wanted to marry and approached her father about funding a rather elaborate wedding. He refused."

He slid another stack of stapled sheets to Anjali. "Tilly's social media posts suggest she didn't take the refusal well. In them, she calls her father several choice names and threatens to cut off his, well, parts of him."

Anjali stopped chewing and pulled the pages closer.

Alex gave her time to glance over them before continuing. "Last, Roger's ex-wife Gloria left him two years ago for a man ten years her junior." He slipped on his reading glasses and squinted at the text below the woman's photo. "When she jetted off to Greece, her Facebook posts informed her friends she was off to live a less stifling lifestyle with her soul mate. She described her new lover's skill set in intimate detail." He leered at the page, then lowered it to the dinette table.

"Gloria Thornton returned to London three months ago divorced, sunburned, and broke. In an email to Roger, she asked for a reconciliation, which he refused. In a later email, she says she understood, but demanded enough cash to start over. Again, he refused but did offer to give her the wedding ring he still wore. In the final email, the last one before Roger blocked her, Gloria says she's staying with her sister in Birmingham and demanded the ring and a lot more or she'd make his life a living hell."

"Birmingham's only about an hour from where I found the finger," I added helpfully.

A full minute passed, during which Anjali sipped coffee and frowned at her plate. "How do you have access to the deceased's emails?"

Alex's crooked grin appeared. "Same way you will, I expect."

I poured myself coffee and settled next to my husband on the dinette's bench. "A few phone calls will tell you where these folks have been over the last couple of days. You may not solve the case, but you could get at least one of those three in an interview room by lunchtime,

I imagine."

Anjali leaned her elbows on the table and covered her face with her hands. After a moment, she shook her head, rubbed her eyes with her fingertips, then raised her face to us. "Who are you people?"

"Vi and Alex Foley, like we told you, dear. You must have looked us up on your databases," I said.

"I did. Everything you told me about yourselves checked out."

I opened my eyes wide, feigning shock. "Why wouldn't it?"

She patted a hand on the printouts in front of her. "How did you get this information?"

"How does anyone get anything anymore, dear? On the internet." I reached across the table and gave her hand a squeeze. "We're good at research."

She ran her free hand through her damp hair, then waved it at Alex's folder. "I can't use this."

"Of course not. You'll do your own research. We've just given you a head start." I glanced up at the microwave clock. "But you'd better get a move on. You've got a lot of calls to make before your eleven o'clock meeting with the detective inspector."

She stood, banged her knee on the underside of the dinette table, and plopped down again.

Alex gathered up the stray printouts and slid them into the folder. "Don't forget these, Detective."

Anjali's hand hovered over the folder, then pulled back. "It's Officer, Mr. Foley."

"Not for long, I'm sure," he said.

She reached for the folder, hesitated again, then scooped it up. Without a word, she slid from the bench and dashed out.

✳✳✳✳✳

We never did hear from Detective Inspector Brannon. With a suspect in custody, he was likely satisfied with our statements. Whatever relationship Alex or I might have had with the victim or his ex-wife ten years ago was unimportant. Gloria Thornton had confessed anyway, so why bother, especially when you're an aging detective with a drinking problem?

Two days later, Alex and I were casting off the mooring lines when Officer Bajwha came running down the little hill leading from the main street to the dock.

She shouted from the towpath. "I can't believe you're leaving without saying goodbye."

"We didn't want to bother you," I called. "You're busy with your case."

"The thing is, I've been assigned another one. Not officially. Brannon's taking leave to deal with his. Well. He needs my help on a few things whilst he's away."

"Congratulations," Alex called.

"You wouldn't be able to stick around for a bit, could you?"

My husband and I shared a glance.

Alex tossed her a line. "Oh, absolutely."

Anjali helped us re-secure the mooring lines, then hopped aboard.

We discussed her new case over tea and biscuits. An hour later, Alex and I watched her climb up the rise to her patrol car.

"What do you think?" I asked. "Can we use this to our advantage?"

"Not in the next book, but I think one day soon Detective Inspector Lou Hastings will find a body somewhere in the Grand Union Canal." He shoved his hands into the back pockets of his jeans. "You're sure she has no idea who we are?"

"Not a clue. I checked her online book purchases. I was surprised to find Officer Bajwha is a fan of the sweet romance. Cute meets and happily ever after endings. Not a thriller or mystery in her library. I doubt she's ever heard of The Case Files of Lou Hastings or V. A. Openshaw."

"Maybe we should tell her before she finds out accidentally. We should at least ask Maddie what she thinks."

"Maddie's our agent, Alex. She's all for anything that sells more books. Do you want to deal with the publicity that would generate? Interviews? Our faces everywhere under stupid headlines like 'Crime Novelists Solve Real Life Who Dunnit.'"

He raised his face to the muddy clouds overhead. "Heavens no. I spent too many years surrounded by too many people. I want to play with my boat on the canal while we knock out three-thousand words a day on the next Detective Lou Hastings." He raised my hand to his lips and kissed my fingertips. "Most of all, I want to be with you, not a bunch of strangers at conferences and book fests."

We turned back to *The Incognito* and climbed aboard her.

"Alex, I want to stay on and help Anjali."

"Why?"

"She'll get a leg up and we'll gather ideas for new material. If I promise we'll keep a low profile, are you with me?"

My husband draped an arm across my shoulders. "Oh, absolutely."

# *Karma's a Bitch*

## *Sharon Richards*

The first killing was the hardest. Not in any moral sense; Margaret had no qualms about that—her targets deserved to die—but it was hard in practical terms.

She hadn't perfected her methods that first time so it was sloppy and she couldn't quite believe she'd got away with it.

Hiding under the bridge in the middle of the night, she waited for him to stagger up to her on the path, then she pushed. He was too drunk to resist, too drunk to even process what was happening to him and, weighed down with his heavy winter coat and boots, it took less than a minute for him to stop thrashing in the freezing, black murk of the Manchester Ship Canal. He had made quite a lot of noise in that minute though, and Margaret knew that if she was going to bring her long-cherished plan into fruition she would have to put more careful thought into the next one.

As time passed she became more adept and, eventually, quite creative in her methods, pinching lots of ideas from police true-crime programmes on the telly.

She didn't have to seek out her targets; people brought them to her. She was proud of the system she'd set up; simple but effective.

**Step 1: Get a burner phone**; cheap, untraceable and easy to dispose of in a hundred and one ways (something else she'd learned from the telly).

**Step 2: Advertise her services.** She visited ladies' toilets in large shops all over the city and stuck a notice on the back of each cubicle door. She'd spent ages designing them, eventually choosing a font she hoped was both caring and professional.

*Domestic Abuse Helpline. You are not alone. Ring this number for practical help. We are waiting for your call.*

She was surprised at how many of those calls originated from the posters in Waitrose and M&S.

**Step 3: Extract as much information as possible from the person calling the number.**

As soon as she engaged with one woman she would remove every flyer until she was ready for the next case. She used a different phone with a different number for each one, gifting each individual with all of her care, attention and hands-on help before moving on to the next; the next set of flyers, the next burner phone, the next woman, the next horrific litany of cruelties.

Hearing their stories was always the hardest part for Margaret, and they cost her many sleepless nights, but it was an essential step. Margaret was nothing if not fair, and she would have hated to be responsible for any miscarriages of justice. So it was only when she was completely satisfied that the person in question did in fact deserve to die that she requested a copy of a recent photo for ID, along with a list of their routines, habits, most frequented haunts, underlying health conditions, and current medications.

Most callers were too upset to even give a second thought as to why a domestic abuse helpline might need such an eclectic selection of information but if anyone did ask, she replied in her soft Scottish brogue, 'Oh, I know dear. It's data collection gone mad nowadays if you ask me. They'll soon be asking for our GCSE results, before we can get an appointment at the dentist.' Her humour, and genuinely warm manner usually teased out the details she needed after that.

**Step 4: Memorise every detail of the above information.**

**Step 5: Destroy the current burner phone.**

**Step 6: Rid the world of one more monster.**

**Step 7: Repeat from step one.**

It annoyed Margaret that the news reports used the word 'Victim' to describe the men she targeted (they had all been men so far and she was relieved about that). These men weren't 'victims', they were perpetrators. Couldn't anyone see that? It was their wives and girlfriends who were the victims; the seemingly endless stream of women who'd finally found the courage to copy down the number in the loo and make the call, their words tumbling out in trembling, hurried whispers, in case he should come home unexpectedly and overhear them.

It rankled too that the news used the word 'murder' to describe the deaths. It might look like murder but it wasn't really—not when you looked at it logically. Murder was taking away life so how could it be murder when she was saving more lives than she took, giving more life than she was taking away? No, it wasn't murder—it was karma, plain and simple.

Margaret was a practicing Nichiren Buddhist of many years (they were all nice people and their simple daily ceremony fitted with her no-nonsense approach to life) so she understood that karma is nothing more than the law of cause and effect. If you do something good, you make a good cause and that inevitably that produces a good effect. If you do something bad, you make a bad cause and that inevitably that produces a bad effect. 'Simples', as they said on her favourite TV adverts.

But what niggled Margaret about the law of cause and effect was the time lag, because the good or bad effects of someone's good or bad actions only ever show up when *the circumstances are right*. In some cases the effects of an action could appear immediately but in others that effect might not show up for days, years, and even lifetimes after the action itself.

People say 'Karma's a bitch' but, to Margaret's mind, she was not a big enough or fast enough one. There were too many lives at stake to let karma take her own sweet time punishing abusive men, so she simply decided to lend a helping hand by speeding the whole process up a bit.

And the project was going swimmingly. She'd just wrapped up her eighth case when she heard a demanding knock at the front door. The man on the step held his ID badge up at face height so that she could verify the details. She blinked at the name: Patrick Colquhoun.

'It's pronounced 'Cahoon'', he announced. 'I'm a detective from Greater Manchester CID. I'm investigating a murder and I have a few questions I'd like to ask you.'

A few doors down, Margaret's neighbour paused from trimming his privets and stared in their direction. 'It might be better if we talk inside,' the detective suggested.

'Yes, yes, of course.' She motioned him in, pointing towards the open kitchen doorway at the end of the hall.

She watched him walk ahead of her, his muscular frame almost filling the narrow space. The word that popped into her head was 'solid' and she found that comforting somehow. Plus, he had the kind of face you can trust, and she wondered if a face like that was that one of the requirements for being a murder detective. If so, he was in the right job. He had a nice face.

In the kitchen, he picked up the kettle, and reached over the sink to fill it from the tap. 'Tea, Mum?'

'Absolutely, son, I'm parched. You know, it's a good job the neighbours know you or they'd think I was being arrested every Wednesday teatime.'

The doorstep routine had begun almost a year ago, the day he'd transferred to the murder squad. He wanted it to be a surprise and hadn't even told her he'd applied. She'd been helping Karma along for about six months at that point. She'd opened the door to his unexpected knock and been confronted with a police ID badge. She greeted that with a swear word he didn't think was even in his mum's vocabulary. Every Wednesday teatime since then, he'd repeated the same gesture and the same words, their little ritual, like a secret handshake between Masons.

She found this weekly 'arrest' comforting somehow, almost as if she were inoculating herself against the shock of when it might happen for real. But this prospect didn't worry her; her work was too important to waste time on ruminating over the future. She was a woman on a mission, doing the world a favour and besides, what was the worst they could do to her? Probably just a few years in an institution for the criminally insane.

She'd thought about what that might entail: it would mean her not being able to go anywhere, not being able to see friends and family. It would mean someone else being in control of her money, someone else deciding what she would wear, what she could eat, when she could eat, when she could sleep and an ever-present background threat of a beating. Well, she'd lived through all that and much, much worse during her 20 year marriage to Pat's father before his death so the prospect of prison held no fears for her. At least this time it would be worth it.

Her husband was the reason Pat had become a policeman. He hadn't been in the force himself; he was a window cleaner who got his kicks from peeping at women through windows. It always amused him that they unwittingly paid him to do it.

Despite all Margaret's attempts to hide the truth from him, Pat was five when he first realised that something scary was happening at home.

Between great racking sobs, he announced one day, 'When I'm big, I'll find all the naughty men and put them in prison.' As he spoke, his little hands tried to wipe the blood from Margaret's forehead.

'That's a great plan, son,' she said. And it really was.

But hers was better.

'Busy day today, mum? You look a bit tired,' Patrick said as he mashed the tea bags in the mugs.

In her mind's eye Margaret had a fleeting image of the dollop of peanut butter she'd slipped into the sandwich of today's target. She'd done it while he was pumping iron with his steroid-bloated body at the local leisure centre. His one and only life-saving adrenaline pen was now safely ensconced in the sanitary towel bin in Sainsbury's. While she was there disposing of the evidence, she'd picked up some lovely strawberry jam. 'Waste not, want not' was one of Margaret's mottos and, rather than throw the remaining peanut butter away, she decided it was high time she tried a  'peanut butter and jelly sandwich' as the Americans called it. A plate of them, cut into party triangles and wrapped in clingfilm waited on the side. They'd do quite nicely for her supper.

'Yes, it's been quite a good day all in all, Pat, and it's even better now you're here. Come here and give me a love.'

He bear-hugged her off her feet. 'Get away with you, you daft beggar,' she laughed.

They drank their tea and started to cook the meal together, just as they did every week, she making enquiries about his work, he about her health, trips out with friends and Buddhist meetings.

'Becky not joining us today, son? It's been ages since I've seen her. Is she alright?'

Margaret loved her daughter-in-law and was beyond happy to see her son finally settled with such a beautiful, clever and genuinely kind-hearted young woman. Over the three years since their marriage Margaret had come to love and treasure Becky like her own.

'She's been crazy busy at work for months and then she got that bug that's going around'.

'Oh, no. Poor wee hen. I'll pop round tomorrow and see if she needs anything.'

'Best not; wouldn't want you to catch it. Not at your age.'

'Cheeky begger.'

When the meal was ready, they decamped to the living room to eat off their knees. As usual, she had a recording of a true crime documentary lined up to watch as they ate.

'I know my programmes are a bit of a busman's holiday for you, son, but I do like them. Never used to; it's only since you got this promotion.'

Pat was flattered and answered her questions willingly and in detail. These conversations were gold dust because his insider knowledge allowed her to use the methods outlined in the show whilst avoiding the mistakes that had inevitably lead to the criminal being arrested by the end of the episode.

She'd asked him very early on about the ever-present CCTV monitors and thanked the lord for Covid because it meant she could walk past them wearing a face mask and glasses (which she bulk-bought in different styles, £1 a pair from *Home Bargains*).

But Pat also told her that the police still glean a lot of clues from the footage even if the face isn't visible; the person's height, their build, any visible scars or tattoos, their style of dress, the way they walk.

Being a tall woman, Margaret knew she could easily pass for a man, so she spent hours perfecting different walks, each so different from her own ladylike steps. On occasion she swaggered or strutted, sometimes she jogged, sometimes she limped on her left leg, a few assassinations later, on her right. Aware of how much evidence can be gleaned from a single shoe print, she bought multiple pairs of different sized men's boots, then wore leg weights and filled her pockets with bags of wet sand to affect the depth of any imprints.

She altered her appearance for each case, buying her props from charity shops: wigs, caps, scarves, umbrellas, gloves and boots, summer hats and long dresses, high viz waistcoats, hoodies and handbags, sometimes even a walking stick or Zimmer-frame. She returned them to a different charity the day after each assassination, to be sold again to a stranger and disappear off the radar forever. She didn't so much destroy the evidence as recycle it; she'd always felt it important to do her bit for the planet.

Each disguise was meticulously thought out, knowing as she did that the cameras would pick up, not the slim, ramrod straight, middle-aged, greying woman with a mincing step that she was, but perhaps a stooping, portly, elderly man in glasses and cap shuffling along on his walker. The officers at police HQ peering for clues on the grainy footage would dismiss what they saw every time and conclude, 'Nothing of any use here I'm afraid, Sarge.'

But it wasn't just her changing appearance that threw the police for a loop. She was particularly proud of the fact that, unlike other serial killers, she hadn't fallen into the trap of developing a regular 'M.O.' (as her programmes called it). Her varied methods made it almost impossible for the police to spot the connection between so many different deaths.

And, most importantly, those weekly conversations with her son, had taught her how abysmally short-staffed and under resourced the police were. They had neither the time nor the manpower to link the murders to each other, let alone link any of them to her. They would never catch her. Of that she became certain and she was absolutely right.

She was just settling down to watch *Strictly* one Saturday night when the mobile rang—the current burner. Number withheld. Margaret knew immediately that it was someone afraid they'd be rung back and the abuser would find out about the call.

She cleared her throat and got the '*Domestic Abuse Helpline, how can we help?*' greeting ready in her head. She'd started experimenting with different accents recently, having just become aware of the role of voice recognition software in criminal investigations. She was aiming for a subtle French that evening. She'd tried Welsh last time but it turned out to be harder than she'd imagined and she'd found it morphing into an unconvincing Yorkshire burr by the end of the conversation.

But the young woman wasn't listening. She talked straight over Margaret as soon as she answered the call, begging for help between great racking sobs.

'You've got to help me. Please help me. It's my husband. I don't know what to do. I'm scared. If he finds out I'm ringing he'll kill me. I can't take it anymore. He's always been a bit possessive but for the past two years he's started with these crazy ideas that I'm always looking at other men. It's getting worse, much worse. I can't go anywhere. He won't let me see my friends anymore; he doesn't even like me talking to them on the phone. I can't even see my mum; he doesn't want her to see the bruises. And he gets so angry over nothing. It used to be just shouting and swearing but he's started hitting me now and it's got much worse in the past couple of months. He's going to kill me one day, I know he is.'

Margaret took a deep breath. She'd heard it all before, so many times, too many times, but she needed to get the full story to be sure and for that she needed the woman to be calm.

'Okay, chérie, it's alright. Everything is going to be good now. I'm here for you and I'm so pleased you have got in touch. I'm Francoise.' She knew that was a cliché but the woman's extreme distress had thrown her slightly and it was the first French-sounding name she could think of.

'I'll need some information in just a minute, chérie, but first tell me; are you safe? Is your husband in the 'ouse or on his way 'ome?'

'No, he's at work. He's on a night shift tonight'. The woman's voice was hoarse; raw from crying—or screaming.

'Très bien. Do you have a chain on the front door?'

'Yes.'

'Why not put that on now, just to be safe, in case he does come back unexpectedly? If he does that and he asks why you've done it, just tell him you 'eard a noise outside and became frightened.'

There was the sound of rapid footsteps.

'That's done,' the woman panted.

'In that case we can take our time and get all the details down and see where we go from today. Let's start at the beginning, chérie. What is your husband's first name?'

'Patrick.'

'Last name?'

'It's pronounced Cahoon but it's spelled C  O  L  Q  U  H...'

# *Drowning Not Waving*

## *T. K. Howell*

Dylan told me that all he needed to do was keep pulling at the threads and eventually the whole thing would unravel. Except sometimes pulling at threads didn't unravel things, it only made the knot tighter. Sometimes that knot might begin to tighten around your own neck. I guess that's what happened to poor Dylan. He couldn't accept that Cindy Garter had simply washed out to sea and never washed back in again.

Without a body, Kevin and Katy Garter had to make do with a memorial plaque for their daughter. They chose the spot down behind the High School where we students had held our vigils. After she disappeared into the unwelcoming blue we laid flowers and wept over guttering tea-light candles then melted into the dark of the playing fields to drink and smoke our pain and confusion away. The whole school was stunned. Cindy Garter wasn't the Queen Bee, because Queen Bees are something that only exist in lazy Hollywood coming-of-age films. But she was popular, well-liked, beautiful, and a talented swimmer. People took it hard: seventeen-year-old girls with their whole lives ahead of them weren't supposed to vanish with the click of the fingers. If it could happen to her, it could happen to any of us.

A month after she was given up for lost, the Garters cleared the mouldering piles of flowers, planted a pear tree, and put a plaque underneath it. Funny, I don't particularly recall Cindy ever being that keen on pears.

The Coastguard had called off the search after two days, but in reality, when they didn't find her within the first hour they knew they were only ever looking for a corpse. Cindy never came ashore, taken out on the riptides. Fish food. Off to finally be at one with the great, wide water. A mermaid, just like she had always dreamed. But Dylan wouldn't have it. There really was no reason for him to start studying tidal charts, the movement of fishing vessels, the pattern of the currents. There was no reason to start driving the ten miles to Belcher Cove for his morning runs, just on the morbid off-chance he'd stumble across her bloated body.

"There's no way. She was captain of the swim team, breaking County records since she was twelve. Nobody that could swim 800m freestyle in sub-nine minutes had any business drowning on Belcher Cove on a clear, calm day, riptide or no riptide. And unless she'd made it more than three miles out, her body should have washed ashore somewhere around Hader's End within the first twenty-four hours. I've studied the tides," Dylan told me after the memorial service. It wasn't the first time, and it wouldn't be the last. The speeches would become longer and more elaborate with every new brick of information and data he fixed into the wall he was slowly building around himself.

"She's gone, Dyl. It's not like you were even that close anymore."

That earned me a scowl. "Close enough, Shiv. Am I the only one that cares about the truth?"

"So what's the truth then?"

"Tiger sharks."

Tiger sharks. It was Tiger sharks for the first few weeks. True, there had never been a shark attack within one hundred miles of Belcher Cove for as long as anyone had bothered to count these things, but he showed me the records: a lone Tiger shark had been spotted out past the Cove on a Summer's evening back in 1985 and then again in 1998. It was Tiger sharks at first, but then Dyl settled on Casper Trebell, and that's when things really started to snowball.

*****

I looked over the seawall at Hader's End. Down there, somewhere, was the spot where they found Dylan, two miles north of the Cove. Bladderwrack pressed into the crannies between the rocks where the breakers hit and shattered. It groped its way through the cold gaps, urged on by the same unseen force that swelled the waves. It had battened onto the rocks in defiance of the cold pummelling waters that beat everything else into submission, the body of Dylan Bugliosi included. There was an uncompromising beauty to the whole scene, the kind of rough, brutal beauty that I admired. A terrible beauty. But then I wasn't there the day they plucked Dyl's bloated and battered body from where it had lodged between the rocks. I guess that might have changed my outlook. I wasn't there even though he'd emailed me the exact location and a two-hour window in which he predicted his body would wash ashore. I wasn't there when he took a row boat out past the last place people said they'd seen Cindy Garter, injected enough of his mom's Tramadol to kill a horse, and then jumped in. Well, he proved he was right in the end, for all the good it did him and Cindy Garter.

I looked down at the darkened rocks and deep green fronds. It seemed they wanted something from me, something that I wasn't yet willing to give. The water harboured so many shaded secrets and I felt that it wanted me to know, wanted me to share my own secrets, to make an exchange. I wondered if this was what Dylan felt before his final leap.

"What do you want me to do about it?" I yelled into the crashing surf. It didn't answer back. It was dusk and there wasn't a soul around, not that I would have cared much if there was. I was cooked, baked, stoned. Again. It was all I was good for, it was all anyone ever wanted from me. Siobhan Lee: the girl who could get you any pill, popper, or powder you wanted. The girl with the family connections. Not Dyl, though. Dyl loved me, in his own weird way. And now he'd left me his tapes. He wanted me to finish it, though it wasn't a thread I particularly wanted to pick at. Because in truth, it had wrapped itself around my neck already.

*No body has yet been recovered,* ran the headlines in our small-town newspaper for a full month after Cindy disappeared. But the facts were simple: the sea had taken her. People had seen her go into the water, but no one had seen her come out again, *ergo.* Dylan was wont to remind me that he'd held that body close once, he'd felt its warmth, its youthful vibrancy, and its *desire* for him—short-lived as it was—before she'd dropped him like dirt and moved onto Casper Trebell the Football hero. Casper Trebell, the rich, handsome All-American kid whose family just happened to have their own speedboat moored down at the quay.

I paid my respects and threw an ounce of weed into the sea. It's what Dyl would have wanted.

*****

He started in on Evie and Willa first. They were Cindy's best friends and they'd been with her that day at the beach. The three of them had always been tight.

I saw Dylan zone in on them down by the memorial one night. He walked with that purposeful, Frankenstein's monster gait of his and I knew there'd be trouble so I shuffled after him into the dark of the playing fields where the two girls were smoking alone. I wrapped my hunter-green jacket tight around myself and hoisted the collar up, trying to shrink inside as Dylan loomed over them.

"You were with her at the party the night before she died, weren't you?" Dylan asked. The girls stood close together as if they had just been whispering into each other's ear. Willa held a cigarette down by her hip and was striking the sort of angular pose that belonged on the cover of a magazine. Evie eyed me coolly and I looked away. She smiled.

"Well, yeah," Willa snapped. "It was at *my* house. You know. You were there too. You and Shiv," she said, jutting her chin at me.

"Cindy had a fight with Casper."

"Yeah. *Everyone* heard. Why are you asking stupid questions? Stop being weird, Dyl. *You were there!*"

"It was nothing," Evie said, her voice smooth, soothing. That was Evie, deep freeze cool. I always liked that about her, even if she thought I was dirt beneath her feet.

"Ten minutes of shouting and then they were all over each other again."

"That's not true. I saw him drive off straight after."

I tried to remember the party, but it was a blur. I stayed in one of the back rooms smoking pot with the Loser's Club and selling pills to the jocks while Dylan jostled for position out there in the middle echelons of the school pecking order. It was rough out there, and I felt much safer having opted out. Whether Casper Trebell did drive off straight after he argued with Cindy or whether the argument had been anything to write home about, I couldn't recall.

"I know you and Cindy were a thing for, like, a week a year back, so you probably don't know how you feel about all this," Evie said, soothing again.

"Yeah, but imagine what it's like for us," Willa said. "We were there, Dyl. We *saw* her swim out and we expected her to just swim right back any minute. We didn't think anything of it. If we'd only raised the alarm earlier... But even after we called the Coastguard I still believed she'd just casually swim back to shore and ask us what all the fuss was about. She saw the warning signs but she just couldn't bring herself to believe she was in danger."

"Casper has a speedboat. He could have-"

"Oh shut *up* Dylan. Give it a fucking rest. Honestly, this is sick. Casper is in pieces. He hasn't left his house since. We talked with Cindy after everyone had gone home that night, just the three of us. She and Casper... it wasn't just, like, about the sex, you know? He'd proposed. Sort of. No ring or anything, but he'd asked."

"Who said that, Casper or Cindy? C'mon, you both know he was seeing Lottie Henderson too, don't you? You know people saw his boat out there that day."

"For Christ's sake, Dyl! He went out in his boat *after* we called the Coastguard. He was helping with the search. Man, you're a piece of shit."

They walked further into the darkness and Dyl made to follow, but I grabbed his sleeve. "They're right, man. You need to get a grip."

"Something ain't right," he said.

The following morning, Evie cornered me at recess and told me to get my friend in order or there'd be trouble. The day after that, the Police called on Dyl and gave him a dressing down for making a nuisance of himself. It didn't take a rocket scientist to work out who had put them up to it.

*"How do you think the Garters feel about you saying this kind of thing? This is painful enough for them."*

When he started with the social media posts, he really caught hell. Expulsion was not off the cards. The other kids started calling him Dyl the Delusional. Snide comments piled up in the corridors.

"Tell us where MH370 is, Dyl."

"Do you know the melting point of steel beams, Dyl?"

"I know a guy who was a crisis actor at Sandy Hook, Dyl."

He let it all bounce off him. "Freedom of speech," he'd parrot like it was some kind of shield that would save him from the slings and arrows and sticks and stones. He wouldn't take the posts down, even when the Principal called him in. Because he, and only he, knew the *truth.*

After that, he started recording everything. And those were the tapes he posted through my door the morning he set out for his last boat trip. It was just like Dyl. Why use a sleek, modern, portable, and discreet cell phone to record Voice Notes when you can carry a chunky Dictaphone in your pocket that whirs while it records?

I blamed the Police at first. There are certain people you shouldn't warn off unless you want them to bite hold and never let go, even as it drags them under. But just as the sea remorselessly pummelled the shore at Hader's End, the guilt ate at me. It was something I should have put a stop to a long time before Dyl ended up in the morgue. I should have seen the signs, but I was too distracted.

I listened to the tapes out of pure masochism. I don't know what I expected, but I was taken aback by Dyl's rambling, his incoherence. Had I been so oblivious to it all that last month? He faltered, he doubled back on himself, he never entirely seemed to know where his monologue was taking him, and seemed surprised when he arrived there. He fluctuated wildly between despondent resignation and euphoric revelation, but in the cold light of day every single one of his 'discoveries' counted for naught.

*"I, er, so I talked to some folk down here... I'm down on the quay south of Belcher Cove and right now as I talk to you I'm staring at a speedboat that folk tell me belongs to the Trebell family. I've got three... er... two guys say they remember the day Cindy drowned and Casper was down here before the time the Coastguard gave for the commencement of their, er,*

*search. The boat is not exactly inconspicuous. It's yellow with black trim, kinda like an angry hornet. God, why would anyone paint a boat this colour? You can believe that when people saw it they sure as hell remembered it. And I got two guys, er, three, now say they're certain the boat was already out on the Cove long before the Coastguard raised the alarm about Cindy. It's spotless, by the way. I'd say it'd been thoroughly cleaned recently."*

I shook my head. Poor Dylan. I could hear the seagulls screeching in the background, but I wondered if he'd ever even spoken to anyone on the quay. There were no interviews, nothing on tape, and he gave no names. Benefit of the doubt might suggest he was trying to protect his sources, but I had to conclude that he had begun to lose the run of himself. I could believe he had fabricated some of the details. There was more on the Trebells and Casper. A lot more. Dylan dug into his mother's run for Commissioner, and his father's business interests. He cornered Lottie Henderson and she spat in his eye. About a week before he took his final voyage, Dyl doorstepped Casper when he knew his parents were out. Or so he explained. The truth of it was that for the first five minutes, Dylan could have been interrogating the sea itself. There was the sound of a doorbell and then Dylan launched into a barrage of unanswered questions, his voice gradually rising.

*"Casper, when did you take out your family speedboat? I have witnesses who say it left its mooring at 12:30, a full hour before Cindy was reported missing."*

No answer.

*"What did you and Cindy argue about the night before at the party? Was it Lottie?"*

No answer.

*"Did you know she was going to be at the Cove that day?"*

No answer.

*"Was she pregnant? Is that why you killed her?"*

Casper, if he was even there, didn't say a word. The silence stretched on uncomfortably. Dylan began to speak more rapidly to fill it. He sounded truly unhinged, like a street-corner hobo preaching to the pigeons.

"*If they test your Jeep or the boat, will they find Cindy's DNA?*" Dylan snapped.

And then Casper spoke. It was only a few words. He spoke impatiently, with a hint of anger. Not unreasonable, but it was crass and I could visualize that smug, entitled face of his.

"*Oh, you'll find both of our DNA on the upholstery. Mostly mine, though.*"

Dylan gasped audibly into the Dictaphone.

"*Now get the hell off my lawn.*" There was the sound of Casper slamming the door in Dylan's face. Dylan tried to piece together his thoughts a few times, but his sentences ran aground. I could imagine him shaking that big head of his in bewilderment.

"*He did it, Shiv. He did it,*" Dyl muttered into the tape. It was the first time he had directed his thoughts at anyone and I realized that every single word on those tapes had been meant for me. The tapes were his final farewell, and he'd chosen me as the only person worth saying goodbye to. Everything around me went very still, very quiet, and very dark for a period that could have been seconds and could have been days. My room at the back of the trailer became a dark cavern and I could have been crying, but Siobhan Lee didn't cry no more, so to hell with that. I wouldn't.

"*There were scratches on his arm, I saw them when he closed the door. And his neck. It was in his eyes, Shiv. You heard the way he talked about her, she was just skin to him, just a piece of ass. She didn't mean shit to him and he got her on that boat, killed her, weighted the body, and dumped her way out at sea. I saw him that morning. I was at Belcher Cove and I saw Casper Trebell pacing the beech, on the phone, ringing someone, and getting no answer. You should have seen how angry he was. I saw him take the boat out but no one believes me. And then I saw you, and that's the bit I can't wrap my head around. Truth is, I was at the Cove because I was looking for you. I came round and your mom said you'd already left with some friends. So I drove out there to find you because, look, I know I was never your type. I know you ain't never been into guys.*"

*But I had to ask, you know? Only, all I found was Casper fucking Trebell until I spotted you getting on a bus back to town. I didn't recognize you at first, you had your hair down. An hour later, the Coastguard was zooming up and down looking for Cindy. What were you doing out there, Shiv? What were you doing?"*

The wings of something dark brushed up against me, a snake with scales like ice writhed on my back. I couldn't listen to it anymore. This wasn't the friend I remembered, but what he had become: a good kid ruined by an unexplainable obsession. I hid the tapes under my bed and tried not to think about them. But there they lay beneath me every night when I went to sleep: inexorable fathoms of darkness that I should have cast a headlamp on.

*****

Senior Year came and I started to wonder if I'd ever get out of High School alive. Slinging hash and pills used to earn me a quantum of respect, but now it put a target on my back. After Cindy, the School suffered a schism and a significant portion of the student body had been swept up in a puritanical landslide. God had been busy over Summer Break making new recruits. I guess teenagers coming face to face with their own mortality react in strange ways.

Casper Trebell had still not come back to school. I wondered about that, and I wondered about Dyl's tapes. I wondered if perhaps Casper had been as rattled as I had by Dylan's relentless pursuit of the boy he believed was Cindy Garter's murderer. I wondered how long it took scratches to heal.

Evie caught up to me after class one afternoon. She didn't say anything at first, just glanced at me from under her pixie cut. Short hair and long, cool silences – Evie could have been a European screen ingénue. There was a time when I would gladly have played her indispensable Girl Friday. We walked on for a few soundless paces, but I couldn't outlast her. She had a quality about her that turned silences into a black hole, dragging things out of you. I coveted it.

"Dylan killed himself," I said. "I feel... I feel partly responsible for that."

"Only partly?" Evie smiled, showing me her perfect white teeth. I eyeballed her, but it didn't bother her none. It was a shitty thing to say, but Evie could always say the shittiest things and make them sound like rainbows and sunflowers.

"Do you think Cindy could have been pregnant?" I asked. Evie didn't answer immediately and settled into one of her long, draining silences. But I was determined to outlast her. We covered half the distance to my bus stop by the time she gave in.

"Maybe," she said, and the cautious tone in her voice told me all I needed to know. I felt momentarily nauseous.

"I'm guessing it would have been Casper's?"

It was Evie's turn to eyeball me. "Of course. Cindy wasn't like that."

"Poor Dylan was pretty set on Casper. And honestly, I almost convinced myself there for a moment listening to him lay it all out."

"Listening?" Evie said and I knew I'd erred.

"He, um, he was recording tapes. I don't know, I think he saw himself as one of those true crime podcast guys, you know?"

"I see. And what are you going to do with this information?"

"Nothing. There's nothing in them. Rambling, that's all."

"Are you certain?"

"Absolutely," I lied. There were nine tapes, thirty minutes per side, but so much of it was Dylan talking about tides and weather patterns and boat movements that it became dully hypnotic. I was finding it hard to sleep and it became something of a ritual to listen to them and smoke a joint to wind down. I wasn't even sure what I had and hadn't listened to. It had all begun to slosh into one.

"Really? But... but what if there could be something in it?"

I gave Evie the sort of sidelong glance I reserved for my Gym teacher and bartenders who asked to see my ID. "What are you talking about?"

Evie smiled again. "I think you should let us hear the tapes so we can decide. I'm thinking of Mr. And Mrs. Garter. And Willa. She gets so upset about it still. Replays the whole thing over and over wondering if we could have said or done anything differently. Honestly, I don't much like being linked to you in this way. She was my friend. And you're, well, a *wild card.* No offense." It was a tiny little dagger into a discrete, roped-off portion of my heart. I wasn't going to pretend it didn't smart, but I'd get over it. "Willa and I, we just don't know what you might do next. And after Cindy and Dylan, well, I don't think the town could take any more."

It sounded like a threat and I raised my eyebrow at Evie. She shook her head. "Sorry, perhaps I didn't phrase that as well as I could have. We just need to know you aren't holding out on us, Shiv. We want the whole thing buried, put to bed. Let us hear the tapes."

"I'll think about it," I said. But by the following morning, it would be out of my hands.

*****

Later that night, I had been walking home alone from my job waiting tables at a bar in town. There was a two-hundred-yard stretch where the road down to the trailers passed through a small copse of woodland. No street lights. Quiet. Gone midnight. If you were going to run someone off the road, it was the perfect place to do it.

I had been dimly aware of the SUV gaining on me, but it was killing the headlamps that gave them away. What had made them do it? Squeamishness? Did they not want to see me smeared all over their hood? I turned to look just as the car swerved and on instinct I jumped sideways into a wide roadside ditch, cutting myself to pieces on brambles. The car came to a stop one hundred yards up and I kept perfectly still, like a stunned deer. I knew deep down that I should have been running.

The driver's side door opened, but then another car came around the bend and the SUV sped off again. I was pretty sure I recognized the SUV. I hid in the undergrowth for what felt like hours until I was certain they'd gone. When I got home, I found my mom in her usual position, passed out in her chair with the TV tuned to the Shopping Network. An empty bottle of gin sat on the table. At the back of the trailer, my room had been tossed. My first reaction was to search under the bed for the tapes. I got on my hands and knees and saw the empty space where they had been at exactly the same moment I registered the movement of a shadowy figure behind me. A dog barked three times in the near distance, there was a searing, tearing pain in my left shoulder and then everything went black.

*****

"The Doctor said you were well enough to speak to us," Detective Sanders said. He was a stocky man, perhaps thirty. His hair was receding and he wore his navy blue suit like a man who was used to wearing something with considerably more buttons and pockets and buckles. I wondered how long he'd been out of uniform. "A skull fracture, three broken ribs. The knife bounced off your shoulder blade and took most of the force out of it. You were lucky."

"If this is what good luck feels like, I'd hate to have a bad day."

"Ha. They said you were a funny one. Smart, too."

"I prefer cunning. My back hurts like hell. My head is... woolly. They said it's been a week?"

"You were in a medically-induced coma for three days. You've been in and out since then, rambling."

"Has anyone been in to see me?"

The Detective looked at the floor and winced. "Your mom was here the first day, once they'd sobered her up."

I tried to nod my head, but it felt like it might fall off. One day. That seemed about right.

"Casper Trebell is under arrest. We found a knife with your blood on it underneath his porch. And then there are Mr. Bugliosi's tapes. Of course, they made it online and then into the local press long before we ever got our hands on them. Town turned ugly. He's better off behind bars right now anyway. Safer."

The sound of the waves on the rocks at Hader's End rang in my head. My brain was flooded by an in-rush of cold, salty water, and all my heaviest, darkest memories were churned up from the seabed of my mind where I had consigned them. What would Dylan have said? He got his man, in the end. It suited everyone to see Casper swing for it. No one would mourn him too much. But that wasn't the way it worked, was it? It was neat, it was convenient. And it was very, very wrong.

"Detective Sanders, I think you better get me a lawyer."

*****

They kept me under guard after that. Three days later I was well enough to travel to the Station to give a full statement. Poor Dyl. I couldn't have told him. I *should* have told him. He'd have been alive and whatever was going to happen to me would have happened anyway. The truth was that by the time Dylan had disappeared down a rabbit hole labelled 'Cindy Garter', I was already a fortnight ahead of him. Every night since the party I saw nothing but her face leering up at me from the chilly depths when I tried to drift off to sleep. Not that she ever went anywhere near the sea.

"If Casper Trebell had stabbed me in the back, do you think I'd be here right now? The guy's six foot two and at least one-ninety pounds. And the bloody knife under his own porch? Even he wasn't that dumb. It was Willa Edwards tried to stab me."

There was no collective gasp from Detective Sanders or his colleagues. My Lawyer twirled his pen nervously, but the Police had already agreed I was free and clear as long as I gave them everything.

"It was her father's SUV that had tried to run me down earlier that night, too. My guess is Evie didn't know about it. She would never have gone for it. Why bother to fit the frame on Casper when Cindy's death was already yesterday's news? The only person who didn't accept their version of events had killed himself. No one was looking at it. I guess guilt does funny things to people."

"Cindy Garter?" Detective Sanders prompted.

I took a deep breath. "She never went into the sea. She never even went to the beach. She died the night of the party, drowned in the pool. Not that I saw any of this, you understand. I was home and passed out in bed by then. I only have what Willa and Evie told me. I never saw her body. If you ask me, she'll be buried within a mile of Willa's place, probably in a shallow grave in the woods. All I know is that she was gone when I went back to the house the following morning, and that was only a few hours later. I don't see Willa and Evie lugging her into a car, driving out of town, and burying her six feet deep in that time. Willa would have panicked and cool as Evie is, she's got arms like noodles."

"Who killed her, Miss Lee? Who killed Cindy Garter?"

"Well... as much as anyone did, I guess it was me. That night, Willa came into the back room where I was hanging out with the Loser's Club and scored three tabs of Acid off me. I was a little surprised. She didn't seem the type but I didn't think much more of it. And then I get a call at about three in the morning. It was Evie. She said they needed me to come back right away, though they didn't give me any particular reason why on earth I should do such a thing. Obviously, I told them to go to hell. At about five, Willa turned up outside my trailer in that big SUV and leaned on the horn until she woke up the whole damn place. I came out and she said she wouldn't quit it unless I got in. What else could I do? I climbed in and asked her what she thought she was doing, but her brain was somewhere else. That short drive back to Willa's house was about the scariest thing I've ever been through. She huddled over the steering wheel, her eyes twitching from side to side as though unseen car-crushing monsters were lurking in the treeline waiting to pounce. She was sweating something crazy. Her arms were caked in mud. Occasionally she made a sort of squeaking noise in the back of her throat."

"She was high?"

"High as cirrus clouds. My guess was that she took a tab and then when nothing happened straight away she took another and then before she knew it, *wham,* it hit all at once and she ended up in a deep pit she couldn't find a way out of. She got me back to her house and Evie was there. She seemed to be on a much more even keel. I guessed she'd missed out on a tab. She was holding a shovel, and just seeing that shovel..." I let out a little shiver at the memory. "Look, you're a Policeman, I would bet a pretty teenage girl caked in mud and holding a shovel at five in the morning has never presaged anything good, right?"

"Not in my experience, no. Go on."

"I didn't see the body. Or the grave. But I got the gist of it. They'd bought the tabs off me to distract Cindy. Her and Casper... yeah, I remember it now. It had been a proper break-up, almost violent. She was in a bad way, so for some idiot reason, they decided to slip a tab into her vodka to take her mind well and truly off things. It was fun at first, Willa said, but then she and Evie crashed out under the stars and when they woke up Cindy was face-down in the pool. They hadn't even bothered to warn her that they'd spiked her drink. God only knows what she thought was happening. I don't know why she ended up in the pool and how she ended up drowning. Willa said it must have been my shitty drugs that had killed her, not that anyone's ever OD'd on the stuff, right? She got all up in my face, I thought she was going to hit me. And then Evie stepped in and told me what would happen if I didn't help them. Who was going to side with the girl with my family name? The known dealer? My drugs had killed her. So I did as they asked. I put on Cindy's swimsuit and jeans, her big summer hat, and her over-sized sunglasses. We were about the same size, same pale skin, both brunettes. Who would even be looking? I drove us all out to Belcher Cove in her car. We swam out a few hundred yards. I swam over to the rocks and came out that way, hidden from everyone on the beach. The girls swam back alone. I walked past them ten minutes later, picked up my bag without saying a word, changed into my own clothes, and caught the first bus coming back to town. They raised the alarm about an hour later. Poor Cindy drowned, but she never went anywhere near the sea. I think they planned to put her body in the water later, but for whatever reason they never did. My guess is they lost their nerve. What happens now?"

"Involuntary Manslaughter, possibly." Detective Sanders tapped his teeth with his pen then shook his head. "Unlikely. If they have a good lawyer, which I'm betting they do, then they'll get it busted down to Obstruction of Justice and Preventing the Lawful Burial of a Body. We might be able to turn them on each other, but if they take the line that it was Cindy's idea to take the LSD, they'll likely do no time. We can't prove otherwise."

I gave a shudder. "But what about Willa? She tried to kill me."

"Did you see her face?"

I paused. "No," I said uncomfortably. "But I... oh God, I *sensed* that it was her. That's not going to play well, is it?"

Sanders shook his head sadly. "No other witnesses. People around you don't tend to see much, do they? No physical evidence at the trailer. Weapon clean but for your blood. Unless she's left a pile of bloodstained clothes in her room, that won't stick either."

"Well, shit."

*****

Casper was out within a day. He was an asshole, no doubt, but he didn't ever do anything worse than treat Cindy like shit and lead her on. The Police released his speedboat from impound and it was firebombed the same night. I like to think it was as much a comment on the paint job. It took the cadaver dogs two days to find Cindy and by then Willa and Evie were already in custody trying to throw me under the bus.

A storm picked up and threw waves at Hader's End, breaking hard over the seawall. Over the next week, the press kept springing up on me out of dirty little nooks and crannies so I went down there to get away sometimes. There had been some unpleasantness down by the trailers.

I told the sea what had happened in the hope that somehow it could get a message to Dyl, wherever he was. I hoped he would forgive me for not telling him. That one was on me, I had to wear it all myself. He might be alive if I had, but then again he might not. Perhaps there was more there that I wasn't seeing, something that had always swirled in deep currents.

The storm didn't break until the Friday when Sanders called on me. The autopsy was in. He thought I better hear the news from him first.

"Good and bad. I think. I don't really know if it's fair to classify it in those terms. Firstly, Cindy *wasn't* pregnant. Small mercies."

A small, but not inconsequential weight lifted off my shoulders. I braced myself. "So what's the bad news? If that's what we're calling it."

"There was dirt in her lungs," he said in a subterranean tone. He waited for me to catch up.

"Well, shit," I said.

"She went in the hole alive. They were probably too cooked to notice. You know what this means?"

"She suffocated. Legally, *they* killed her?"

"We could go for Murder. Manslaughter for certain now. You're going to have to see this through. You'll come under a lot of pressure."

I grimaced. Siobhan Lee: Witness for the Prosecution. Well, I'd be damned. What would Daddy say? Outside, the sky was still dirt-grey, but the wind had dropped to a murmur. Down at Hader's End, the waves would be settling and somewhere Dylan Bugliosi would be laughing his head off. I would have to see it through to the end, the sea wouldn't have it any other way.

"Just tell me when Sanders, I'll be there."

# *Urban Wasteland*
## *Maroula Blades*

For months, Rory planned the robbery of the decade. He needed four men to carry out his well-laid scheme, which should be executed with no glitches. But he knew the foibles of men. And he bore them in mind when choosing his partners in crime.

"Hey Rory, close the door," said Mike.

"Stop moaning, will you, and move away from the heat; it can't circulate with your big butt in the way," said Rory, rubbing the cold from his hands.

"Did you get my message, Rory? What do you think; it's a good plan, isn't it?"

"Hold your horses. I haven't said yes to anything and as far as this plan goes, the layout sucks. We have to take more precautions. We need two lads to help us out."

"Oh man, I didn't want to split the booty between four. I need every penny what's in them sacks."

"This is the new plan. Like it or lump it, but I'm not lifting a finger until there's a tick by each of those damn points. Got it? You can run your sad arse idea on your own for all I care."

Rory slapped the papers down in a coiled heap on an old oil drum. And then he placed his tall frame by of the gas heater. Mike went to the window, took out a cigarette, and lit it.

"Okay, Rory, you win, you're the Boss."

Mike booted the wall of the garage. A clang of steel thunder echoed.

"Good, I'm glad that's settled. Let me see, we need a driver and a heavy bloke too."

"I'm a skilful driver. What about me?"

"Nah, I need you to cover my back. You're as dopey as hell, but I trust you with me life. Craig Thomas is a wicked driver. I've used him before on a job. He's a reliable bloke, and he doesn't ask too many questions. His cousin Dave, the Bull, is a hard nut, but he's good when the going gets hairy. He broke a guy's face in a Battersea Pub three months ago because the bloke looked at his sister, all horny like. Bull laid him up in hospital for three weeks with a crushed jaw and a broken collarbone."

"You're kidding, aren't you?"

"Nah, mate, Bull did a month's stretch in Brixton for GBH. He's out now. Bull's looking for work. He's a troll, a mean bastard, but he's cool. I've just got to keep him in check."

"Yeah, they're just what the Doc ordered. I'll get in touch with them tomorrow, Rory."

"Nah, Mike, I'll get in touch with them. Let's get some rest. Tomorrow will be a kicking day. If you want something to do, tidy this stinking garage. There's less mess in a pigsty. We need a brighter light and a blackboard. And don't forget the bloody chalk."

"Yeah, Rory, I'm on it."

"Good. I'm hitting the sack. See you tomorrow at 2.00 p.m. sharp."

Rory left the garage, banging the door, slicing Mike's 'goodnight'. Mike had a hard time cleaning. A 10-force gale wind lifted sheets of corrugated steel; rubbish spewed around. It was a paper chase. Mike's fourteen stone sweated. It was hard work. A nonchalant rat caught his eye.

"Come here, you little critter. Who gave you the okay to come in here snarling with your saggy, hairy arse? Take that."

Mike threw a big spanner, which missed the rat, but hit two drums of litter. They fell like skittles, emptying over the floor. The wind ruled the waste once more.

"What a bloody mess."

Mike spent the best part of the evening getting the place in shape. After he had finished, he plunged into a tired sofa with a bottle of beer in one hand and a slice of pepperoni pizza in the other. Mike slumped like a sack of potatoes, watching the American series Hawaii Five O, created by Leonard Freeman. He scented the air with terror belches.

Sleep crept in, hitting his blue eyes closed, leaving a half-eaten slice of pizza in his hand, which fell to the floor. The rat came back, chewed its fill, and then pattered to a hole in the skirting board.

Rory was fifteen minutes early the next day. He was reliable, punctual, and precise. He was in the game since his teens. Rory had never been caught. People knew him about town as the *Overall Man*. The slightest detail he didn't leave to chance. They took his word like the gospel.

"Hey, man, where are you?" said Rory, entering the garage, carrying a cardboard tray with hot drinks and a bulging greaseproof bag.

"Alright, Rory?"

Mike came out of a pungent toilet, doing up his zip. His perforated vest stopped below the navel, showing his dark hairs running into his jeans.

"Oh man, spare me; it's too early for this shit."

Rory turned around, massaging his eyeballs, walking to the blackboard. He scrutinised the emptiness as if he wanted to find something precious in the vacuum.

"What, what, what have I done?"

Mike tried to tuck tyres of flesh and clothes into his jeans, but it was hopeless. It all came tumbling out again. Mike was an undesirable, foul smelling fellow with a big heart.

"Oh, forget it. That's some cruel weather out there. I hope it cools off. Here's a custard doughnut and a cappuccino for your woes. There's an extra one in the bag, if you want it."

"Cool. They're my favourites. From my eighth birthday in the orphanage, I always got one as a present. Those people who look after us kids were evil buggers. Some nights, I slept on the floor with just the clothes on my back."

"I know, mate. Don't stress it; it was a long time ago."

While they ate, Bull and Craig entered.

"That's brutal weather outside. Alright, mates, where's the action?" Bull said, punching the air.

"Steady on. Save it for the morons who get in the way," said Rory.

"Mike, get four stools. Here's the detail. You all need to soak it up before we talk business. This is how it goes."

Rory drew diagrams on the blackboard, labelling every structure. He was fast and competent. He had studied technical drawing at college for two years. Mike returned, groaning under the weight of chrome stools. Bull helped him. In silence, they studied the blackboard.

"Blinking Nora," said Craig, "You're not thinking of hitting Bradbury's, are you? They have loads of security blokes down there. They run about like bugs on the weekends."

"Yeah, you're right, but not during transit. Look here," replied Rory.

Rory pointed to a section of writing on Craig's paper. Craig nodded approval.

"I've been over these details with a frigging tooth pick, plus I've cased out the joint for three days on the bloody trot in this mad weather. I know when the buggers pick their noses and use the bog. We will hit them hard on Saturday, along the Acker Road. It's a quiet strip that goes near the reservoir in Streatham, South London. We could hide the cash there too in a cast-off pipe. It's just wasteland. The odd maintenance worker steps foot over there once every six months."

"Yeah, I'm with you. What about taking heavy metal with us?" Bull asked. "The security geezers carry stun guns. They can zap you with 350 volts — your dick will fall off."

Bull's adrenaline level was rocketing. He crossed his bulbous legs as if to protect his manhood.

"No guns, Bull. It's not a hard job," said Rory. "We don't want a goner on our hands. With guns, it's another ball game all together. You get an extra twenty years if you're nabbed with them."

"I don't plan going back in the can, Boss. I don't want to stand there, bollock frigging naked. As well loaded as they are, but they won't get me out of trouble. Mavis, the barmaid at the Orange Pub, always takes a barrel of me nuggets home on a Saturday night. She always left screaming for more bull's-eyes, get it?"

Everyone laughed apart from Rory.

"No guns, Bull. Either you're in my corner or you're in my way. Does everyone understand?"

Rory was crocodile mad. Bull was stomping all over his beloved territory, splashing about in his most prized lake. Rory's brown eyes shot out as if he was waiting under water for the snatch. He was ready to strike with his sharp teeth and serrated tail. Bull sensed the danger of the death roll and cowered. There was a unanimous, "Yes."

"Study the plans, boys. We'll have a rehearsal on Friday. No more booze until the job's done and keep your traps shut. If I get wind of this on the streets, I'll flush these frigging plans down the bog. Got it?"

"Yeah, mate, whatever you say," said Craig, "You're the Boss."

Bull was testing Rory's authority. Rory had an ambitious streak, but not for stupidity. His father always complained that he took after his dead mother. She was a wild one who died a premature death parachuting. Her main parachute failed to open and the reserve one was jinxed, too. She landed broken, a tangled kookaburra in wire meshing, which surrounded the reservoir back then. Red streams covered her alabaster face. Rory used to follow the flight of her colourful, winged parachute by bike. She was like an untamed exotic bird, reaching out to kiss and nibble the sky. However, on this day, she dropped from the blue like a brick. Rory found her shattered. Since that day, Rory became obsessed with the wasteland. Every night he walked by the reservoir, running a palm along the fence. Sometimes he left a rose or a bright wooden parrot by the memorial plaque erected in his mother's memory.

*****

On Thursday evening, Rory met Mike to go over the plan. The rainstorm troubled Rory.

"I've been watching the weather forecast. We're in for some fucked up weather. I'm thinking of calling off the job. It could prove tricky on the road, especially with hailstones mashing about the place."

"Oh nah, Rory, I had my sights set on a Caribbean holiday this year. You know, sunning myself with two passion fruits, wearing skimpy bikinis. Drinking pina coladas until sunrise."

Rory rolled his eyes and yawned. Mike continued, "My gob is watering just thinking about them hot nights. Oh mate, you're breaking my heart with this news, don't do it."

Mike grabbed his chest as if he felt a colossal pain.

"OK, meatball, you've got a green light. Listen, I'm worried about Bull. Watch him. If you notice anything, tell me. Did you get the clothes, stockings, hardware and the car?"

"Yeah, everything's ready, Boss. I've sprayed the Ford blue and changed the number plate. Don't worry about Bull; I'll be on his backside like a fly on a turd."

"Good, mate, see you tomorrow at 2.00 p.m. prompt."

"Catch you later, Rory, you're rock solid."

After Rory left, Mike browsed through a Trinidadian travel guide in the kitchen. Hunger pangs got the better of him. He smiled as he opened the freezer, reaching for a frozen chicken curry, which he then put into the microwave. The dial was on the ten-minute mark. Mike took a bottle of beer and then continued to walk to his seedy sitting room. The slice of pizza was still on the floor from the night before with tiny teeth marks decorating edges. The place reeked of stale air. Mike's furry friend hid behind the sofa. It waited for morsels, except for its poor bottom, which deposited pellets on the rug. Mike opened a can of peanuts. He threw them into his mouth while watching the news, shaking his head. Nuts fell all around the sofa. The dark creature feasted, using its fangs to crack and chew. The bell rang in the microwave. Mike ran to the meal, rubbing his greedy hands together. His belly wobbled like a huge water-filled balloon. He was a glutton and so was his hairy flatmate. Later in the evening, they ate popcorn and crisps non-stop for an hour and a half. Then they both curled up on the spot where they had binged, snoozing until the next morning.

Mike rose to the sound of birdsong from the silver birch outside. He walked around the back of the couch and felt something warm with bristles under his foot. He shouted, "You're an ugly rat."

Mike spat at the scampering animal; it wasn't fast enough. Mike hit it with a fat mucus ball on the back of the head. The rat shuddered.

"Ha, that will teach you, you little critter. I will buy some Edam cheese and stuff it with poison today. You won't get fat on that shit;

you'll just be dead."

The rehearsal went without a glitch. Craig proved his steady hands on the gears. Rory threw surprise obstacles at the speeding Ford, testing Craig's reaction time. He didn't falter once. He had the talent to be a Formula One racing driver. Rory drove the car back to the garage while Craig walked the length on the Acker Road. He wanted to note every concrete nook and cranny. He came upon a row of wooded parrots. Some stood faded while others were colourful, like his mother's lipsticks. He laughed, picking up a somewhat new bird, tucking it away for keeps.

Back at the garage, Bull tried out his bullying tactics on Mike. Mike imitated a security man. He ended up sobbing flat on his back with a black eye as big as a hornet's bonnet. After 'acting out', Mike put a fatty clump of meat on his nasty bulge, which he later cooked.

"That went well, guys. The weather held up," said Rory. "If it goes like that tomorrow, we shall be well away with one hundred grand each."

"Yeah," they cheered.

Rory said, "Hey Mike, that's a mean-looking shiner you've got there."

"Don't worry about it, mate," said Mike, lowering his head.

"I'm hungry like a wolf for that cash," said Bull. "I'll buy me a little place to start up a boxing club. My lad Tony's showing promising jabs. I've been training him since he was six. A red and blue sack swings from his bunk bed; he's got gloves to match. He's a little pit bull terrier, rock hard."

Bull looked as proud as Lucifer while he told the gang of his son's boxing abilities. He added, "My Dad was a drunk, and my Mum was flighty. If you know what I mean," Bull winked. "I want to take it up a notch for my son. I never had much; he should have more."

"Craig, what you going to do with your wonga?" Mike asked.

"I don't know. My Mum's getting on. She always wanted a fur coat and to own her council flat. When the job's over, I want to help her with a mortgage. She works too hard for pennies. And with the rest, I'll go to the Canaries and treat myself to a bit of high society, and my Mum to a mink coat."

"Alright, you lot, stop bloody dreaming," said Rory. "There's a long way to go before we're kings. Come on, sling your hooks; it's late. Remember what I said: no firearms, no blabbing or drinking."

Rory felt something strange in the air. He had no tangible reason for it. On the way home, he stopped at a florist and bought a white rose, tinged with pink. And a vivid wooden bird from the quaint shop called Seeds, where he often bought knick-knacks. He glared at the rose as if it was haunted. Perhaps the faint red hue fascinated him; it weaved through every petal. He tucked the flower in the fence surrounding the reservoir near his mother's plaque and pressed the bird's feet into the soil. Rory stood in the dark, singing a nursery rhyme while clapping and stomping his feet.

Craig and Bull went to the Orange Pub. Craig drank bitter lemon. Bull had a pint of lager.

"Watch it, Bull," said Craig. "You heard what Rory said. He's got eyes and ears everywhere. I'm heading off home now to get a good night's kip. You should do the same."

"Yeah, yeah mate. Don't worry."

Bull had been winking to Mavis while she pulled draughts of lager. He was admiring her muscular forearms.

"I'm almost finished, Bully," whispered Mavis in a bushy ear hole, "Do you want a little company tonight or do you have to run home to the Wifey?"

"Nah, I'm all yours tonight, darling. A little slap and tickle never did anyone any harm. Hear that? It's pelting down outside, but I'll keep you warm, Angel."

Mavis suffered a laughing fit. She was howling, turning on the waterworks. Rivulets ran down her chubby cheeks as the rain crashed against the windows. The pub's shield banged an eave like an annoying clock. The wind raced the street. A bell rang.

"Last orders, ladies and gents," cried Mavis, smudging mascara around her green eyes.

Back at the garage, Mike double-checked the equipment. He was nervous. He was a hamstring away from his freedom in the sun. His unpleasant flatmate was also restless. Mike caught the rat sneaking around the blackboard. He was just about to slam a sheet of metal down on its bushy head when he stopped midway, saying, "After tomorrow, you can have the whole crib for yourself, your lucky beastie."

The night was tumultuous, wind up-rooted trees, set off car alarms, and tore down electricity cables. The fire brigade had exhausted all its men. Hundreds of people were homeless, seventy-five people were missing, and ten people died.

The following day, everyone was punctual at the garage. Dark circles outlined their eyes. Sleep had been a stranger to all of them. Craig inspected the Ford to see whether he had overlooked something during the rehearsal. They checked the details and synchronised watches. They changed into navy overalls. No one talked or smoked in the car. Bull had a mouth full of extra strong mints to disguise the smell of alcohol. He had a splitting headache. Outside he seemed cool, but inside he was a shock of nerves. Rory handed out American tan stockings, which they stretch over their menacing faces. The heavens seemed livid about something. The rain was crashing down in sheets. Between the windshield wipers there were huge hailstones and twigs. The debris clawed the window screen. Condensation hindered Craig's vision.

"I can't see a bloody thing, Boss. It's the worst storm in decades, so the weather man said on the box last night."

"Here's the Acker Road, Craig," said Rory. "Run the car into that side road, just over there."

"Where?"

"There, you blind bat."

Craig turned a sharp left and then swung around to face the road again. They waited in the bleak; skirts of air whistled around them. Sirens pierced the dark. The storm was in control. In the gale, the rescuers had their work cut out for them. Because of the poor weather, Rory had calculated the security van being late. They sweated for twenty minutes; their hands glistened. Bull's limbs jittered. Mike lifted his tan stocking, his face a pool of perspiration.

Craig tapped out a rock rhythm on the steering wheel. Rory's eyes stayed fixed on the saturated grey. Headlights emerged from out of the gloomy space.

"Go, Craig, go," screamed Rory.

Craig revved up the motor. The car skidded off on a collision course with the van. Craig manoeuvred a perfect 180-degree turn in front of the vehicle. The van driver's reaction was too slow. He fumbled at the wheel. The van skidded off the road, landing on its side in a gully.

"Move out," shouted Rory.

They approached the van with caution. Two wheels still spun. Hail as big as sharks' eyes hammered their face. The driver's door was open; he had fled. Bull banged on the van. Rory scoured the scene; he couldn't a trace the driver.

"Get the fuck out of there or I'll blow the doors," said Bull.

Bull was mad as hell. The doors swung open; two uniformed men jumped out. Bull hit them to the ground with a baseball bat behind the knees. A man bled from the gash on his skull. He fell face first on the tarmac. Blood thinned in the rain. Bull knelt down, pulled the man's hair, lifting his head. The wounded man pinched his eyes closed. Blood stuck like a parasite to Bull's boots.

"Easy, Bull, just watch them. Okay?" Mike said.

"You're a useless cretin. It's your lucky day. You were just about to feel the steel in my cuff."

Bull hissed the words. He released the bleeding head. It thumped on the street. Rory jumped into the van. Mike stood behind him, holding a crowbar. They both retrieved two swollen white money sacks. In the van, they handcuffed the security men. Craig sprinted to the car. Rory saw the missing driver running out from behind a tree.

"Watch out, Craig."

But it was too late. By the time Craig turned around, the driver pumped him with electricity. Craig lay unconscious. His body writhed in spasms. Frozen rain pounded him. A yellow wooden parrot's head poked out of a pocket.

Bull let out a battle scream. He pulled out a sawn-off shotgun from under his jacket. Two big cartridges fell, smoking to ground. They hit the man hard in the chest. He lay with his legs jerking. A bloody fountain squirted out of his torso. Sirens pierced through the rain.

"Bloody hell, Bull, you're an idiot," yelled Rory. "You've done it now. Mike, get the car. Bull, get Craig. Hurry guys. I'll meet you back at the garage. I'm going to hide the loot over there."

Rory pointed to the reservoir.

"Split," cried Rory.

The Ford speeded off. Rory ran and jumped over the fence. Mud slid. The money sacks resembled clumps of earth. A tree branch hit Rory full in the face, ripping his forehead. Blood dripped into his eyes. Blinded, he inched from tree to tree. There was a loud cracking sound, and then gushing water echoed. Great bodies of mud moved, as if seething with anger under his feet. Rory tried to steady his foothold. He pressed his heels into the soil. Suddenly, the tree lined ridge Rory stood on fell. A torrent of sludge swallowed everything.

Mike was great at the wheel. Craig still lay unconscious, shaking at intervals. His head was in Bull's lap.

"Mike, Craig needs a doctor," said Bull, "He's in a bad way."

"I know; I'll take him to my Mum's. She was a nurse."

Just as Mike said this, the rat jumped out of a pocket of darkness onto Bull's shoulder.

"What the fuck!" Bull punched and screamed. "There's a frigging animal in here. Stop the bloody car, will you? It's scratching and biting my flipping face."

Mike hit the brakes. He bruised his ribs on the steering wheel. Bull jumped out. They searched the car. And sure enough, Mike's scraggy, fat friend was shivering next to a sneering, wooden parrot in a dim corner behind Craig's boot. The rat had its tail against a dead end. Bull made a shield from a piece of cardboard. He found it on the back seat. Sirens rang closer. He encircled the rat. Mike held the safeguard in place as Bull's huge hands lifted the creature to his eye level, saying, "You're a nasty, big bastard."

"Hurry, will you?" Mike yelled.

Bull spat in the rat's face. It winced, and then he threw it to the ground. The rodent lay twisted. Mike knelt down to stroke it as the last breath squeaked out of its body. They entered the car again. A blue revolving light spun the dark.

"We're okay. It's just a fire engine, said Bull."

"Good."

Mike was about to speed off when a jagged light streaked the sky. The lightning struck a conifer tree; it fell. It was all over in a second. A large bough crashed onto the car bonnet. The windscreen flew in shards. Mike's face and throat caught glass. Craig fell, banging his head on the driver's seat, never to regain consciousness. Bull was groaning, trapped in the back. Oil was leaking. Strobe lights and sirens came nearer. Headlights burned. Three firefighters stopped to cut the metal body of the Ford. A firefighter radioed for help. They hauled out two bloody corpses. A chubby, dead man lay next to a deformed rat. A fireman wiped the stony faces clean. They put the corpses into black body bags. Help came as hot-headed police. They arrested Bull with his shotgun tucked under his jacket. He suffered four broken ribs from overzealous batons charging on him.

*****

The following day, the sun rose early. It pierced an opaque sky. On the radio, the weather forecast reported that the aftermath of the storm was one of pure chaos. An urban wasteland stretched for miles.

In the Acker Road, a crooked plaque hung on a half-scorched tree. Leaves of blue paint peeled from its bark. The tree bled white tears. A flock of bright, wooden birds trod water and a grubby rose petal lay on a rodent's back.

# *Porcelain Angel*
## *David William Johnson*

Hinges squawked. Spender stumbled through the door as if someone had shoved him in the back. Collapsed into a sagging chair whose springs poked through the muslin, his skinny body resembled a question mark. He held his head in his hands and rocked back and forth like a downhill skier at the starting gate. He made a keening sound. I waited.

"Sometimes it helps to talk," I said. His arrival interrupted my appraisal of the weekend's purchases. I was assigning prices to each object in a box of mixed porcelain and glass. I bid eight pounds ten and was quite pleased. The lot contained a figure made in Dresden worth five times what I paid for the box. A porcelain angel. I was admiring her beauty when Spender burst in. I set her on the shelf reserved for favourites.

Spender raised his shaved head. His eyes were frightened. He retrieved a stained handkerchief from his jacket pocket and wiped snot from his nose.

"I had an accident," he said.

"How serious?"

"I think I might 'ave killed somebody," he said.

He sighed as if the energy required to recall details might be beyond him. He gasped twice and continued. "It 'appened on the M23, on our way back from Brighton.

Spender travelled with the three other members of The Kingdom. Sometimes a roadie joined the group to lug instruments and amplifiers in exchange for access to drugs and female fans. Kingdom was on the road almost every weekend, struggling to stay afloat during a sea change in pop. Four skinny lads hurling epithets and spittle at the audience caused a stir at the Nashville Rooms that was reported the *New Musical Express*. In recent weeks Spender slept less and took more speed.

"Were you high?" I asked.

"Had a few pints and smoked in the van."

"Popped pills?"

"I did."

"You were driving?"

"A' course I was driving," he spat. "Lazy cunts fell asleep. Can't keep their trousers up without me."

More slowly, as if wanting to be careful with his words, "Just after the roundabout, I caught sight a' someone out of the corner of me eye. Bloke stepped waving his arms. I tried to swerve 'round him, thought I made it, but heard a bump and yell."

"A yell? What did he yell?"

His head fell back into his hands. "Not that sort of yell."

"More like a scream then?"

"What difference?" he said. "Will you help me go look?"

"What do you mean, help you go look? Look for what?"

"The bloke."

I stared at Spender's bristled head until he raised his eyes to meet my stare. "So you are telling me that you did not stop?"

He nodded.

"Bloody hell," I said.

I did not think long about the situation. Spender was my mate. "Let's get going then," I said, putting an arm around his shoulders. I reached for my jacket with my free hand and ushered his bony frame toward the door. I turned the sign to Closed. My angel would be waiting for my return.

*****

I opened my shop in 1971, four years after I came to England from the States to research an eccentric British quack who feuded with Henry Fielding. As I spent days straining my eyes in dim light in the North Library of the British Museum, I began to consider a difficult choice. I realized the churning in my stomach was about more than unfamiliar curry.

One evening upon entering my local, The Lamb on Lamb's Conduit Street, an inebriated transplant from the north attacked me about Vietnam as if I were the secretary of state. His accent rendered his screed almost unintelligible, but I understood the drift. When I began to defend a United States policy that I did not understand, he invited me outside and decked me with a punch. He returned to the pub and I retreated home. I began to think harder about the images I had in my head: orange clouds of napalm defoliating forests, a monk setting himself on fire, children screaming as they ran from exploding bombs. In January of my fellowship year, the North Vietnamese invaded South Vietnam, killing many young men like me.

My stomach upsets grew more frequent, sometimes sending me to the nearest public loo. An artistic sort, I was estranged from my ambitious family. When I met a single mother who loved to dance to Ray Charles, I clung to her for several months until I could stand on my own as a potential ex-pat. The relationship did not last beyond May, but my decision felt permanent. I met Spender in August as we queued up outside the Marquee Club to hear Ten Years After. He was oblivious to world affairs and treated me as a kindred spirit who loved the blues. He was mystified that I would leave the States because so much music was happening there, yet was the first Brit who showed signs of being a real friend.

Our friendship carried on through my early ex-pat depression, his alcohol abuse, and my becoming a boringly predictable shopkeeper while he struggled to find work in various bands. Despite his erratic behaviour and a blossoming drug habit, he earned my deep gratitude during my flu bout, checking on me sometimes twice a day as I spent two miserable weeks in bed in bed in the squalor of my second-floor flat. When I had difficulty breathing, he took me to hospital.

That summer, Spender toured the U. S. as bass player with a prog band. Their second single broke into Billboard's Top 100, but charting singles and the band were gone in ten months. While on tour, Spender changed his name to Dylan, as I had changed mine to Derek after becoming an ex-pat. While the band waited to take the stage at the Fillmore as support act for the Grateful Dead, a prankish roadie dosed Spender's Coca Cola with acid. He made it to the end of the set before collapsing. Sid Herring, the group's manager, poured him onto a flight to London, where he arrived in a near-catatonic state. Having received Sid's phone call, I was waiting for Spender at Heathrow and drove him to London City Hospital. After four days, the doctors put him in a detox program. The prog band continued its tour, making a name in the U. S. that would have resulted in a second tour had the group managed to stay together. Abandoned by his bandmates, Spender credited my hospital decision as a turning point in his life.

We were mates now. There was no need — or time – to think about what to do.

*****

Before leaving for Bristol, Spender showed me the dent and crust of something that could have been dried blood near the left front headlight of his Ford Transit. We took my car, leaving the van in the alley behind my building. I pulled over onto the verge near where Spender thought he might have hit the man. We knew we did not have much time before the police would arrive to check the car. Frustrated by high weeds and underbrush below the level of the motorway, Spender thrashed his hands against his hips. I felt my mouth become dry and heart beat against my chest. We separated to cover more ground. Moving forward through the vegetation, our heads turning like conning devices, unsure what we were looking for: a body, a human imprint on the leaves, a path through bushes where someone had walked or crawled away, or….

"Bloody fucking hell!" Spender shouted, summoning me to his side with frantic waves. I moved slowly, not sure I wanted to see. As I approached, I saw the small body wearing a red cardigan and yellow-striped bellbottom pants. Edging next to Spender, I looked down at a girl of perhaps sixteen, black hair tucked under an Irish fisherman cap. A patch of white accented the black like the stripe on a skunk. Her face appeared to have an Asian cast.

The girl lay on her right side, left hand raised slightly above her due to the angle of her arm resting on her hip. Dried blood was visible on a sliver of exposed skin below the cardigan. Several flies buzzed around the wound.

"We need to get out of here," Spender said. "There's no telling…."

"Are you sure, mate?"

Spender looked at me in raw fear. Surprising both of us, he tiptoed around the girls' legs to squat in front of her. He put his face so close to hers that their noses almost touched. He went rigid for several seconds, quivering in his haunches, then looked at me in disbelief. "I think she's breathing," he whispered. "Danny," he said, calling me by my American name. "What should we do?"

I recoiled from his use of "we," but kept my head.

"Let's split and call the police from the nearest phone box," I said – a plan I had formulated in those few seconds Spender squatted by the girl

Spender appeared to hesitate. I grabbed him by a shoulder. "Get up! Get moving. We'll be summoning help within minutes. That is absolutely the best thing we can for her."

"Are you sure we should leave her, Danny?"

"I'm sure. Do you want to live your young life in jail?"

"All right, then," he said, rising to his feet while keeping his eyes on her face. "Let's go. Let's get out of here."

He ran toward my car. "Slowly!" I shouted. He slowed to a brisk walk, and I followed him at a slower pace, unzipping and zipping my fly. Should someone notice, we were two guys stopping to take a piss.

Spender remembered a telephone box just ahead. I did the talking. I spoke with my mouth against the crook of my arm. I was feeling weight on my shoulders and pressure on my chest. My voice came out constricted. I reported seeing a hit and run and gave the location. Then I hung up. Spender jiggled from one leg to the other outside the box, striking his fists against his hips. He had to piss.

*****

Working open the stubborn lock the next morning, I inspected the premises from counter to shelves to table displays to assure myself everything was in order. Satisfied, I resumed my inspection of the figurines. Finishing that task seemed the most natural way to begin the morning. Back in business, I could breathe.

Task completed, I set the angel on the lowest shelf behind the register station, where I kept the most fragile items. I moved her a bit to the left, then turned her a hair. Satisfactory. I am compulsive. She needs a name. I will call her Yoko.

The next day, Spender dropped by to tell me he saw a report on the nightly news about a hit and run accident on the motorway: an unidentified motorist struck a woman who was walking along the hard shoulder. The woman, age seventeen, was being treated for broken ribs and insect bites. Police asked anyone who had information about the accident to call a phone number.

Spender took the van to a shop owned by the brother of a dealer friend. The brother had been roughed up during questioning on an assault charge and was no friend of the police. Spender told his new bandmates that the van leaked a lot of fluid that morning; to drive it further risked freezing the engine. Spender was the leader of the band, so his mates believed him. He drove them to their next two gigs in his father's van from the flooring business. No one commented on a news report. No mate gave off a scent of suspicion. Spender blamed his irritability and long silences on fatigue.

After a week passed, then a month, Spender and I began to believe our luck. Life went on. I moved the angel to a higher shelf and would not sell it despite the pleas of a porcelain collector who offered double the original price.

"No longer for sale, I'm afraid."

"Why do you have it out then?"

"I've come to be fond of her. I call her Yoko."

"Suit yourself," the collector huffed.

Before he could slam the front door, a shortish man wearing a dark suit and black fedora shot out his arm to prop the door open. The collector left without looking. The newcomer waited a couple of beats, took a step in, and closed the door carefully behind him.

About my height and unsmiling, he came to the counter. He

appeared to be looking at a point above my right shoulder where there was nothing but faded green wallpaper.

"May I help you?" I said.

"Would you be the owner?"

"Why yes, I would."

"And your name is…?"

"Derek. Derek Quinn."

The visitor reached inside his coat pocket and produced a photograph. He slid the photo flat across the counter. I recoiled from this sudden invasion of my space.

"I am Detective Inspector Hetherington from Metropolitan Police. I am looking for this man in connection with an investigation. Would you happen to recognize him?"

Cracked at the edges, the photo was a police mug shot of a man with round cheeks, copious black hair, and a bruised lip. Pakistani or Indian, I thought. Don't know him. But he looked familiar.

"I'm not certain," I said. "A lot of people come into the shop. Perhaps here or around the city. I get out a bit."

Inspector Hetherington gazed at me steadily and said nothing. Time slowed.

"All right, then," he said after the long pause. He reached into his back pocket for his wallet, and handed me his card. "Be sure to call me if something jogs your memory."

He walked slowly toward the door as if thinking of something, then turned. "Oh, yes. Would you happen to know a man named Michael Spender?"

I looked down at the counter. I was sure my face flushed. "He's a friend."

"I expect to be speaking with him very soon," the inspector said. "Are you sure you don't know the man in the photograph?"

"He looks familiar," I admitted. "Possibly a friend of a friend."

"We're getting somewhere then. Would it help if I told you his brother runs an auto repair shop?"

Oh my God, I thought. The man who repaired Spender's van. We met once or twice at Spender's local pub.

"May I ask what this investigation is about?" I stuttered.

"A motor vehicle-pedestrian accident," Inspector Hetherington said, having eased halfway back toward the counter. He pulled a small black notebook from his side pocket. "Name?"

"I don't...."

"Not the man's name. Your name. I understand your legal name is not Derek."

"Daniel," I said, tapping my right-hand nails on the counter. "Daniel Quinn."

"United States citizen?"

"My application to become a British citizen is in process."

"I see. You wouldn't want to be sent home then, would you?"

"What do you mean?"

"Did your friend Spender drive the vehicle that struck a young woman on the motorway about five weeks ago?"

I pictured myself curling into a foetal position behind the counter, yet remained standing. Behind the counter, my left leg twitched.

"Yes," I said.

"Did he tell you he was the driver?"

"I believe so."

"Yes? No?

"Yes."

"Did you return with Spender to the M23 in search of the victim?"

"Yes."

"Would you meet me at the New Yard at 4?"

"Certainly," I said. "I will close early and be there at 4."

"All right, then."

He turned and left, leaving the door ajar.

*****

I took the underground to Waterloo and exited onto Victoria Street. I suppressed the impulse to call Spender. Inspector Hetherington seemed methodical. Spender would hear from him soon enough.

As I entered the steel and glass building, I was aware that I already was distancing myself from Spender. Hetherington's question passed through my brain repeatedly, like the revolving police insignia outside the building: Would I rather be a witness or an accomplice?

A uniformed bobby told me the inspector could be found down the hall in the interview room. "I appreciate your punctuality," Hetherington said as I entered. "Please take a seat." Opposite the wooden visitor's chair, with a thick-legged wooden table in between, was the cushioned chair with arms that Hetherington occupied. It squeaked as he pulled up to the table.

"Now then," he said, his pen poised above a white legal pad. "Begin at the beginning, and tell me what happened."

I intended to recite the facts as I knew them in as neutral a tone as I could muster. I hoped to present himself as a reliable witness dismayed by the awful circumstances. To my growing unease, Hetherington's questions often began with "So, you and Spender…" did this or did that.

"So you and Spender separated after stepping off the hard shoulder into the shrubbery so you could cover more ground in your search for the victim?"

Pause. "We did, I guess."

Hetherington jotted a couple of lines on the legal pad. "You did," he repeated.

After an hour of Hetherington's questioning, I no longer felt any loyalty to my friend. After two hours, I left the building in a state of numb shock. Spender would be arrested. I would be called to testify against him. I was certain.

Before leaving the building, I returned from a bathroom break to find Hetherington standing up to stretch, looking more human than he had before. This slight hint of ease gave me the courage to ask something that occurred to me as I pissed: What was the significance of the man in the photograph?

"Not sure yet," Hetherington said, remaining standing. A smile played at the corners of his mouth like a flash card signaling a better mood. "We happened to have a police photo of the gentleman. Prior arrest. I showed it to you to prompt your memory. Which it did."

Still standing, he dismissed me with instructions. "No contact with Spender or his friends. If he comes to your place of business, tell him you would rather not talk to him just now. No discussion of this interview with anyone, including wife, partner, significant other, the man in the street. And *do not* under any circumstances leave the jurisdiction of the Metropolitan Police Service without notifying me by phone or in person. Do you understand?"

I nodded. "Yes. I understand."

"And well you should. This is a grave matter. Leaving the scene of an accident after causing personal injury. Her injuries are more serious than reported in the news. The broken ribs punctured a lung, causing internal bleeding. She could have died in the shrubbery if you had not alerted us to her presence – the sole mitigating fact in an otherwise damning display of stupid cruelty. Keep that mind as you tend shop. You may go."

Hetherington ushered me into the hall as a burly man with red hair seasoned by grey passed us on his way to the interview room. He acknowledged Hetherington with a nod, and shut the door behind them with a backhanded shove that I could not help but feel was directed toward me.

*****

Lin-Yan Yang rose through an anaesthetic fog. Diaphanous letters of fine grey vapour shimmered against a light blue sky. *Heal.* She could hear the word as well as see it. Its tone was resonant, commanding. She emerged from the fog to realize that she was in the recovery room of a hospital. Her friend Mina visited and offered her a bed in her flat for the time when Lin-Yan would be released. Mina would sleep on the couch. Since she had returned two months ago from China, Lin-Yan had crashed in friends' flats, mostly on couches. In September, she would move back into her dormitory. She and her friends often went out to hear punk bands at the Nashville Room. They were among the crowd on the night the fight broke out between a hyperactive new band and members of the audience. In the grainy photograph that appeared in the following week's *New Musical Express*, Lin-Yan's pale, delicate features were visible in the lower left corner.

In hospital, Lin-Yan became a minor celebrity. The detective inspector came to question her as soon as she was able to speak. He returned every other mid-afternoon to continue seeking her recollections.

"Making good progress, I see," he said cheerily, as he always did, on the seventh afternoon when he found her sitting up in bed, reading *Siddhartha.*

"Thank you for kindness, sir. I feel much better soon."

On the eleventh day, she left the hospital. A nurse pushed the wheelchair out to the semi-circular drop off/pick up area where Mina's boyfriend John stood by his car. Mina remained at the flat, cleaning the bedroom and changing linen for Lin-Yan's arrival.

*****

During the interview at the New Yard, Inspector Hetherington and Chief Inspector Mende confronted Spender with the testimony of an unidentified witness that he left the scene of a hit and run accident, and offered him two years in prison with possible time off for good behavior.

In front of him, the inspectors considered an appropriate punishment.

"If she were my daughter, I'd marinate his balls in a fruit jar on my mantel," Hetherington offered.

"Too good for the bastard," Mende amended. "I'd require him to spread his legs so I could crush his nuts with the left front tire of his vehicle."

"Very Old Testament, chief."

Backlit by the green-shaded light dangling above the interview table, Mende's red curls looked like flames. Fearing that he might be attacked in prison, Spender begged his father to retain a barrister to defend him. The barrister made much of Spender's return to the scene that saved the victim's life, and the prosecutor agreed to six months. There was no trial.

Spender's martial arts skills were rusty but adequate. He managed to repel two attackers in his first week in prison, breaking the second man's nose with a fist. For his own safety, the warden transferred him to a prison in the north, where he told fellow prisoners he was serving time for robbing a pub.

*****

During Spender's imprisonment, the porcelain angel occupied a place of honour in the centre of the bottom shelf behind the counter. Each time I noticed it, the image of the girl lying on the ground came to mind like a photograph. I tried not to feel guilty or apprehensive about Spender, who may have learned that I was the witness spoke with detectives. After all, I rationalized, Spender was a few hours too late to grasp the import of the terrible accident he had caused.

Two years later, toward the end of a bleak February afternoon, I was almost finished inventorying costume jewellery I had bought in a batch at auction. Jewellery sales provided a steady stream of small profit. Pocket watches brought to me every few weeks by an Indian man who knew the trade did better. That morning I had sold a Hamilton watch in a gold-plated case for a hundred fifty quid to a barrister. With my back bent to my task, I heard the door rattle behind me, then squeak open. I turned to face a stocky man of middle height wearing a green cloth coat and black cap. He appeared Asian. I felt as if I had seen him before. After carefully closing the door, he stood looking at me in an appraising way.

"May I help you?" I said.

"Are you Mister Quinn?" he asked.

"I am. Yes. How may I help you?"

"I would like to speak with you," he paused, "about a personal matter. You have done a great favour to…." He seemed to be searching for the right word.

He stepped forward to the counter and held out a business card. "I am Yang Ming," he said. "My daughter is Lin-Yan Yang."

I reached out to accept the proffered card and held it chest high in front of me as I read it – a gesture I understood to demonstrate respect toward my Asian visitor. Lettered in both Chinese and English, the card identified Mr. Yang as owner of an export/import business. Ah…he wants to sell me something. I placed the card face up on the counter in front of me. I slipped into negotiating mode. His words took me to a different space.

"Police say you came to help my daughter."

"Came to her rescue. Yes, I suppose I did."

Of course the girl had a father. Of course he would come to London to check on the well-being of his daughter. Of course he would speak with the police about the accident. But wasn't it like I was in the witness protection program, or something like it? Inspector Hetherington was an unpredictable man.

"I wish in some small way to…pay back your help," said Mister Yang slowly.

"There is no need of that, sir," I said in a neutral tone. The elevation of my role in this sorry episode to that of good Samaritan was unexpected. I was not sure I trusted the change. "I did what any man would do."

Mister Yang smiled. "But you are not in jail."

"Evidently," I said, surprised by his humour.

"May I buy from you?"

"Of course."

"What to buy?"

I thought for a moment. The choice became obvious. I reached for the porcelain angel, and placed it on the counter next to his business card.

"Statue of goddess!" he exclaimed.

"A sort of statue," I said, "and not of a goddess. But hard to find, and in perfect condition. It is an angel. A winged messenger from a god. A guardian of the young."

"The young?"

"Such as your daughter, sir. During these long months, I thought of the angel as watching over your daughter as she recovered. I hope her recovery is complete."

"Yes, better," he said. "Much better" His smooth brow furrowed as he pondered the rest of what I said. "Watching her like a guard. Very nice."

Reaching into the outside pocket of his blazer, he extracted a silver money clip thick with currency. He licked his fingertips and counted out five twenty-pound notes, which he placed on the counter next to his business card. "Enough for angel?

"More than enough, sir." I paused to see if he might want change.

"Wrap it, please," he said, with the proprietary voice a customer might use after making a significant purchase. Mister Yang had satisfied his sense of obligation.

As I wrapped the porcelain object in protective layers of newspaper and a double thickness of brown paper, he continued to speak to me. His words sounded almost scripted.

"My daughter is now afraid. The accident has changed her. She has friends, but they are young. She needs someone older to be her friend, to accompany her to places. She loves music. She has beautiful voice and wants to sing. Would you accompany her sometimes to be her friend…so she is not afraid?"

"To hear music?"

"Yes, and to go to theatre. She loves English play."

I got what he was suggesting, but did not get it. I was speechless. He must have anticipated my uncertainty.

"Police told me you are a good man. That you would help Lin-Yan with what happened to her, like you did before."

"I guess I have no choice then," I said as cheerfully as I could muster. Out of the blue, Inspector Hetherington had called to remind me that my file was still open. In our last meeting, he said he would hold off dealing with my role in covering up the accident until Spender served his time. If I behaved myself and performed what he loosely referred to as a "service," he would close the file. My record would be clean. When I asked Hetherington what my service would entail, he said he would discuss the matter when the time came.

Apparently, Mr. Yang had met with Hetherington, who phoned the next day to describe my service assignment. I was to chaperone Lin-Yan Ying to clubs and theatres. He added, "…and perhaps other service as the need may arise. I want you to report back to me every two weeks to assure me that everything is as it should be." Everything?

*****

When I came by her flat, Lin-Yan answered the door. Her hair was longer, with shoulder-length ends curled inward. She looked older than when I had glimpsed her lying on the ground like a discarded doll. In the intervening months, she had gained a bit of weight, and looked like a young woman. Except she still dressed as an aspiring punk, wearing a red shirt with metal studs and a brown leather skirt fastened by an oversized safety pin.

"Thank you for taking me," she said in a soft voice. She reached for a black leather jacket on a coat peg, inserted her right arm, and let me hold the jacket for her left. "We go now?"

"Yes, let's" I said.

On the tube and walking to the club, I made attempts at conversation. Lin-Yan responded to each by turning her face toward me with an agreeable smile and saying "I see what you mean."

We merged into the pedestrian flow on Oxford Street. I did not notice the queue of twenty or more people waiting to enter the club until Lin-Yan walked faster, as if to head off any more getting ahead of us. That was the first sign of her excitement. She looked up at me with the same agreeable expression, and a sparkle in her eyes. "Wow," she said.

Doors opened fifteen minutes after we arrived. The queue behind us now equalled the one in front. Clearly the KB Band had a following. As the line moved forward, Lin-Yan jumped up to get a better look at the door. "I cannot believe!" she exclaimed.

"What? That we are here? Well, we are. Watch your step." We had reached the stairs leading down to the performance floor.

The venue operated as a club. We paid a pound apiece at the door. No sooner had we entered the dingy room with a black-and-white tiled floor than I felt a tap on my right shoulder. Startled, I looked right. Spender stood to my left, snickering. "Fooled ya!" he shouted above the sound system that played a recent hit from the Electric Light Orchestra – much more to my taste than the band Lin-Yan wanted so much to see.

I felt a surge of adrenalin. "What are you doing here?"

"Surprised, are ya? Sure y'are. You came to see me, what? — Oh, that's right. You never came to see me. Not once in two years months? I could have bloody well died there for all you knew, ya cunt."

He ogled my companion. "And who have we got here? Don't I know you from somewhere?"

"Spender!" I warned, putting my arms out as if to keep him back. "You need to leave us alone. Now. I'll catch up with you another time."

"Catch up with me, ya sorry cunt? I have more of right to be here than you do. I play bass with the support group."

"Bass?"

"Good enough for Jimmy Page when he was a Yardbird. Good enough for me in Step 13."

I turned toward Lin-Yan. She now stood several feet away, her expression neutral, her hands clasped across her stomach. She stared toward the vacant stage.

"Be that as it may, Spender, you must keep your distance," I said. I leaned toward him. "I'm doing community service, asshole," I hissed. "Hetherington's idea."

He looked puzzled. "Ya don't say. Copper dating service?"

"Not a dating service," I said. "Debt to society."

"Bollocks," Spender shouted over his shoulder. "Tell your inspector that I work here. You and your Chinese friend are guests." A look had passed between them that I did not understand.

I wanted to leave, but Lin-Yan insisted on staying. "Kate is my favorite," she said of the singer she came to see. We stood at the back of the room throughout Spender's performance. The name of his band was Elsinore. "Hamlet's castle!" I shouted to Lin-Yan through the screeching. She did not hear. Spender gyrated on the opposite side of the stage from us, thrusting the long neck of his base toward several girls who stood close.

Lin-Yan's favourite took the stage to applause and joyous shouts. A slender girl whose pale young face stood out against waves of black hair down to her shoulders, she kept her eyes closed when she sang. Her sidemen were respectful, playing much softer than Elsinore, and the girl's crystal voice delivered lyrics with clarity. There was a reference to Wuthering Heights. Her set was over, and she looked at the audience for the first time with a shy smile. A girl with a garland in her hair bent forward to give her flowers.

"Was she as good as you hoped?" I asked Lin-Yan as we ascended the stairs to a deserted Oxford Street.

"Yes. I like her very much."

Self-conscious because of the awkwardness of my situation, made more awkward by the confrontation with Spender, I escorted Lin-Yan home in silence.

Her flat was on the second floor. I could hear music inside. Mina must be home. As we stood by the door to her flat, Lin-Yan lifted her brown eyes to mine for the first time that evening. "Very much fun for me, Derek," she said. "I hope you have fun." I assured her that I did. I wished her good night and turned to go. "Bye," she said softly. I heard the music get louder, then softer as I paused on the landing below.

*****

I live above my shop – a convenient location, yet sometimes a liability when a person I would rather not see comes looking for me. I know what readers might be thinking: that Spender waited for me inside the entrance to my building with a bludgeon in his hand. Or that he and his accomplice broke into my flat, and I noticed a suspicious light as I walked down my street toward the building. In fact, I noticed nothing until a heavy-set man with a knit cap pulled down to his eyes blocked my way, and a man (presumably) behind me locked my arms with his and jerked my arms upward. This sudden and violent pressure produced a pain in my right shoulder that was excruciating. I began to scream, but the man behind released my left arm and slapped his gloved hand over my mouth. A quick series of punches to my midriff and sternum knocked the breath out of me. As I crumpled to the pavement, I heard a faint crack.

*****

Two days later, after hiding out in Hampstead with a friend who was fond of me and loved my shop, I reported the assault. Hetherington rang the next morning, asking me to meet him at 3 p.m. at the New Yard.

He shut the door of his small office, whose confines made two people meeting a cosy affair. But close quarters were preferable to the sterile, over-lit environment of the interrogation room, where I felt acutely uncomfortable at our last meeting.

He looked up from a pile of paperwork next to a stack of manila folders. "Well?" he said.

"No room for the chief inspector today," I observed, stalling.

"I will keep him apprised," Hetherington said, reaching for his white legal pad, on which he appeared to have made some notes. Without breaking contact between his eyes and mine, he tapped the pencil eraser on his desk twice and asked, "Are you quite sure that Friday night was your only contact with Mister Spender?"

"Quite sure."

"Any problems at your place of business? Disgruntled customer? Someone to whom you owned money?"

"Not to my knowledge," I said.

"That was a yes or no question."

"No."

"Yin-Lan is quite attractive, as we both know. Did anything take place between you and her that might have offended her—"

"Absolutely not."

"—or her father?"

"Not that I know of." Equivocation must have been all right for this question. "I have no way of knowing, of course."

"Inscrutable?"

I smirked, recalling an old cartoon in *Playboy* magazine: a nude Oriental woman corrects a man who mistakes the word "inscrutable" for a more sexual term.

"Did I say something funny?" Hetherington asked.

"No," I said lamely. "Don't know what I was thinking."

"Nervous tic, perhaps," he replied.

He leaned back his chair in the little room allowed him, and reached for the top folder. Placing the folder on top of the notepad, he removed a photograph of a man. He handed it to me.

"Was he one of them?"

"Wait. Is this the same man whose picture you showed me at the shop?"

"I repeat. Was he one of the men who assaulted you?"

I looked at the prominent eyebrows and dark eyes beneath. "He may have been," I said slowly. "It was dark."

"Not completely," Hetherington said. "There was a bit of a moon."

Now that he mentioned it, I recalled noticing the quarter moon on my walk home from my tube stop.

"His name is Dariush," Hetherington said. "His brother is Datsuke. They own an auto repair shop in East London."

Spender's friends. Their names triggered a memory of the glove slapped across my mouth. Grease. Gasoline. Some smell that could have come from a garage. I said as much to Inspector Hetherington. He took in the information without expression, except for a slight glimmer of interest in his eyes. I was becoming familiar with his expressions – and lack of them.

He let his chair down toward his desk and tapped the pencil eraser twice. "I visited him some time ago as I said I would," he said.

"You mean on the day you first came into my shop?"

"Yes. And visited him as I intended. He was under suspicion."

"Of what?"

"You don't need to know the details. A crime. All I need to know from you is whether you can say, with a great degree of certainty, is that this is one of the men who assaulted you."

I thought for a minute. What I saw of the man's face. The remembered smells of gasoline and grease on the glove. I was seventy-five percent certain and said so.

Hetherington seemed to know that was all he would get from me that afternoon. He stood up. I stood as well, surmising the interview was over. He turned to his desk, rather than toward me, and replaced the photograph in its folder. I realized the folder must be for Dariush. It was several pages and at least one photograph thick, enough to suggest a criminal with a record.

"You can let yourself out," Hetherington said, facing the window. "Please close the door." Had I, or something related to my visit, irritated him to rudeness? I closed the door, and tried to put his manner out of my mind.

*****

As a boy growing up near Ipswich, Hetherington was obsessed for more than a year with assembling picture puzzles. His favourite was a hunting scene called "Tally Ho!" A man in a bright red coat sat astride a magnificent chestnut horse and raised his hat to signal the start of the hunt. A pack of eleven brown and black hounds leapt into action. The chase was on!

Hetherington remembered how upset he was the day a crucial piece was missing. He searched everywhere around the dining room table. Inexplicably, the piece never turned up. He became upset, then depressed, and abandoned his puzzles for model boats. Undercurrents of the upset feeling had come back during his investigation of the M23 hit and run. After the shop owner left his office, he was convinced of it: a piece was missing.

He thought back to his meeting with Bahreini brothers late in the afternoon after he visited the keeper at his shop. As he stepped over wood shavings thrown down to absorb slicks of engine oil, the first thing Hetherington noticed about the brothers was that they moved in the indolent, confident manner of lions. Slow, measured steps, and unhurried arm and hand movements as they hammered out dents on the chassis of aging maroon Jaguar.

The older brother, Dariush, whom Hetherington recognized from an earlier encounter, turned his large head and smiling face in the direction of the visitor. His hair was black and bountiful. He said nothing.

His younger brother glanced for an instant at Hetherington without interrupting the pace of his work. Dariush and Hetherington stood looking at each other for an awkward amount of time, as if not wanting to show weakness by being the first to say something.

"May I speak with you, Mister Bahreini?" Hetherington began.

"Do I know you?" Dariush responded.

"We met once about a year ago. To do with the report of a missing van."

"I don't remember such a meeting," said Dariush.

"Police matter," Hetherington said, putting forward his badge. "Refresh your memory?"

"Yes, inspector. I remember you now. You thought I might have stolen the van. But I borrowed it from a friend who only just bought it. There was a mix up. I came to the station and we talked. I thought we resolved the matter."

"There is a new matter," Hetherington said. "Last night the same vehicle may have been involved in a hit and run accident. The victim is in hospital. I thought the driver might have taken the van to your shop."

Dariush acted surprised. "Here? You can look around. There is no van here."

"So I see," Hetherington said. "Where is your friend? Has he moved?"

"He is somewhere. Who knows? He is a musician. Rolling Stone!" Pleased with his own joke, Dariush grinned. Kneeling in front of the Jaguar's empty headlight socket, his brother snorted.

Hetherington was unsmiling. He recalled their first meeting, when Dariush exuded the same confidence and charm while being questioned about a missing vehicle, likely stolen, and now owned by a traveling musician who had a receipt for its purchase from the man who reported it missing.

"All right, then," Hetherington said, handing Dariush his card. "Call me immediately if you hear from him."

"Certainly, inspector. Good luck in your search."

He turned toward the Jaguar and said something to his brother in Iranian. Datsuke nodded, glanced in Hetherington's direction, and kept hammering.

*****

Lin-Yan and her flat mate Mina sat close to each other on the green corduroy couch. On the small television, a caricature-like Spaniard in a Monty Python skit burst through the wall to announce that "No one expects the Spanish Inquisition!" Mina giggled as her thin fingers groomed Lin-Yan's black hair. In recent weeks, Lin-Yan had allowed her hair to grow long – a manifestation of an increasing disregard for her appearance. Her face showed traces of the pinched emotions she had been feeling. As Mina groomed her, Lin-Yan began to cry small tears that traced tiny moist trails on her cheeks. In Mina's estimation, and to her concern, her flat mate looked more distressed than on the afternoon she was released from the hospital.

"I am so sorry, my beautiful girl," Mina said. "Please tell me what is on your mind? Is it your father again?"

Lin-Yan began to cry harder. Mina pulled her close and hugged her. "He is a very cruel man," she said, "to treat his loving daughter so coldly."

Lin-Yan put her hands over her eyes and shook her head. She was seeing something that Mina did not. Her sadness was not the fault of her father, who was distant but devoted. Nor was it any single circumstance that Lin-Yan cared to tell her flat mate about. Lin-Yan sensed that Mina felt she was a friend of hers, yet she was not, really. Lin-Yan was aware that she was much like her father, keeping people from coming too close, holding secrets in her mind and heart. True, her father had made her a go-between for his one of his businesses – in Lin-Yan's view, the most disturbing one. He ought to more considerate of the safety his only daughter, she felt. Had he forgotten that not long ago, her doing what he wished her to do had almost cost her life? Sometimes she weakened and considered the possibility that she should not judge her father too harshly because he brought her to London for college and was able to support her from money made connecting poppy growers in Afghanistan with drug refiners in Pakistan and dealers in England. The product could remain opium or be refined into heroin. Lin-Yan had learned that there were plenty of people in London, including several of her acquaintances, who craved these bricks and packets. It made her uneasy that Mina was one of them. For months, gentle Lin-

Yan managed to deflect assertive Mina's hints that they experiment with substances together. Mina's hints had become suggestions timed to coincide with Lin-Yan's most vulnerable times. Tonight, Lin-Yan felt terribly lonely, and let Mina cook the heroin in their tiny kitchen and slip the needle into her vein as she trembled against the foot of the couch. When her depression and loneliness returned, she began to cry.

On the television, actor John Cleese took ungodly long steps in a black coat and bowler hat as a member of the Ministry of Silly Walks. The telephone rang in the bedroom, where the women had their beds and shared a dresser.

"I'll get it," Mina volunteered, patting Lin-Yan's cheek. She oozed from the couch and became unbalanced for a moment. She picked up on fifth ring.

"What a surprise," she said cheerily. "Good to hear your voice, but you are being a bad boy. Our message was quite clear. You are not to come around here or call. No, she cannot come to the phone." She paused to listen. Her voice became stern. "He would be very, very angry with you if he found out you had not listened to him. There would be consequences. So keep your distance. Refrain from calling. Do as you have been told."

She hung up the phone and fell onto Lin-Yang's bed. "Come here, lovely girl," she wailed. "Please."

Lin-Yan resolved not to respond. She flipped face down on the couch, wishing the last months had never happened. She heard Mina's footsteps and felt the light touch of her hand brushing her the back of her head. She buried her head deeper into the faded yellow cushion. It made a nice match with the couch. For that moment, the cushion was her best friend. Mina left her side, going to her own bed. Lin-Yan felt the warmth of her mother, who had died when she was five, wrap her body in a cocoon of comfort and safety. Within minutes she fell asleep, not waking until the following noon, when Mina was at work and she was wonderfully alone. This feeling was quite different than the terrible loneliness of last night. She went to the bathroom and took a shower. Gentle whispers from her mother remained with her as she dressed. She knew what she would do.

*****

The day was overcast, and warm for September. Because of the dampness and intermittent showers, I anticipated a slow afternoon. I turned without enthusiasm to the cartons of miscellaneous ceramic items I purchased at auction two days ago. Perhaps there would be two or three overlooked pieces that had enough value to justify what I had paid for the lot. Having sealed shut the cartons with tape, I opened the front right drawer of the counter to choose a razor knife. I owned two, and most often went with duller one. I sliced my finger with the sharper. Fortunately the cut was not deep, but bled as if it were worse. I cut halfway along the tape joining the top flaps of the largest carton when I heard the door rattle. The person was having some difficulty – perhaps a child or old woman.

I took a half-dozen steps to the door and pulled it open. To my considerable surprise, Lin-Yan stood in front of me, wearing an umber sweater and red bandana tied across her brow.

"Hello, Derek," she said, looking into my eyes. "I need to talk."

"Of course," I said, ushering her inside with my arm. "Have a seat." She was light, so my old chair squeaked less than usual. She folded her hands in front of her and leaned forward. I eased my butt against the counter for support. Her body language suggested that she had thought about what she wanted to say, and my part would be to listen.

She cried a few tears and wiped her eyes with the back of her hand. "I lied, Derek. I deceived you. I am so sorry." More tears, a wipe, and she continued. "I delivered drugs to Spender. I was in his van the night before you found me. Sometimes I was his girlfriend. My father told me to spend time with Spender because he knew many musicians. The musicians would want to buy my father's drugs.

"For almost a month I did this, going with Spender and his friends to the clubs where they played. I knew being Spender's girlfriend was not good for me, but did not want to go against my father. He pays for my apartment and education. He gives me money to live on. Sometimes it seems that he wants me to have a good time, like going to clubs with you. Other times I feel like his servant. You are the only man I can talk to."

She cried again, longer this time – long enough for me to feel the need to put my arm around her shoulders and tell her that I understood. She looked across the counter as she spoke, as if focusing on my rows of figurines.

"We had a fight in the van," she said. "Spender was high and driving reckless. The other guys were asleep. I thought I could tell him that I needed a vacation from these trips. I wanted to think about what I was doing. He asked me if I did not want to sell drugs. I said I did not sell drugs. I delivered them. Then he asked me if I was tired of being his girlfriend. I did not know how to answer him. I said maybe. He looked at me as if he hated me, and told me to get out of the van. I sat still, hoping if I did nothing, he would feel better.

"He drove for about a mile when Faz shouted to him 'Get rid of the cunt. She's nothing but trouble.' I started to cry. Spender slapped me across the face and said 'Shut up.' I could not control myself. I kicked him. He pulled over and stopped. He came around to my side and pulled me out. I screamed at him that I was not a cunt. When he got back in the van and started the engine, I ran in front to make him stop. He…hit me! I fell into some bushes. I tried to get up, but could not. The pain was like a knife. I felt sick to my stomach and passed out."

I was confounded by her story. Would Spender do such a crazy thing? Not in my experience, but I had never seen him with a woman.

Lin-Yan continued to talk. She told me about her roommate and the drugs, and that she did not want to go back to Mina's apartment. She asked me if she could stay with me until she figured out what to do. With a jumble of feelings, I offered to turn my apartment over to her for a day or two. I could stay with my friend in Hampstead. She asked me to stay with her because she was afraid. I felt a protectiveness toward her that might have led to sex, if I was attracted to women that way. I was moved that she had come to me to help. Like most men, I derived a certain satisfaction from playing the role of the white knight.

In hindsight, what bothered me most about Lin-Yan's revelations was her assertion that Spender was a dealer. I knew he was a user, and could be an asshole, but did not think he was foolish enough to take an enormous risk. As Lin-Yan slept that night in my bed, I found myself unable to sleep no matter what position I assumed on my couch. I lay there looking at the ceiling, assessing my circumstances. Spender had proved to be an unreliable friend. Lin-Yan was sweet in her Oriental way, yet remote – and, to be candid, not particularly intelligent. The only people I respected during the past months were the detectives; and the only enterprise that mattered to me was my shop. I formulated a course of action that would let me get back to what I liked. In the morning, I would take Lin-Yan to breakfast and urge her to mend fences with Mina; in the afternoon, I would go to the New Yard and give Hetherington my final report.

*****

"If I understand you correctly," said Hetherington, gazing at me over his customary stack of files, "you are saying that this hit-and-run business was more in the realm of a drug deal gone bad."

I nodded.

"And you think that if I questioned them separately, Mr. Spender and the Chinese girl would implicate each other." I nodded again. "And that, if pressed, one or the other would likely identify the girl's father as the supplier of the drugs."

"Yes," I said. "Mister Yang imports hashish, opium, and heroin from Afghanistan and Pakistan. His daughter runs bricks and packets of product to Spender. Spender takes it on the club circuit and sells to musicians, staff, groupies…pretty much anyone, from the look of it."

"Three-step process," Hetherington said. "Four if you count the producers. All that bother to get high for a bit. Costly, too. I prefer the occasional pint at the local."

Hetherington shuffled his files for a moment, then extracted the photograph of Dariush Bahreini. "We're letting him carry on for the time being," he said, holding the photo between two fingers like a playing card. "His brother as well. Lack of evidence. Just as well. They are bound to come to our attention again. I will be sure to let you know."

He stood up, leaned forward, and extended his hand. "Good job," he said. "We thank you for cooperation. Consider your service concluded."

His cool, thin fingers could have belonged to a pianist rather than a detective. I could feel my palms sweat. "Should I close the door?"

"Oh, by the way, how is business at your shop?" Hetherington asked. His timing felt deliberate. I was halfway out the door. I stopped.

"Doing well," I said. "Londoners looking for a bargain. Couples from the country coming to town, asking how much their Edwardian bed warmer might fetch. The odd tourist poking his head in to ask directions." I tried to smile. "I get by."

"Good. Good. Business will pick up, I'm sure. And your citizenship application? Any word?"

"I haven't heard from the Home Office in some time," I said. "I assume the positive."

"Sounds like the right attitude," Hetherington said. "I am sure you will hear something soon."

Tapping his fingertips on the files, he said "Must get to these."

"Of course," I said. "I'll be going now." I was able to breathe normally only several minutes after I left the building. The day was overcast with a chill. I wore my green cardigan but regretted that I had not thought to carry my Burberry.

# If You Can Smell It,
# You're Probably Already Deep in It

## Harris Coverley

The Toyota hatchback rolled to a stop against the curb on Matlow Lane, Ben Carr slamming the brake pedal and heaving the handbrake on.

"Fuckin' thing!" he groaned. He checked his cardboard cup of flat white and saw that in the holder before the gearstick it had flopped over to its right, drizzling out.

"Awh fuck's sake!"

He corrected it before licking his sugared thumb, immediately regretting the taste of sweat and dust.

Tyler Ward had been holding his coffee with the lid on and had avoided any spillage.

"Easy bruv, easy, yer gotta go easy with that brake," he said, taking a sip from the peaked hole in the top.

"I know, and I know I keep sayin', but this car's like a fuckin' motorised shopping trolley. Since I lost the Ford I've been fucked."

"Yer just gotta keep it easy with the braking."

"Yeah, yeah, I'll try, I'll try…"

Carr checked the time on the dashboard: it was exactly 10:15. It was fifteen minutes to go.

"Quarter of an hour," he said to Ward, and the other nodded.

Carr picked up his coffee and wiped chaotically at the spill on the plastic before the gears with a napkin.

"The thing is I'm pissed more because I know this is a good cup of coffee."

"Yeah, not bad," said Ward, slurping.

"I'd say McDonalds do the best takeaway coffee, which is somethin' I don't think I'd say, like, a few years back or whatever."

"Really?"

"Well, yeah, when yer consider the competition like."

"Like what?"

"Well, I know Subway sandwich do the fuckin' worst, I'm pretty fuckin' sure about that."

"Never 'ad a coffee from there."

"Oh, it's the fuckin' worst."

"Yeah?"

"Bitter and over-milked, it's shite."

"I thought yer got a flat white there."

"Yeah, but their white coffee is shit. Like it's brewed with the sweat off a bollock."

Ward carried on drinking, before adding: "I don't really drink that much coffee me."

"I have two or three a day now."

"Yeah…"

"Keeps me goin'…getting older."

"Yer fuckin' twenty-five mate."

"Still fuckin' older…"

Ward got out his phone and checked the time for himself.

"Half ten Barnes said?"

"Half ten, yeah."

Ward perused his social media while Carr looked up and down the street, barely irradiated by the grim discoloured day. It was fairly unassuming: shitty, but an *austere* as opposed to a *garish* kind of shitty. The terraces were tall and thin, mid-Victorian, brown and red, with little front gardens, some bare, some filled with garbage and broken furniture, some packed with green torrents erupting over their edges.

As per Barnes's instructions, they had parked five doors up from number 24, the house of Connell and a few of his boys.

"Usual shithole," said Carr staring at a damp ashen stain on the wall beneath the guttering of a house on the other side of the road.

"Mmmm," intoned Ward, still looking at his phone.

Carr tapped on the bottom of the wheel.

A minute had passed.

Ward finally put down his phone and unwrapped the remains of his Breakfast Muffin which he had been storing in the door pocket to Carr's chagrin—a greasy pocket could stink out the whole vehicle for days.

"Yer still eatin' that thing?" asked Carr.

"Yeah," replied Ward with a full mouth.

"Finished mine before we left car park."

"I know yer fat bastard."

"Hey, easy, easy…"

Carr slapped his gut.

"Still two stone lighter than a year ago…commitment paid off."

There was a pause as Ward finished the last of his sandwich.

"All right that," he said.

"It's garbage though."

"*You* suggested it."

"I know, I know, but it's *easy* yer know, too easy."

"Mmm, yeah."

A cyclist in full luminous red and gold attire came down the street from behind them and both young men watched as he rocketed past, turned the left corner in a snap, and was gone.

"Couldn't do that shit, fuck that shit."

"Naw mate, fuck that shit."

"Y'know," continued Carr, "prob'bly still reelin' from Saturday."

Ward lightened up and grinned: "Yeah mate, that was good that."

"Good time, good time…nearly pulled y'know."

"Wha'? When?"

"That girl at the kebab shop."

"She was fuckin' pissed up."

"Aye, but she was willing."

"She was drunk an' loud."

"Cute and loud."

"She was making a show of it…"

"I liked her little black star tattoo on her shoulder, it was cute."

"No fuckin' way mate…"

"Yeah, but how about you and that woman?"

"She was all right 'er."

"Fuck me mate, she had a face like a stubbed out fag."

"It weren't that fuckin' bad—"

"It fuckin' was mate."

"It weren't though fuckin'—yer said yer like older women."

"Yeah, older, not geriatric—"

"Right—"

"Not fuckin' survived Chernobyl or whatever it was—"

"Right—"

"If anything, I thought she looked a little bit like yer mum."

"Awh fuck off."

"No really."

"No seriously, mate, I'm not fuckin' 'avin' that, I swear down…"

"All right, all right…maybe not…so much…"

Ward looked at Carr suspiciously, then turned his eyes front, and then back down to his smartphone.

They sat in silence for a minute.

Carr checked the time: it was 10:21.

"Did yer," he started to ask Ward. "Did yer, err, did yer bring anything?"

"Like what?" replied Ward, not looking up.

"Like, a, erm, *protection*, or anything?"

"We're not *fuckin' 'em*."

"No, not like that dickhead—yer know what I'm sayin'. A knife or some shit like that."

Ward reached into the pocket of his hoodie and pulled out a Stanley knife, cold silver and rusting red at the edges. Its slide stiff and dry, he flicked out the blade, dull as the clouds above.

Carr breathed out: "I don't know…"

"Wha' d'yer mean?"

"I mean, like, it's fuckin' difficult to think of it…what if they search us before we go in and they find that?"

"Naw."

"I mean, but what if they fuckin' did?"

"Not gonna happen, honestly mate."

"No, can't do it."

"What?"

"No knives—too much of a risk."

"Fuckin' seriously bruv?"

"Put the knife in the glove box, outta sight, outta mind."

"No way mate, not with these cunts…"

"Seriously, I'm not doing it if we're gonna give 'em an excuse to fuck us up or whatever. Not doin' it."

"Yer gonna fuckin' turn yer back on that cash?"

"Seriously mate, I'm gonna drive off now."

Carr turned the key short of starting the engine and the dashboard lights flashed on red and blue, warning of several broken sensors and of an annual engine check overdue by 574 days.

"I'll do it."

"Yer fuckin' wouldn't."

"Get rid of the fuckin' knife, it's too fuckin' much."

"I'll fuckin' get out."

Ward put his hand on the door latch.

"Barnes wants both of us—just one, no fuckin' job."

"Yer don't fuckin' know that."

"D'yer fuckin' wanna to test 'im? That fuckin' loopy cunt?"

Carr and Ward stared each other out for what felt to them like an hour, but was really only a matter of a few seconds.

Carr did not expect to win—he had traditionally always been the weaker of the two in their friendship, more easily led, more easily trapped.

To his surprise, Ward relented.

He took his hand off of the latch and opened the glove compartment. With a scratching growl he slung it into hard plastic scoop and slammed it shut.

Carr realised he could have been smug, gloating—but he needed to keep Ward close, especially when it was a matter of minutes before everything was going to go down.

He put his hand on Ward's shoulder: "Look mate, it's just better this way, believe me."

Ward closed his eyes and gently hit his head against the seat cushion: "But what if things turn to shit?"

"Yer said yerself they're not gonna search us. Maybe if yer were gonna bring the knife, maybe then, in their heads, they'll just assume we're armed anyway maybe?"

"Then why not just bring the fuckin' knife then?"

"No, no, let's not risk it."

"I don't fuckin' get it…"

"Just better, can't risk a big fuck up."

"Then what do we do *if* things fuck up?"

"Yer know, yer said on the phone three days ago this was in the fuckin' bag, fuckin' easy as shit."

"I know yeah, but y'know, it's not always the case…"

Carr rubbed his face, already exhausted.

"Right, tell yer what…"

"Yeah?"

"If things fuck up, we fuckin' run, right?"

"Run?"

"Yeah, run like fuck. Don't ask questions. Fuck Barnes, fuck Connell, fuck everybody else, fuck the stuff, fuck the money."

Ward looked off into the road.

Carr carried on: "Yer got that scar still from that mad twat with the bottle right? Yer don't want another…or a fuckin' bullet wound."

"Come off it mate—they don't have fuckin' guns these pricks."

"Don't matter, don't wanna find out."

"Yeah, yeah…"

"So, okay—things fuck up, we run, yeah?"

"Yeah."

They rocked closed fists together and the pact was agreed.

Carr checked the time: 10:26.

Four minutes or less.

He looked down the street. The entire place was empty of life. Not even did some scraggy black cat make his regular rounds, nor did a lone woodpigeon peck at a lump of fetid organic matter in the gutter before the grate. It was just them in his car and the tender wind lapping at the naked skeletal branches of the elm at the end of the row.

Carr again tapped on the wheel, Ward back at his phone.

"Did they get back to you about that job?" Carr asked Ward, suddenly remembering.

"Which was that?" replied Ward, not looking up.

"The one with the, with the, err, glass people was it?"

"The window glaziers?"

"Yeah, those guys, did they get back to you on that or what?"

"Naw mate, I'm not fuckin' doin' that."

"But you said it was good money?"

"Naw mate, it's fuckin' shit."

"Why? What went wrong?"

"They just wanted somebody for a like a month, it's fuckin' shit."

"Right, yeah…"

Carr felt jealous—at least Ward had been offered a job by somebody decent. Carr had not worked (legally anyhow) for two years, and multiple people were beginning to ask questions, to pry, to worry.

There was movement at the end of the pavement—two men, one tall, one short.

Carr checked the time on the clock: 10:27.

He waited.

It was them. They were early.

"'Ey up," he said, and tapped Ward on the shoulder. "They're 'ere."

"Fuck me," breathed Ward, and slid his phone into his pocket.

They got out and walked down to outside 24 Matlow Lane to meet them.

Matthew Barnes was the leader of a very petty group, but dressed strangely well: a nice shirt, keeping it casual with no tie, a brown leather jacket, clean dark jeans, and decent shoes. His hair was cut short but not shaved, and his stubble was well-groomed.

His go-to muscle, Craig Nolan, on the other hand, at over six foot tall, wore a gruesomely bright yellow two piece tracksuit, striped with white, his huge feet in even brighter green-blue trainers, with the haircut that Carr in his head privately dubbed the "Shithead" for its shaggy pile on top of the skull above the smoothly shaved sides and back.

By contrast, Carr and Ward appeared excessively hirsute and unkempt, almost like transients, in their torn jeans, Ward's hoodie and Carr's shagged-out autumnal jacket.

Carr had never liked Barnes, and had half a mind to slap that leering mug even then.

"All right gentlemen?" Barnes grinned. "You remember Craig don't you?"

There was an exchange of mumbled greetings and Barnes drew them in, talking quietly: "Everybody clear on the plan? Craig you come in with me, you two, stand either side of the door in the hall after its shut."

"Yep," said Ward.

"Gotcha," said Carr, eyeing Barnes's brow, searching for any tell-tale sweat.

"And I wanna tell yer," continued Barnes, "I want you to pay a-fuckin'-ttention, right? Stay still, stay quiet, stay alert, and everybody gets out easy easy. That means no phones."

He reached in and tapped the solid rectangular bulge in Ward's front pocket.

"I know you Tyler—keep it in the pocket."

Ward genially nodded.

Barnes checked his golden (but not actually gold) watch.

"Let's do it."

As a foursome they walked through the garden and up the steps.

Barnes rapped four distinctly loud times on the door's window pane.

It creaked open and there stood a man even taller than Nolan in a black tracksuit with Buscemi eyes and a weird bowl cut of a hairdo. He was the ugliest being both Carr and Ward believed they had ever seen on two legs.

Barnes smiled toothily: "Hi, here to see Greg at half ten."

"Mr Connell is inside," grunted the human monolith, and pulled the door fully open to let the posse in.

For a brief second on the top step Carr, the last in, had an overwhelming urge to make a run for it. He thought about what Ward had said minutes earlier about them not fucking Connell and his associates—however, fucking them in a different way *was* in fact the plan. As far as Greg Connell and his men were concerned, this was a drug deal and a formal setting of territorial boundaries. In actuality, Barnes and Nolan were there to rob Connell and make it clear who was now the boss in the local area. It was a bold and brutal move—and they were slap-bang in the middle of the shitstorm at the shitshow.

But Carr repressed the impulse—he had made an agreement and a pact, he was going to fulfil it. He had gone through so much of his life regraded as a pussy, and he had to prove otherwise, at minimum to himself. Besides, it was a hundred pounds just to stand there at a door, not lift a finger, and give Barnes the appearance of strength.

The hallway was bare, no art, no mirror, not even a slim desk or table, the walls cracked and in dire need of a plaster and paint. The floor was covered with a grimy layer of industrial carpet, stained dried blood brown.

"Mr Connell's in 'ere," said the big man, indicating to the door into the front room.

Through the open door Carr and Ward could see Connell himself, willowy, older, and balding, in jeans and an undershirt sat on the couch against the far wall.

"Matthew," said the boss, "good to see you!"

"Good to see you Greg," replied Barnes.

"You know Big Jimbo?"

"Yes, of course…"

Carr and Ward stood still as Barnes and Nolan entered the room, followed by the towered Jimbo.

Before the door closed Barnes turned to them, smiled and winked.

The two men took up their positions either side of the door, Ward to the left, Carr to the right, as muffled conversation continued beyond.

"I fuckin' told you we wouldn't be searched," mumbled Ward.

"*Shuuuuu…*" went Carr. "He told us to keep *quiet.*"

"Awh bollocks to it…"

Ward settled down though, and they tried to listen in on the exchange.

The door was old and solid, as were the walls. There was a gentle rumble of speech, no shouting, no screaming, just normal talk vibrating through with the odd hiatus.

Carr looked forward to the blank wall before looking over to Ward. He could tell instantly that he was itching to glimpse at his phone.

"Don't do it."

"Do what?"

"Look at yer phone."

"I'm fuckin' not…"

"Yer fuckin' want to though."

"How the fuckin' 'ell would you know?"

"I can fuckin'—"

Carr's ramble was interrupted by a clear raising of voices from the room.

"What the fuck?" asked Ward.

"Shuuush," Carr hissed, waving his hand and turning his ear to the door. They listened.

From the hubbub within broke through the odd word and phrase. There was a "FUCK!", followed soon by a "FUCKIN' BASTARD!", topped after a moment by a "FUCKIN' JOKIN' BRUV!"

Something of glass smashed in the room, at which both Carr and Ward flinched.

There was a rapid shuffle of feet and furniture. A yell. A scream. A table tipped over.

Another "FUCK!" came through.

There was a loud popping bang and the wood of the door splinted outwards from the middle.

"What the fuck?!" yelled Ward.

"Let's get the fuck outta here!" Carr bellowed.

"Wait, maybe—" began Ward, but he was interrupted another popping bang.

"Arrgh FUCK!" he cried and grabbed his arm.

There was no confusion now—Carr could see where the bullet had come through the wall and through Ward's left upper arm, already streaming blood, with a trajectory straight into the opposing partition.

"SHIT!" he yelled. "Shit! Shit! Fuck! Shit!"

"RUN!"

"RUUUN!"

As the gun went off again Carr released the Yale lock and hustled Ward out of the house.

Stumbling, Ward fell against the garden gate as Carr glanced through the front window. The last bullet had shattered it into a spider web, but he could still see the battle inside, a fight to the death over the control of what had to be the only shooter.

"Fuck it!" Carr said. "Keep going! Back to the car!"

Ward managed to open the gate and the two bowled through, up the pavement, Carr keeping Ward upright and finally getting the latter into the passenger seat.

Carr raced around to the driver's side and got in, not daring to look back at the insanity back down the street.

As he started the engine he could not help but scold Ward: "You fuckin' said they wouldn't fuckin' 'ave guns!"

Gripping his flesh, Ward groaned: "They fuckin' weren't s'posed to!"

"Well what the fuck was that then?! A fuckin' party popper?!"

"Oh fuck off yer cunt!"

"You fuck off! Gettin' blood on me fuckin' seat!"

"Get fuckin' off!"

Carr slammed the accelerator and they jolted away, averting their eyes from the doomed house.

Carr drove for several minutes, stopping by a fenced off wasteland across from an estate.

"Let me have a look," he said to Ward, and he compliantly slid off its hoodie.

"It's not as bad mate…" he said weakly. "It's stopped bleeding."

Ward held his arm and Carr could see he was correct: the bullet had passed fully and cleanly through the flesh on the outer edge of his arm. The two little circular wounds, wiped with a spare napkin, had indeed stopped running with blood.

The muscle was swollen, but Ward's movement of the injured arm was fine—he could flex it and his hand worked normally. The pain appeared no worse than that of a sprain or a bad bruising.

"Yer one lucky motherfucker," said Carr, wiping his hands. "But I think you should still go to A&E…"

"Naw mate fuck that," Ward replied, cramming his ruined hoodie into a plastic bag.

Carr was in no mood to argue—the threat seemed to have passed anyway.

They sat for a moment as the sun broke through the clouds and gave them a blessed white light.

"Yer a real fuckin' gangsta now with bullet wounds…"

"Right, fuckin' too right…"

Carr looked over at Ward and saw the wound was still stable.

"What do want to do now?" he asked.

"Yer know," Ward said, looking about. "I'm getting hungry again."

"Yer fuckin' jokin' right?"

"Naw, I need to build me strength up I guess."

"After that shit? Are you sure yer okay?"

"Yeah, yeah, like yer always joke, it's just a flesh wound."

"Fuck me…where do you want to go?"

Ward whistled.

"Back to McDonalds?"

"*Really*?"

"Why not?"

Carr could not come up with a good rejoinder. It was not even midday and he was completely spent.

"All right then…back to fuckin' Mickey D's…"

"McChicken Sandwich I'm thinkin'…"

"Now you've given me the idea…do yer think they'll give a shit about all the blood?"

"When do those poor bastards give a fuck about anythin' in a car?"

"Yeah, yeah…"

As he drove, his eyes tired, his friend's blood under his fingernails, Carr knew he needed to get himself a proper job and soon.

The thought then came to him: "Yer gonna 'ave to replace that seat cover y'know."

"Awh fuckin' 'ell mate," croaked Ward, shaking his head.

## The Usual Unusual Suspects

***Daniel Marshall Wood*** leads a double life as proprietor of Edgefield B&B in Sharon Springs, NY and in NYC as editor of corporate investigation reports — as well as an identical twin. He is a member of Mystery Writers of America, with a number of mystery short stories published online and in print magazines.

***Gerald Elias*** leads a double life. He is the author of the critically acclaimed Daniel Jacobus mystery series that takes place in the dark corners of the classical music world, other novels, and many short stories and essays.

Elias is also an internationally recognized musician who has been a violinist with the Boston Symphony and music director of the Vivaldi by Candlelight concert series in Salt Lake City since 2004. He divides his time between the shores of Puget Sound in Washington and the Berkshire Hills of western Massachusetts, where he continues to expand his literary and musical horizons.

*https://geraldeliasmanofmystery.wordpress.com/*

He has also appeared in *Crimeucopia – One More Thing To Worry About* with *Last Night.*

***S.E Bailey***'s stories have appeared in the American magazines *Thuglit, Switchblade* and *Mystery Tribune* as well as the *Noirville* anthology from *Fahrenheit Press.* He's currently working on a historical crime fiction novel when he isn't toiling at the day job.

He also appears in *Crimeucopia – Say What Now?* with *Sureshot,* and *Crimeucopia — Boomshakalaking! Modern Crimes for Modern Times* with *So Clear it Burns.*

***Alexander Frew*** comes from farming and mining stock in the county of Ayrshire, Scotland. He went to the same Academy as Sir Alexander Fleming, the man who discovered penicillin, but it is fair to say that on leaving at the age of fifteen he failed to make the same societal impact. He wrote poetry and short stories in the 80s, then joined Borderline Theatre in the 90s and had several plays performed in an old church in Ayr. He also started *South West Writers*, and had three books for children published at the turn of the century. This led exactly nowhere, and after a fallow period he started self-publishing and produced a series of poetry booklets, CD's and performances in conjunction with the group.

After having an adventure story accepted by Hale in 2012, Alex has published some twenty books in the Western genre. He has also had a science fiction book published by *Mocha Memoirs Press*. His first, and greatest love, is the short story and he is trying to get better because it is harder to write a short story than a short book. His short story, ***Darkness Before Noon***, appeared in *Crimeucopia – The Cosy Nostra*, and his *Rebel Seed (Joe Flint book 1)* Western story is part of *Crimeucopia — Dead Man's Hand*.


***Kelly Lewis*** comes from Devon, likes long walks and cats, detests telephone cold callers, dogs, and certain people who use the expression 'Janner' within her hearing. Her work has appeared in various magazines, including *The Hub, Bottle, 3 x 5* and *Expressions* to name a few.


***Carew S. Bartley*** is originally from eastern Kentucky. After receiving a bachelor's degree in neuroscience from the University of Richmond and a J.D. from Georgetown, he returned to Richmond, Virginia to work as an attorney. His fiction has been published with *Hearth & Coffin Literary Journal* and *365tomorrows*, and his law-related articles with *Reuters, JD Supra*, and the *Georgetown Legal Ethics Journal*.

*Madeleine McDonald* finds inspiration walking on the chilly, windswept beach of her Yorkshire home. As a former precis-writer, she enjoys the challenge of writing flash fiction. Her short stories have been broadcast on BBC radio, and published in various anthologies and journals. Her historical novel, *A Shackled Inheritance*, is available from Amazon Kindle. Madeleine's *Not the Dog* appears in *Crimeucopia — One More Thing To Worry About*, and *I Can See Clearly Now* in *Crimeucopia — Tales From The Back Porch*.

*Edward Lodi* has written more than 30 books, both fiction and nonfiction, as well as a poetry chapbook. His short fiction and poetry have appeared in numerous magazines and journals, such as *Mystery Magazine*, and in anthologies published by *Cemetery Dance, Main Street Rag, Rock Village Publishing, Superior Shores Press*, and others. His story *Charnel House* was featured on *Night Terrors* Podcast. His *Death on a Pedestal* appears in *Crimeucopia - The I's Have It*, and his *Under the Table* appears in *Crimeucopia - We'll Be right Back — After This!*

*Michaele Jordan* was born in LA, educated in New York, and lives in Cincinnati. She's worked at a kennel and AT& T, at a Hebrew School and a church. She's a bit odd. Now she writes, supervised by a long-suffering husband and two domineering cats.
She's written two novels, Blade Light (serialized in JimBaen's Universe) and Mirror Maze (sadly, now out of print since the demise of Pyr Books). Her work has appeared in the *Magazine of Fantasy and Science Fiction, Abyss & Apex*, and *Buzzy Mag*. Horror fans will enjoy her *Blossom* series, from *The Crimson Pact* series.
Her website, www.michaelejordan.com, is undergoing reconstruction, but just grab a hard hat, and come on in.

*J. Aquino* is an attorney and retired journalist whose fiction has appeared in numerous anthologies. He is the author of *Truth and Lives on Film: The Legal Problems in Depicting Real Persons and Events in a Fictional Medium, 2nd edition June*

2022, https://mcfarlandbooks.com/product/truth-and-lives-on-film-2/ and *The Radio Burglar: Thief Turns Cop Killer in 1920s Queens*, September 2022, https://mcfarlandbooks.com/product/The-Radio-Burglar/

**David Rich**'s third novel is **The Mirrored Palace** (Adelaide Books). His first two books were *Rollie Waters* thrillers: **Caravan of Thieves** and **Middle Man** (Dutton/Berkley).

David spent the early years of his writing career in Hollywood, where he wrote the feature film, **Renegades**, starring Kiefer Sutherland and Lou Diamond Philips, as well as episodes of **MacGyver**, **StarGate-SG1** and other shows. In addition, David has written three plays: **The Interview**, **The Rescue**, and **W.A.R.** (*Women's Armed Resistance*).

He also teaches fiction and screenwriting in a graduate program in Connecticut

**Kelly Zimmer** read her first Agatha Christie mystery at age thirteen. Since then, she's lived on a steady diet of murder, thrillers, horror, and suspense novels. For most of her adult life, Kelly labored in a stifling corporate atmosphere in the wonderfully bizarre and diverse landscape of Florida, USA.

Visit Kelly on her website at www.kellyzimmerauthor.com or on Instagram @kellyzimmerauthor.

Kelly's *Conestoga Number Four* appears in *Crimeucopia – The 'I's Have It*, and she is the author of the Emi Watson novels, *Not Deep Enough*, and *The Magic In Me*.

**Sharon Richards** is a retired clinical psychologist, who is now a full-time performance storyteller. She has run the Success Stories storytelling club in Manchester for 14 years and was nominated for Cheshire Woman of the Year as a result. The Storytelling website link is: www.thesuccessstoriesclub.wordpress.com.

In what little spare time she has left, she has written 2 young adult novels *Deathly Inheritance* and *Pirates Out Of Time* which have both been shortlisted for writing prizes. She is happily married to Bill, "the nicest man on the planet", and has two adult sons.

As you may have guessed from her story, Karma's a Bitch, she is a Nichiren Buddhist!

**T. K. Howell** lives on the banks of the Thames and manages ancient oak woodlands, tending to trees that are older than most countries. His writing is often inspired by mythology and folklore and can be found at various genre and literary spaces including *Space and Time Magazine, Mystery Tribune, Mystery Magazine,* and *Brigid's Gate.*

**Maroula Blades** is an Afro-British multidisciplinary artist living in Berlin. In June 2023, she was awarded a grant for a novella-in-progress from the UK Society of Authors Foundation and the K. Blundell Trust, and in April 2023, a multimedia project grant from the Jan Michalski Foundation for Writing and Literature in Switzerland. She was selected for the 2021 *Initial Special Grant* from the Academy of Arts in Berlin. In 2020, *Chapeltown Books,* UK, published her short story collection, *The World in an Eye,* available on Amazon, Barnes & Noble, and other online platforms. In 2019, Maroula was nominated for the German *Amadeu Antonio Prize* for her multimedia, bilingual educational project titled *Fringe.* Her works were published in *The Caribbean Writer, Bacopa Literary Review,* the *Perito Prize Anthology, Words with Jam, Here Comes Everyone Magazine, Abridged, The London Reader, Ake Review, Midnight & Indigo,* and *Peepal Tree Press,* among other magazines and anthologies. Regularly, Ms. Blades gives bilingual (in English and German) poetry workshops in Berlin schools and high schools. Her multimedia projects were presented at many international literary festivals in Germany. Maroula's *The Sting* appears in *Crimeucopia—Tales From The Back Porch.*

**David William Johnson** is primarily known for his nonfiction works, but has been known to write crime fiction when he gets an idea.

His most recent stories have appeared in a New Hampshire

compilation, *Voices of Crackskull's* (Crackskull's Coffee & Books) Living Room Publications.

His biography of Mississippi blues musician Booker "Bukka White" will be published in 2024 by the *University Press of Mississippi.*

Of *Porcelain Angel* and Spender, he says that the character "arrived one day and demanded a role. He happened to manifest in London, where I spent the summer of 1967 as a research assistant in the British Museum Library. Spender preferred to be in London circa 1974, just before the arrival of punk. He is an alright musician, but a bad driver."

**Harris Coverley** has more than ninety short stories published or forthcoming in *Penumbra, Hypnos, JOURN-E,* and *The Black Beacon Book of Horror* (Black Beacon Books), amongst many other places. A former *Rhysling* nominee, he has also had over two hundred poems published in journals around the world. He lives in Manchester, England.

"**Art, history and mystery in one thrilling read.**"
*New Jersey Link*

**The Gallery of Beauties** by Nina Wachsman
**Available on Amazon and Barnes & Noble**

Learn more at https://venicebeauties.com/

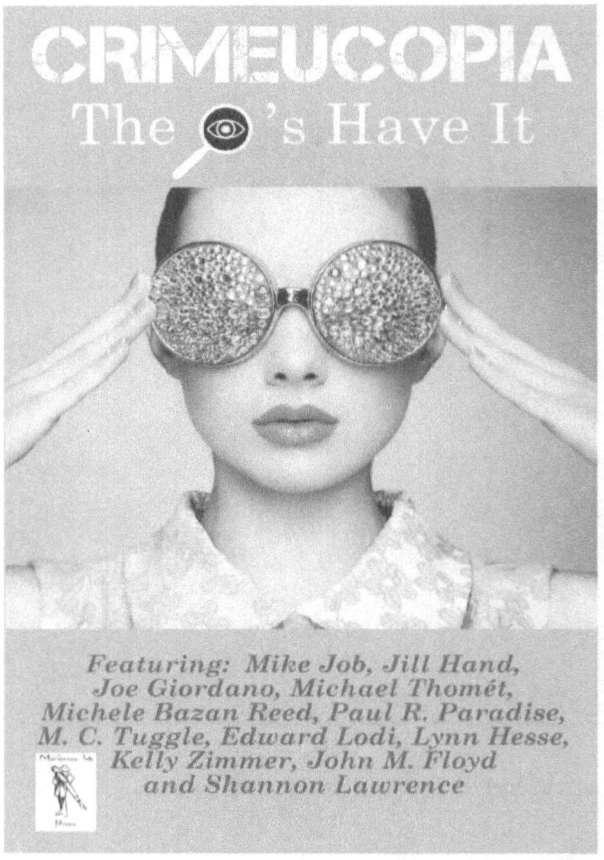


Investigators and investigations are the mainstay of most Crime fiction sub-genres. Everything from the original *Golden Age* of country houses and the amateur sleuth, through to the high tech ultra-modern 21st Century – a place where the cyber investigators sometimes appear to be baffled by old-fashioned motivations of power and greed, and human foibles such as love and revenge.

So is there any real difference between the Private and the Public Sector investigators? Not much, if writers are to be believed, and the two can often be found straddling both sides of the 'what's legal procedure?' fence.

Of the twelve authors contained within, eleven are voices new to the world of Crimeucopia - and although the theme is *Investigators*, the material ranges from Cosy, through to not too Hardboiled - and most are touched with a vein of humour, be it light or dark. Rather like a box of chocolates…

Paperback ISBN: 9781909498327  eBook ISBN: 9781909498334

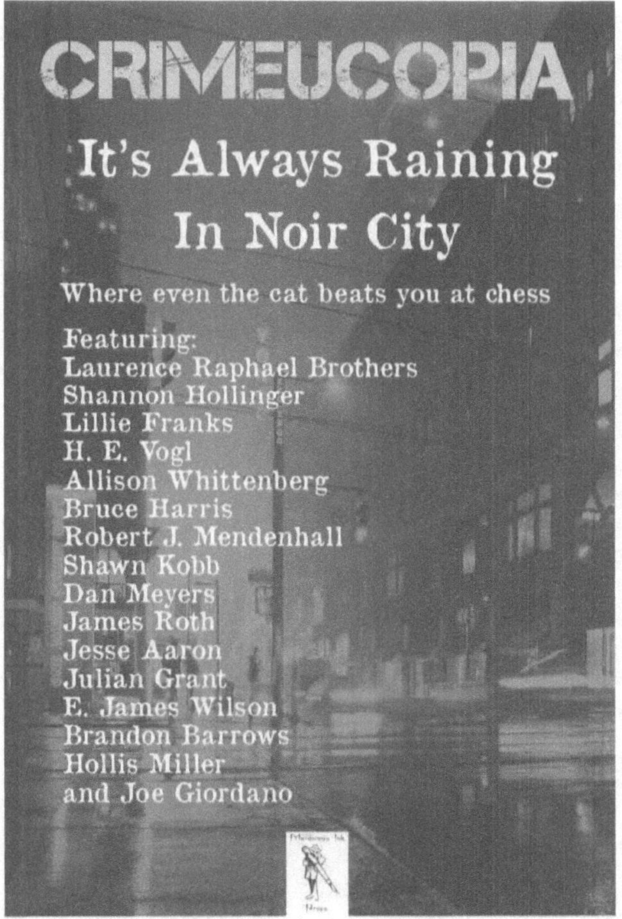


Is the Noir Crime sub-genre always dark and downbeat?  Is there a time when Bad has a change of conscience, flips sides and takes on the Good role?

Noir is almost always a dish served up raw and bloody - Fiction bleu if you will. So maybe this is a chance to see if Noir can be served sunny side up - with the aid of these fifteen short order authors.

All fifteen give us dark tales from the stormy side of life - which is probably why it's *always* raining in Noir City....


Paperback Edition  ISBN: 9781909498341
eBook Edition ISBN: 9781909498358

Small town, big city, watercooler or the back of that 1950s beat-up
Chevy Bel Air with the leather back seat that your parents told you
never to get familiar with. It doesn't matter where you hear it, gossip
is 100% pure ear addiction – and knowledge is, after all, power when
all's said and done.

So why don't you settle down, get yourself comfy, and pour yourself
a drink – long and tall, or just short and nasty, the choice is yours –
and let these 16 story tellers spin their tales as only they know how.


Paperback Edition  ISBN: 9781909498365
eBook Edition ISBN: 9781909498372

# CRIMEUCOPIA

When the theme is no theme at all, you've just got to ask the question

## Say What Now?

*Featuring:*
Peter Ullian,
S. E. Bailey,
N. M. Cedeño,
Edward St Boniface,
Jan Glaz,
Eleanor Luke,
Momodou Bah,
Eve Fisher,
John M. Floyd,
Joan Leotta,
Glen Bush
and DL Shirey

Sometimes editors are forced to reject submissions through no fault of the author. It could be a wonderfully written manuscript, but if the editor cannot place it, then what do they do?

MIP has been lucky in its flexibility and its "Can we start a new project with this?" attitude. Some of the dozen authors contained within are seasoned professionals, having been published in the likes of Alfred Hitchcock's, Ellery Queen's, or other notable publications, while some are making their publishing debuts as Crimeucopians. And while the quality throughout remains exceedingly high, the subject spectrum is the widest we've published so far. But that's only fitting when you consider that the theme of this Crimeucopa is that of No Theme At All.

And in true Murderous Ink fashion, with a dozen authors to choose from, you're bound to find something you'll like, and something you didn't know you'd like until you've read it.

Paperback Edition ISBN: 9781909498389
eBook Edition ISBN: 9781909498396

This is the first of several 'Free 4 All' collections that was supposed to be themeless. However, with the number of submissions that came in, it seems that this could be called an *Angels & Devils* collection, mixing PI & Police alongside tales from the Devil's dining table. Mind you, that's not to say that all the PIs & Police are on the side of the Angels....

Also this time around has not only seen a move to a larger paperback format size, but also in regard to the length of the fiction as well. Followers of the somewhat bent and twisted Crimeucopia path will know that although we don't deal with Flash fiction as a rule, it is a rule that we have sometimes broken. And let's face it, if you cannot break your own rules now and again, whose rules can you break?

Oh, wait, isn't breaking the rules the foundation of the crime fiction genre?

Oh dear....

New Crimeucopians *Aran Myracle, Alexei J. Slater, Gerald Elias, Terry Wijesuriya, Issy Jinarmo, Larry Lefkowitz,* and *Vinnie Hansen* smoothly rub literary shoulders with a fine collection of familiar Crimeucopia old hands: *Bob Ritchie, Michele Bazan Reed, Nikki Knight, N. M. Cedeño, Wendy Harrison, Andrew Darlington, Madeleine McDonald, Joan Leotta, H. E. Vogl* and *Jesse Aaron.*

All 17 tell tales that will make you realise there's always going to be One More Thing To Worry About....

With 16 vibrant authors, a wraparound paperback cover, and pages full of crime fiction in some of its many guises, what's not to like?
So if you enjoy tales spun by
Anthony Diesso, Brandon Barrows, E. James Wilson, James Roth,
Jesse Aaron, Jim Guigli, John M. Floyd, Kevin R. Tipple, Maddi Davidson,
Michael Grimala, Robert Petyo, Shannon Hollinger, Tom Sheehan,
Wil A. Emerson, Peter Trelay, and Philip Pak
then you'd better get
CRIMEUCOPIA - Strictly Off The record
by the sound of it!

Boomshakalaking is a variant of the expression Boomshakalaka, currently recognised as a boastful, teasingly hostile exclamation that follows a noteworthy achievement or an impressive stunt — the meaning similar to *in your face!*

Which is why this anthology is subtitled *Modern Crimes for Modern Times*, because most, if not all, are not your 'regular' crime fiction pieces — in fact some quite happily dance along the edges of multiple genres and styles, while others skew it like it is.

Of the 14 who appear in this anthology, 8 are new Crimeucopians, and even we have to admit that this is one of the most diverse Crimeucopia anthologies so far, and still sits under the umbrella of Crime Fiction.

As with all of these anthologies, we hope you'll find something that you immediately like, as well as something that takes you out of your comfort zone — and puts you into a completely new one.

In other words, in the spirit of the Murderous Ink Press motto:

*You never know what you like until you read it.*